THE
BURNING
HOUSE

THE
BURNING
HOUSE

Short Stories by

ANN
BEATTIE

RANDOM HOUSE
NEW YORK

Portions of this book have previously appeared in the following: *Ms., Vogue,* the *Atlantic Monthly,* the *Carolina Quarterly,* and the *Washington Post Sunday Magazine.*

The following stories originally appeared in *The New Yorker:* "The Burning House," "Greenwich Time," "Waiting," "The Cinderella Waltz," "Running Dreams," "Afloat," "Gravity," "Girl Talk," "Like Glass," "Desire."

"Jacklighting" originally appeared in *Antaeus.*

Grateful acknowledgment is made to Ram's Horn Music for permission to reprint lyrics from "Forever Young" by Bob Dylan. Copyright © 1973, 1974 Ram's Horn Music. All rights reserved.

Library of Congress Cataloging in Publication Data
Beattie, Ann.
The burning house.
I. Title.
PS3552.E177B8   813'.54   82–5292
ISBN 0–394–52494–2   AACR2

Manufactured in the United States of America
Typography and binding design by J. K. Lambert
2 4 6 8 9 7 5 3

First Edition

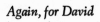

Again, for David

CONTENTS

LEARNING
TO FALL

Ruth's house, early morning: a bowl of apples on the kitchen table, crumbs on the checkered tablecloth. "I love you," she says to Andrew. "Did you guess that I loved you?" "I know it," he says. He's annoyed that his mother is being mushy in front of me. He is eager to seem independent, and cranky because he just woke up. I'm cranky, too, even after the drive to Ruth's in the cold. I'm drinking coffee to wake up. If someone said that he loved me at this moment, I'd never believe him; I can't think straight so early in the morning, hate to make conversation, am angry at the long, cold winter. Andrew and I are both frowning at Ruth's table and she—as always—is tolerating us. "More coffee?" Ruth asks me. I nod yes, and let her pour it, although I could easily get up and walk to the stove for the pot. "What about brushing your hair?" she says to Andrew. He gets up and leaves the room, comes back with her wooden brush and begins to brush his hair. "Not over the table, please," she says. He has finished. He puts the brush on the table and looks at me. "We're going to miss the train," he says. "There's plenty of time," Ruth says. Andrew looks at the clock and sighs loudly. Ruth laughs. She rubs her finger around the top of the open honey jar and sucks it. "Come on," I say to Andrew. "You're right. I'd rather be early than late." I ask Ruth: "Anything from the city?" If she did want something, she wouldn't say—she hates to take things, because she has no money to buy things in return. Nor does she want many things around: the kitchen has only a table and four chairs. What furniture she has came with the house. "No, thanks," she says, and turns off the radio. She says again, as we go out the door, "Thanks." She has a hand on each of our backs as I open the door and cold floods into the house.

Once or twice a month, on Wednesdays, Andrew and I take the train from Connecticut to New York, and I walk down the streets and into stores and through museums with him, holding his little hand, which is as tight as a knot. He does not have friends his own age, but he likes me. After eight years, he trusts me.

Today he is wearing his blue jeans with the Superman patch on the knee. If Superman launched himself from Andrew's knee, he would be flying a foot or so off the ground. People would think that small figure in blue was a piece of trash caught by the wind, a stick blowing, something to gather their hems against.

"I'm hungry again," he says.

Andrew knows that I don't eat during the day. He says *again* because he has already had oatmeal at home and a pastry at the fast-food shop across from the train in Westport at ten o'clock, and now it's only twelve—too early to eat another meal—and he knows I'm going to say: "*Again?*"

Andrew. The morning before the night he was born, Ruth and I swam in Hall's Pond. She loved it that she could float, heavy as she was, about to deliver. She loved being pregnant and wanted the child, although the man who was the father begged her to have an abortion and finally left her six months before Andrew was born. On the last day that we swam in Hall's Pond, she was two weeks overdue. There wasn't a sign of the pain yet, but her tension made me as dizzy as the hot sun on my head as I stood in the too-cold water.

And that night: holding her hand, my hand finally moving up her arm, as if she were slipping away from me. "Take my hand," she kept saying, and I would rub my thumb on her knuckles, squeeze her hand as hard as I dared, but I couldn't stop myself from grasping her wrist, the middle of her arm, hanging on to her elbow, as if she were drowning. It was the same thing I would do with the man who became my lover, years later—but then it would be because I was sinking.

Andrew and I are walking downhill in the Guggenheim Museum, and I am thinking about Ray. Neither of us is looking at the paintings. What Andrew likes about the museum is the view, looking down into the pool of blue water speckled with money.

I stand beside him on the curving walkway. "Don't throw coins from up here, Andrew," I say. "You might hurt somebody."

"Just a penny," he says. He holds it up to show me. A penny: no tricks.

"You're not allowed. It could hit somebody in the face. You could hurt somebody, throwing it."

I am asking him to be careful of hurting people. When he would not be born, an impatient doctor used forceps and tugged him out, and there was slight brain damage. That and some small paralysis of his face, at the mouth.

He pockets the penny. His parka has fallen off one shoulder. He doesn't notice.

"We'll get lunch," I say. "Take your pennies and throw them in the pool when we get down there."

He gets there before me. I look down and see him making his wishes. I doubt that he knows yet what to wish for. Other people are throwing money. Andrew is shy and just stands there, eyes closed and squinting, holding his pennies. He likes to do things in private. You can see the disappointment on his face that other people are in the world. He likes to run with his arms out like the wings of a plane; he likes to be in the first seat in the train compartment—to sit with only me where three seats face two seats across from them. He likes to stretch his legs. He hates cigarette smoke, and the smell of perfume. In spring, he sniffs the breeze like an old man sniffing cognac. He is in the third grade at the elementary school, and so far he has had only slight trouble keeping up. His teacher—who has become Ruth's friend—is young and hopeful, and she doesn't criticize Ruth for the notes she writes pretending that Andrew has been ill on the day the two of us were really in New York. Andrew makes going to the city fun, and for that —and because I know him so well, and I pity him—I almost love him.

We go to his favorite place for hamburgers—a tiny shop on Madison Avenue with a couple of tables in the front. The only time we sat at a table was the time that Ray met us there. Andrew liked sitting at a table, but he was shy and wouldn't say much because Ray was there. The man behind the counter knows us. I know that he recognizes us, even though he doesn't say hello. We always order the same thing: I have black coffee (advertised as the world's best); Andrew has a bacon cheeseburger and a glass of milk. Because Ruth has taught him to make sure he looks neat, he wipes the halo of milk off his mouth after every sip. His hands get sticky from the milk-wet napkin.

Today it is bitter cold, and I am remembering that hot and distant summer. I have hardly been swimming in eight years —not since Arthur and I moved downstate, away from Hall's Pond. When we were in graduate school together, Ruth and I would go there to study. She would have her big, thick

Russian novels with her, and I was always afraid she would drop one into the water. Such big books, underlined, full of notes, it would have seemed more than an average tragedy if she had lost one. She never did. I lost a gold chain (a real one), and my lighter. One time my grocery list fell out of my book into the water and I saw the letters bleed and haze and disappear as it went under.

We went there earlier in the day than other people—not that many people knew about Hall's Pond then—so we always got to sit on the big rock. Later in the day, people would come and sit on the smaller rock, or stand around on the pier going out to the water. Some of the people swam naked. One time a golden retriever jumped onto our rock, crouched, and threw its head back and howled at the sky, then ran away through the woods, its feet blackening in the wet dirt by the water's edge. Ruth was freaked out by it. She wrote a poem, and in the poem the dog came to give a warning. Not an angel, a dog. I stared at the poem, not quite understanding it. "It's meant to be funny," she said. When the dog ran off, Ruth had put her hands over her mouth. The next summer, when I married Arthur, she wrote a poem about the bouquet I carried. The bouquet had some closed lilies, and in the poem she said they were like candles—as big as Roman candles to her eye, as if my bunch of flowers were going to explode and shower down. I laughed at the poem. It was the wrong reaction. Now, because things have come apart between Arthur and me, it has turned out to be prophetic.

"What's up now?" Andrew says, laying down the cheeseburger. He always eats them the same way, and it is a way I have never seen another child eat one: he bites around the outside, eating until only the circle at the center is left.

I look at my watch. The watch was a Christmas present from Arthur. It's almost touching that he isn't embarrassed to give me such impersonal presents as eggcups and digital watches. To see the time, you have to push in the tiny button on the side. As long as you hold it, the time stays lit, changes. Take away your hand and the watch turns clear red again.

"We're going to Bonnie's studio. She's printed the pictures Ruth wanted. Those pictures she took the Fourth of July— we're finally going to see them."

I feel in my pocket for the check Ruth gave me to pay Bonnie.

"But where are we going?" he says.

"To Spring Street. You remember your mother's friend with the long hair to her waist, don't you? You know where Bonnie lives. You've been there before."

We take the subway, and Andrew sits in the crowded car by squeezing himself onto the seat next to me and sitting on one hip, his left leg thrown over mine so that we must look like a ventriloquist and a dummy. The black woman sitting next to him shifts over a little. He stays squeezed against me.

"If Bonnie offers you lunch, I bet you take it," I say, poking the side of his parka.

"I couldn't eat any more."

"You?" I say.

"String bean," he says to me. He pats his puffy parka. Underneath it, you would be able to see his ribs through the T-shirt. He is lean and would be quite handsome except for the obvious defect of his mouth, which droops at one corner as if he's sneering.

We are riding on the subway, and Ruth is back at the tiny converted carriage house she rents from a surgeon and his wife in Westport. Like everything else in the area, it is over-priced, and she can barely afford it—her little house with not enough light, with plastic taped over the aluminum screens and the screens left in the windows because there are no storm windows. Wood is burning in the stove, and herbs are clumped in a bag of gauze hung in the pot of chicken stock. She is underlining things in books, cutting coupons out of news-papers. On Wednesdays she does not have to go to work at the community college where she teaches. She is waiting for her lover, Brandon, to call or to come over: there's warmth, soup, discoveries about literature, and, if he cares, privacy. I envy him an afternoon with Ruth, because she will cook for him and make him laugh and ask nothing from him. She earns hardly any money at the community college, but her half-gallons of wine taste better than the expensive bottles Arthur's business friends uncork. She will reach out and touch you to let you know she is listening when you talk, instead of suggesting that you go out to see some movie for amusement.

Almost every time when I take Andrew home Brandon is there. It's rare that he goes there any other day of the week. Sometimes he brings two steaks. On Valentine's Day he brought her a plant that grows well in the dim light of the kitchen. It sits on the window sill behind the sink and is weaving upward, guided by tacks Ruth has pushed into the window frame. The leaves are thick and small, green and heart-shaped. If I were a poet, those green leaves would be envy, closing her in. Like many people, he does envy her. He would like to be her, but he does not want to take her on. Or Andrew.

The entryway to Bonnie's loft is so narrow, painted bile-green, peeling and filthy, that I always nearly panic, thinking I'll never get to the top. I expect roaches to lose their grip on the ceiling and fall on me; I expect a rat to dart out. I run, silently, ahead of Andrew.

Bonnie opens the door wearing a pair of paint-smeared jeans, one of Hal's V-neck sweaters hanging low over her hips. Her loft is painted the pale yellow of the sun through fog. Her photographs are tacked to the walls, her paintings hung. She hugs both of us and wants us to stay. I take off my coat and unzip Andrew's parka and lay it across his legs. The arms stick out from the sides, no hands coming through them. It could be worse; Andrew could have been born without hands or arms. "I'll tell you what I'm sick of," Ruth said to me not long after he was born, one of the few times she ever complained. "I'm sick of hearing how things might have been worse, when they might also have been better. I'm sick of lawyers saying to wait—not to settle until we're sure how much damage has been done. They talk about damage with their vague regret, the way the weatherman talks about another three inches of snow. I'm sick of wind whistling through the house, when it could be warm and dry." She is never sick of Brandon, and the two steaks he brings, although he couldn't come to dinner the night of Andrew's birthday, and she is not bitter that Andrew's father has had no contact with her since before the birth. "Angry?" Ruth said to me once. "I'm angry at myself. I don't often misjudge people that way."

Bonnie fixes Andrew hot chocolate. My hands are about to shake, but I take another cup of coffee anyway, thinking that it might just be because the space heater radiates so little heat in the loft. Andrew and I sit close together, the white sofa spreading away on either side of us. Andrew looks at some of Ruth's photographs, but his attention drifts away and he starts to hum. I fit them back in the Manila envelope, between the pieces of cardboard, and tie the envelope closed. He rests his head on my arm, so that it's hard to wind the string to close the envelope. While his eyes are closed, Bonnie whispers to me: "I couldn't. I couldn't take money from her."

She looks at me as if I'm crazy. Now it's my problem: how am I going to give Ruth the check back without offending her? I fold the check and put it in my pocket.

"You'll think of something," Bonnie says softly.

She looks hopeful and sad. She is going to have a baby, too. She knows already that she is going to have a girl. She knows that she is going to name her Ora. What she doesn't know is that Hal gambled and lost a lot of money and is worried about how they will afford a baby. Ruth knows that, because Hal called and confided in her. Is it modesty or self-preservation that makes Ruth pretend that she is not as important to people as she is? He calls, she told me, just because he is one of the few people she has ever known who really enjoy talking on the telephone.

We take the subway uptown, back to Grand Central Station. It is starting to fill up with commuters: men with light, expensive raincoats and heavy briefcases, women carrying shopping bags. In another couple of hours Arthur will be in the station on his way home. The Manila envelope is clamped under my arm. Everyone is carrying something. I have the impulse to fold Andrew to me and raise him in my arms. I could do that until he was five, and then I couldn't do it any more. I settle for taking his hand, and we walk along swinging hands until I let go for a second to look at my watch. I look from my watch to the clock. They don't agree, and of course the clock is right, the watch is not. We have missed the 3:05. In an hour there is another train, but on that train it's going to be difficult to get a seat. Or, worse, someone is going to see that something beyond tiredness is wrong with Andrew, and we are going to be offered a seat, and he is going to know why. He suspects already, the way children of a certain age look a little guilty when Santa Claus is mentioned, but I hope I am not there when some person's eye meets Andrew's and instead of looking away he looks back, knowing.

"We're going to have to wait for the next train," I tell him.

"How come?"

"Because we missed our train."

"Didn't you know it when you looked at your watch at Bonnie's?"

He is getting tired, and cranky. Next he'll ask how old I am. And why his mother prefers to stay with Brandon instead of coming to New York with us.

"It would have been rude to leave earlier. We were only there a little while."

I look at him to see what he thinks. Sometimes his thinking is a little slow, but he is also very smart about what he senses. He thinks what I think—that if I had meant to, we could have caught the train. He stares at me with the same dead-on stare Ray gives me when he thinks I am being childish. And, of course, it is because of Ray that I lingered. I always mean not to call him, but I almost always do. We cross the terminal and I go to a phone and drop in a dime. Andrew backs up and spins on his heel. His parka slips off his shoulder again. And his glove—where is his glove? One glove is on the right hand, but there's no glove in either pocket. I sound disappointed, far away when Ray says hello.

"It's just—he lost his glove," I say.

"Where are you?" he says.

"Grand Central."

"Are you coming in or going out?"

"Going home."

His soft voice: "I was afraid of that."

Silence.

"Ray?"

"What? Don't tell me you're going to concoct some reason to see me—ask me to take him off, man to man, and buy him new gloves?"

It makes me laugh.

"You know what, lady?" Ray says. "I do better amusing you over the phone than in person."

A woman walks by, carrying two black poodles. She has on a long gray fur coat and carries the little dogs, who look as if they're peeking out of a cave of fur, nestled in the crook of each arm. Everything is a Stan Mack cartoon. Another woman walks across the terminal. She has forgotten something, or changed her mind—she shakes her head suddenly and begins to walk the other way. Far away from us, she starts to run. Andrew turns and turns. I reach down to make him be still, but he jerks away, spins again, loses interest and just stands there, staring across the station.

"Fuck it," Ray says. "Can I come down and buy you a drink?"

More coffee. Andrew has a milkshake. Ray sits across from us, stirring his coffee as if he's mixing something. Last year when I decided that loving Ray made me as confused as disliking Arthur, and that he had too much power over me and that I could not be his lover anymore, I started taking Andrew to the city with me. It hasn't worked out well; it exasperates Ray, and I feel guilty for using Andrew.

"New shoes," Ray says, pushing his leg out from under the table.

He has on black boots, and he is as happy with them as Andrew was with the pennies I gave him this morning. I smile at him. He smiles back.

"What did you do today?" Ray says.

"Went on an errand for Ruth. Went to the Guggenheim."

He nods. I used to sleep with him and then hold his head as if I believed in phrenology. He used to hold my hands as I held his head. Ray has the most beautiful hands I have ever seen.

"Want to stay in town?" he says. "I was going to the ballet. I can probably get two more tickets."

Andrew looks at me, suddenly interested in staying.

"I've got to go home and make dinner for Arthur."

"Milk the cows," Ray says. "Knead the bread. Stoke the stove. Go to bed."

Andrew looks up at him and smiles broadly before he gets self-conscious and puts his hand to the corner of his mouth and looks away.

"You never heard that one before?" Ray says to Andrew. "My grandmother used to say that. Times have changed and times haven't changed." He looks away, shakes his head. "I'm profound today, aren't I? Good it's coffee and not the drink I wanted."

Andrew shifts in the booth, looks at me as if he wants to say something. I lean my head toward him. "What?" I say softly. He starts a rush of whispering.

"His mother is learning to fall," I say.

"What does that mean?" Ray says.

"In her dance class," Andrew says. He looks at me again, shy. "Tell him."

"I've never seen her do it," I say. "She told me about it—it's an exercise or something. She's learning to fall."

Ray nods. He looks like a professor being patient with a student who has just reached an obvious conclusion. You know when Ray isn't interested. He holds his head very straight and looks you right in the eye, as though he is.

"Does she just go plop?" he says to Andrew.

"Not really," Andrew says, more to me than to Ray. "It's kind of slow."

I imagine Ruth bringing her arms in front of her, head bent, an almost penitential position, and then a loosening in the knees, a slow folding downward.

Ray reaches across the table and pulls my arms away from the front of my body, and his touch startles me so that I jump, almost upsetting my coffee.

"Let's take a walk," he says. "Come on. You've got time."

He puts two dollars down and pushes the money and the check to the back of the table. I hold Andrew's parka for him and he backs into it. Ray adjusts it on his shoulders. Ray bends over and feels in Andrew's pockets.

"What are you doing?" Andrew says.

"Sometimes disappearing mittens have a way of reappearing," Ray says. "I guess not."

Ray zips his own green jacket and pulls on his hat. I walk out of the restaurant beside him, and Andrew follows.

"I'm not going far," Andrew says. "It's cold."

I clutch the envelope. Ray looks at me and smiles, it's so obvious that I'm holding the envelope with both hands so I don't have to hold his hand. He moves in close and puts his hand around my shoulder. No hand-swinging like children— the proper gentleman and the lady out for a stroll. What Ruth has known all along: what will happen can't be stopped. Aim for grace.

JACKLIGHTING

It is Nicholas's birthday. Last year he was alive, and we took him presents: a spiral notebook he pulled the pages out of, unable to write but liking the sound of paper tearing; magazines he flipped through, paying no attention to pictures, liking the blur of color. He had a radio, so we could not take a radio. More than the radio, he seemed to like the sound the metal drawer in his bedside table made, sliding open, clicking shut. He would open the drawer and look at the radio. He rarely took it out.

Nicholas's brother Spence has made jam. For days the cat has batted grapes around the huge homemade kitchen table; dozens of bloody rags of cheesecloth have been thrown into the trash. There is grape jelly, raspberry jelly, strawberry, quince, and lemon. Last month, a neighbor's pig escaped and ate Spence's newly planted fraise des bois plants, but overlooked the strawberry plants close to the house, heavy with berries. After that, Spence captured the pig and called his friend Andy, who came for it with his truck and took the pig to his farm in Warrenton. When Andy got home and looked in the back of the truck, he found three piglets curled against the pig.

In this part of Virginia, it is a hundred degrees in August. In June and July you can smell the ground, but in August it has been baked dry; instead of smelling the earth you smell flowers, hot breeze. There is a haze over the Blue Ridge Mountains that stays in the air like cigarette smoke. It is the same color as the eye shadow Spence's girlfriend, Pammy, wears. The rest of us are sunburned, with pink mosquito bites on our bodies, small scratches from gathering raspberries. Pammy has just arrived from Washington. She is winter-pale. Since she is ten years younger than the rest of us, a few scratches wouldn't make her look as if she belonged, anyway. She is in medical school at Georgetown, and her summer-school classes have just ended. She arrived with leather sandals that squeak. She is exhausted and sleeps half the day, upstairs, with the fan blowing on her. All weekend the big fan has blown on Spence, in the kitchen, boiling and bottling his jams and jellies. The small fan blows on Pammy.

Wynn and I have come from New York. Every year we borrow his mother's car and drive from Hoboken to Virginia. We used to take the trip to spend the week of Nicholas's birthday with him. Now we come to see Spence, who lives alone in the house. He is making jam early, so we can take jars back with us. He stays in the kitchen because he is de-pressed and does not really want to talk to us. He scolds the cat, curses when something goes wrong.

Wynn is in love. The girl he loves is twenty, or twenty-one. Twenty-two. When he told me (top down on the car, talking into the wind), I couldn't understand half of what he was saying. There were enough facts to daze me; she had a name, she was one of his students, she had canceled her trip to Rome this summer. The day he told me about her, he brought it up twice; first in the car, later in Spence's kitchen. "That was *not* my mother calling the other night to say she got the car tuned," Wynn said, smashing his glass on the kitchen counter. I lifted his hand off the large shard of glass, touching his fingers as gently as I'd touch a cactus. When I steadied myself on the counter, a chip of glass nicked my thumb. The pain shot through my body and pulsed in my ribs. Wynn examined my hands; I examined his. A dust of fine glass coated our hands, gently touching, late at night, as we looked out the window at the moon shining on Spence's lemon tree with its one lemon, too heavy to be growing on the slender branch. A jar of Lipton iced tea was next to the tub the lemon tree grew out of—a joke, put there by Wynn, to encourage it to bear more fruit.

Wynn is standing in the field across from the house, pacing, head down, the bored little boy grown up.

"When wasn't he foolish?" Spence says, walking through the living room. "What kind of sense does it make to turn against him now for being a fool?"

"He calls it mid-life crisis, Spence, and he's going to be thirty-two in September."

"I know when his birthday is. You hint like this every year. Last year at the end of August you dropped it into conversation that the two of you were doing something or other to celebrate *his birthday.*"

"We went to one of those places where a machine shoots baseballs at you. His birthday present was ten dollars' worth of balls pitched at him. I gave him a Red Sox cap. He lost it the same day."

"How did he lose it?"

"We came out of a restaurant and a Doberman was tied by its leash to a stop sign, barking like mad—a very menacing dog. He tossed the cap, and it landed on the dog's head. It was funny until he wanted to get it back, and he couldn't go near it."

"He's one in a million. He deserves to have his birthday

remembered. Call me later in the month and remind me."
Spence goes to the foot of the stairs. "Pammy," he calls.

"Come up and kill something for me," she says. The bed
creaks. "Come kill a wasp on the bedpost. I hate to kill them.
I hate the way they crunch."

He walks back to the living room and gets a newspaper and
rolls it into a tight tube, slaps it against the palm of his hand.

Wynn, in the field, is swinging a broken branch, batting
hickory nuts and squinting into the sun.

Nicholas lived for almost a year, brain-damaged, before he
died. Even before the accident, he liked the way things felt. He
always watched shadows. He was the man looking to the side
in Cartier-Bresson's photograph, instead of putting his eye to
the wall. He'd find pennies on the sidewalk when the rest of
us walked down city streets obliviously, spot the chipped finger
on a mannequin flawlessly dressed, sidestep the one piece of
glass among shells scattered on the shoreline. It would really
have taken something powerful to do him in. So that's what
happened: a drunk in a van, speeding, head-on, Nicholas out
for a midnight ride without his helmet. Earlier in the day he'd
assembled a crazy nest of treasures in the helmet, when he
was babysitting the neighbors' four-year-old daughter. Spence
showed it to us—holding it forward as carefully as you'd hold
a bomb, looking away the way you'd avoid looking at dead fish
floating in a once nice aquarium, the way you'd look at an
ugly scar, once the bandages had been removed, and want to
lay the gauze back over it. While he was in the hospital, his
fish tank overheated and all the black mollies died. The doctor
unwound some of the bandages and the long brown curls had
been shaved away, and there was a red scar down the side of
his head that seemed as out of place as a line dividing a highway out west, a highway that nobody traveled anyway. It
could have happened to any of us. We'd all ridden on the
Harley, bodies pressed into his back, hair whipped across our

faces. How were we going to feel ourselves again, without Nicholas? In the hospital, it was clear that the thin intravenous tube was not dripping life back into him—that was as farfetched as the idea that the too-thin branch of the lemon tree could grow one more piece of fruit. In the helmet had been dried chrysanthemums, half of a robin's blue shell, a cat's-eye marble, yellow twine, a sprig of grapes, a piece of a broken ruler. I remember Wynn actually jumping back when he saw what was inside. I stared at the strangeness such ordinary things had taken on. Wynn had been against his teaching me to ride his bike, but he had. He taught me to trust myself and not to settle for seeing things the same way. The lobster claw on a necklace he made me was funny and beautiful. I never felt the same way about lobsters or jewelry after that. "Psychologists have figured out that infants start to laugh when they've learned to be skeptical of danger," Nicholas had said. Laughing on the back of his motorcycle. When he lowered the necklace over my head, rearranging it, fingers on my throat.

It is Nicholas's birthday, and so far no one has mentioned it. Spence has made all the jam he can make from the fruit and berries and has gone to the store and returned with bags of flour to make bread. He brought the *Daily Progress* to Pammy, and she is reading it, on the side porch where there is no screening, drying her hair and stiffening when bees fly away from the Rose of Sharon bushes. Her new sandals are at the side of the chair. She has red toenails. She rubs the small pimples on her chin the way men finger their beards. I sit on the porch with her, catcher's mitt on my lap, waiting for Wynn to get back from his walk so we can take turns pitching to each other.

"Did he tell you I was a drug addict? Is that why you hardly speak to me?" Pammy says. She is squinting at her toes. "I'm older than I look," she says. "He says I'm twenty-one, because I look so young. He doesn't know when to let go of a joke, though. I don't like to be introduced to people as some child prodigy."

"What were you addicted to?" I say.

"Speed," she says. "I had another life." She has brought the bottle of polish with her, and begins brushing on a new layer of red, the fingers of her other hand stuck between her toes from underneath, separating them. "I don't get the feeling you people had another life," she says. "After all these years, I still feel funny when I'm around people who've never lived the way I have. It's just snobbishness, I'm sure."

I cup the catcher's mitt over my knee. A bee has landed on the mitt. This is the most Pammy has talked. Now she interests me; I always like people who have gone through radical changes. It's snobbishness—it shows me that other people are confused, too.

"That was the summer of sixty-seven," she says. "I slept with a stockbroker for money. Sat through a lot of horror movies. That whole period's a blur. What I remember about it is being underground all the time, going places on the subway. I only had one real friend in the city. I can't remember where I was going." Pammy looks at the newspaper beside her chair. "Charlottesville, Virginia," she says. "My, my. Who would have thought twitchy little Pammy would end up here?"

Spence tosses the ball. I jump, mitt high above my head, and catch it. Spence throws again. Catch. Again. A hard pitch that lets me know the palm of my hand will be numb when I take off the catcher's mitt. Spence winds up. Pitches. As I'm leaning to get the ball, another ball sails by on my right. Spence has hidden a ball in his pocket all this time. Like his brother, he's always trying to make me smile.

"It's too hot to play ball," he says. "I can't spend the whole day trying to distract you because Wynn stalked off into the woods today."

"Come on," I say. "It was working."

"Why don't we all go to Virginia Beach next year instead of standing around down here smoldering? This isn't any tribute to my brother. How did this get started?"

"We came to be with you because we thought it would be hard. You didn't tell us about Pammy."

"Isn't that something? What that tells you is that you matter, and Wynn matters, and Nicholas mattered, but I don't even think to mention the person who's supposedly my lover."

"She said she had been an addict."

"She probably tried to tell you she wasn't twenty-one, too, didn't she?"

I sidestep a strawberry plant, notice one croquet post stuck in the field.

"It was a lie?" I say.

"No," he says. "I never know when to let my jokes die."

When Nicholas was alive, we'd celebrate his birthday with mint juleps and croquet games, stuffing ourselves with cake, going for midnight skinny-dips. Even if he were alive, I wonder if today would be anything like those birthdays of the past, or whether we'd have bogged down so hopelessly that even his childish enthusiasm would have had little effect. Wynn is sure that he's having a crisis and that it's not the real thing with his student because he also has a crush on Pammy. We are open about everything: he tells me about taking long walks and thinking about nothing but sex; Spence bakes the French bread too long, finds that he's lightly tapping a rock, sits on the kitchen counter, puts his hands over his face, and cries. Pammy says that she does not feel close to any of us— that Virginia was just a place to come to cool out. She isn't sure she wants to go on with medical school. I get depressed and think that if the birds could talk, they'd say that they didn't enjoy flying. The mountains have disappeared in the summer haze.

Late at night, alone on the porch, toasting Nicholas with a glass of wine, I remember that when I was younger, I assumed he'd be our guide: he saw us through acid trips, planned our vacations, he was always there to excite us and to give us advice. He started a game that went on for years. He had us close our eyes after we'd stared at something and made us envision it again. We had to describe it with our eyes closed. Wynn and Spence could talk about the things and make them more vivid than they were in life. They remembered well. When I closed my eyes, I squinted until the thing was lost to me. It kept going backwards into darkness.

Tonight, Nicholas's birthday, it is dark and late and I have been trying to pay him some sort of tribute by seeing something and closing my eyes and imagining it. Besides realizing that two glasses of wine can make me drunk, I have had this revelation: that you can look at something, close your eyes and see it again and still know nothing—like staring at the sky to figure out the distances between stars.

The drunk in the van that hit Nicholas thought that he had hit a deer.

Tonight, stars shine over the field with the intensity of flashlights. Every year, Spence calls the state police to report that on his property, people are jacklighting.

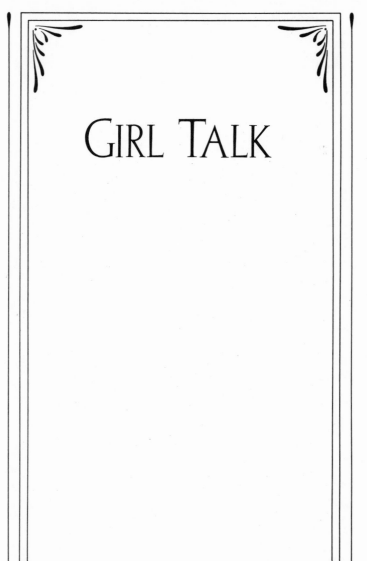

GIRL TALK

Barbara is in her chaise. Something is wrong with the pool—
everything is wrong with the pool—so it has not been filled
with water. The green-painted bottom is speckled with golden-
rod and geranium petals. The neighbor's cat sits licking a
paw under the shade of the little mimosa tree planted in one
of the raised boxes at one corner of the pool.

"Take a picture of that," Barbara says, putting her hand on
top of her husband Sven's wrist. He is her fourth husband.
They have been married for two years. She speaks to him
exactly the way she spoke to her third husband. "Take a picture of a kitty licking its paw, Sven."

"I don't have my camera," he says.

"You usually always have it with you," she says. She lights
an Indonesian cigarette—a *kretek*—waves out the match and
drops it in a little green dish full of cherry pits. She turns to
me and says, "If he'd had his camera last Friday, he could
have photographed the car that hit the what-do-you-call-it—
the concrete thing that goes down the middle of the highway.
They were washing up the blood."

Sven gets up. He slips into his white thongs and flaps down the flagstone walk to the kitchen. He goes in and closes the door.

"How is your job, Oliver?" Barbara asks. Oliver is Barbara's son, but she hardly ever sees him.

"Air-conditioned," Oliver says. "They've finally got the air-conditioning up to a decent level in the building this summer."

"How is *your* job?" Barbara says to me.

I look at her, at Oliver.

"What job are you thinking of, Mother?" he says.

"Oh—painting wicker white, or something. Painting the walls yellow. If you'd had amniocentesis, you could paint them blue or pink."

"We're leaving up the wallpaper," Oliver says. "Why would a thirty-year-old woman have amniocentesis?"

"I hate wicker," I say. "Wicker is for Easter baskets."

Barbara stretches. "Notice the way it goes?" she says. "I ask a simple question, he answers for you, as if you're helpless now that you're pregnant, and that gives you time to think and zing back some snappy reply."

"I think you're the Queen of Snappiness," Oliver says to her.

"Like the Emperor of Ice Cream?" She puts down her Dutch detective novel. "I never did understand Wallace Stevens," she says. "Do any of you?"

Sven has come back with his camera and is focusing. The cat has walked away, but he wasn't focusing on the cat anyway; it's a group shot: Barbara in her tiny white bikini, Oliver in cut-off jeans, with the white raggedy strings trailing down his tan legs, and me in my shorts and baggy embroidered top that my huge stomach bulges hard against.

"Smile," Sven says. "Do I really have to say smile?"

.   .   .

This is the weekend of Barbara's sixtieth birthday, and Oliver's half brother Craig has also come for the occasion. He has given her an early present: a pink T-shirt that says "60." Oliver and I brought Godivas and a hair comb with a silk lily glued to it. Sven will give her a card and some orchids, flown in from some unimaginably far-off place, and a check. She will express shock at the check and not show anyone the amount, though she will pass around his birthday card. At dinner, the orchids will be in a vase, and Sven will tell some anecdote about a shoot he once went on in some faraway country.

Craig has brought two women with him, unexpectedly. They are tall, blond, silent, and look like twins but are not. Their clothes are permeated with marijuana. When they were introduced, one was wearing a Sony Walkman and the other had a tortoiseshell hair ornament in the shape of a turtle.

Now it is getting dark and we are all having spritzers. I have had too many spritzers. I feel that everyone is looking at everyone else's naked feet. The twins who are not twins have baby toes that curl under, so you can see the plum-colored polish on only four toes. Craig has square toenails and calluses on his heels which come from playing tennis. Oliver's long, tan feet are rubbing my legs. The dryness of his soles feels wonderful as he rubs his feet up and down the sticky sweat that has dried on my calves. Barbara has long toenails, painted bronze. Sven's big toes are oblong and shapeless, the way balloons look when you first begin to blow them up. My toenails aren't polished, because I can hardly bend over. I look at Oliver's feet and mine and try to imagine a composite baby foot. As Sven pours, it is the first time I realize that my drink is gone and I have been crunching ice.

In our bedroom, Oliver cups his hands around my hard stomach as I lie on my side facing away from him and kisses my hair from underneath, slowly moving down my spine to where his lips rest on one hipbone.

"My glass of ice water just made a ring on the night table," he says. He takes a sip of water. I hear him sigh and put the glass back on the table.

"I want to get married," I mumble into the pillow. "I don't want to end up bitter, like Barbara."

He snorts. "She's bitter because she kept getting married, and when the last one died he left almost everything to Craig. She's bored with Sven, now that his pictures aren't selling anymore."

"Oliver," I say, and am surprised at how helpless I sound. "You sounded like your mother just then. At least talk sense to me."

Oliver slides his cheek to my buttock. "Remember the first time you rubbed my back and it felt so good that I started laughing?" Oliver says. "And you didn't know why I was doing it and you got insulted? And the time you got drunk and sang along with Eddie Fisher on 'Wish You Were Here' and you were so good I laughed until I got the hiccups?" He rolls over. "We're married," he says. He slides his cheek to the hollow of my back. "Let me tell you what happened on the crosstown bus last week," he goes on. "A messenger got on. Twenty or so. Carrying a pile of envelopes. Started talking CB chatter to the baby on the lap of a woman sitting next to him. The woman and the baby got off at Madison, and between there and Third he started addressing the bus in general. He said, 'Everybody's heard of pie in the sky. They say Smokey in the Sky. Smokey the Bear's what they call the cops. But you know what I say? I say Bear in the Air. It's like "Lucy in the Sky with Diamonds"—LSD. LSD is acid.' He had on running shoes and jeans and a white button-down shirt with a tie hanging around his neck."

"Why did you tell me that story?" I say.

"*Anybody* can get it together to do something perfunctory.

The minute that messenger got off the bus he tied that tie and delivered that crap he was carrying." He turns again, sighs. "I can't talk about marriage in this crazy house. Let's walk on the beach."

"It's so late," I say. "It must be after midnight. I'm exhausted from sitting all day, drinking and doing nothing."

"I'll tell you the truth," he whispers. "I can't stand to hear Barbara and Sven making love."

I listen, wondering if he's putting me on. "That's mice running through the walls," I say.

Sunday afternoon, and Barbara and I are walking the beach, a little tipsy after our picnic lunch. I wonder what she'd think if I told her that her son and I are not married. She gives the impression that what she hasn't lived through she has imagined. And much of what she says comes true. She said the pool would crack; she warned Craig that the girls weren't to be trusted, and, sure enough, this morning they were gone, taking with them the huge silver bowl she keeps lemons and limes in, a silver meat platter with coiled-serpent handles, and four silver ladles—almost as if they'd planned some bizarre tea party for themselves. He'd met them, he said, at Odeon, in the city. That was his explanation. Craig is the only person I know who gets up in the morning, brushes his teeth, and takes a Valium blue. Now we have left him playing a game called Public Assistance with Sven, at the side of the pool. Oliver was still upstairs sleeping when I came down at eleven. "I'll marry you," he said sleepily as I climbed out of bed. "I had a dream that I didn't and we were always unhappy."

I am in the middle of rambling on to Barbara, telling her that Oliver's dreams amaze me. They seem to be about states of feeling; they don't have any symbols in them, or even moments. He wakes up and his dreams have summarized things. I want to blurt out, "We lied to you, years ago. We said we got married, and we didn't. We had a fight and a flat tire and it rained, and we checked into an inn and just never got married."

"My first husband, Cadby, collected butterflies," she says. "I could never understand that. He'd stand by a little window in our bedroom—we had a basement apartment in Cambridge, just before the war—and he'd hold the butterflies in the frames to the light, as if the way the light struck them told him something their wings wouldn't have if they'd flown by." She looks out to the ocean. "Not that there were butterflies flying around Cambridge," she says. "I just realized that."

I laugh.

"Not what you were talking about at all?" she says.

"I don't know," I say. "Lately I catch myself talking just to distract myself. Nothing seems real but my body, and my body is *so heavy*."

She smiles at me. She has long auburn hair, streaked with white, and curly bangs that blow every which way, like the tide foaming into pools.

Both sons, she has just told me, were accidents. "Now I'm too old, and for the first time I'd like to do it again. I envy men for being able to conceive children late in life. You know that picture of Picasso and his son, Claude? Robert Capa took it. It's in Sven's darkroom—the postcard of it, tacked up. They're on the beach, and the child is being held forward, bigger than its father, rubbing an eye. Being held by Picasso, simply smiling and rubbing an eye."

"What wine was that we drank?" I say, tracing a heart in the sand with my big toe.

"La Vieille Ferme blanc," she says. "Nothing special." She picks up a shell—a small mussel shell, black outside, opalescent inside. She drops it carefully into one cup of her tiny bikini top. In her house are ferns, in baskets on the floor, and all around them on top of the soil sit little treasures: bits of glass, broken jewelry, shells, gold twine. One of the most beautiful is an asparagus fern that now cascades over a huge circle of exposed flashbulbs stuck in the earth; each summer I gently lift the branches and peek, the way I used to go to my grandmother's summer house and open her closet to see if the faint pencil markings of the heights of her grandchildren were still there.

"You love him?" she says.

In five years, it is the first time we have ever really talked. Yes, I nod.

"I've had four husbands. I'm sure you know that—that's my claim to fame, and ridicule, forever. But the first died, quite young. Hodgkin's disease. There's a seventy-percent cure now, I believe, for Hodgkin's disease. The second one left me for a lady cardiologist. You knew Harold. And now you know Sven." She puts another shell in her bikini, centering it over her nipple. "Actually, I only had two chances out of four. Sven would like a little baby he could hold in front of his face on the beach, but I'm too old. The body of a thirty-year-old, and I'm too old."

I kick sand, look at the ocean. I feel too full, too woozy, but I'm getting desperate to walk, to move faster.

"Do you think Oliver and Craig will ever like each other?" I say.

She shrugs. "Oh—I don't want to talk about them. It's my birthday, and I want to talk girl talk. Maybe I'll never talk to you this way again."

"Why?" I say.

"I've always had . . . *feelings* about things. Sven made fun of me when I said at Christmas that the pool would crack. I knew both times I was pregnant I'd have boys. I so much didn't want a second child, but now I'm glad I had him. He's more intelligent than Craig. On my deathbed, Craig will probably bring some woman to the house who'll steal the covers." She bends and picks up a shiny stone, throws it into the water. "I didn't love my first husband," she says.

"Why didn't you?"

"His spirit was dying. His spirit was dying before he got sick and died." She runs her hand across her bare stomach. "People your age don't talk that way, do they? We fought, and I left him, and that was in the days when young ladies did not leave young men. I got an apartment in New York, and for so many weeks I was all right—my mother sent all the nice ladies she knew over to amuse me, and it was such a relief not to have to cope. That was also in the days when young men didn't cry, and he'd put his head on my chest and cry about things I couldn't understand. Look at me now, with this body. I'm embarrassed by the irony of it—the dry pool, the useless body. It's too obvious even to talk about it. I sound like T. S. Eliot, with his bank-clerk self-pity, don't I?" She is staring at the ocean. "When I thought everything was in order—I even had a new beau—I was trying to hang a picture one morning: a painting of a field of little trees, with a doe walking through. I had it positioned where I thought it should go, and I held it to the wall and backed up, but I couldn't quite tell, because I couldn't back up enough. I didn't have any husband to hold it to the wall. I dropped it and broke the glass and cried." She pushes her hair back, twines the rubber band she has worn on her wrist around her hair again. Through her bikini I can see the outline of the shells. Her hands hang at her sides. "We've come too far," she says. "Aren't you exhausted?"

We are almost up to the Davises' house. That means that we've walked about three miles, and through my heaviness I feel a sort of light-headedness. I'm thinking, I'm tired but it doesn't matter. Being married doesn't matter. Knowing how to talk about things matters. I sink down in the sand, like a novice with a revelation. Barbara looks concerned; then, a little drunkenly, I watch her face change. She's decided that I'm just responding, taking a rest. A seagull dives, gets what it wants. We sit next to each other facing the water, her flat tan stomach facing the ocean like a mirror.

. . .

It is night, and we are still outdoors, beside the pool. Sven's face has a flickery, shadowed look, like a jack-o'-lantern's. A citronella candle burns on the white metal table beside his chair.

"He decided not to call the police," Sven says. "I agree. Since those two young ladies obviously did not *want* your crappy silver, they're saddled with sort of pirates' treasure, and, as we all know, pirate ships sink."

"You're going to wait?" Barbara says to Craig. "How will you get all our silver back?"

Craig is tossing a tennis ball up and down. It disappears into the darkness, then slaps into his hands again. "You know what?" he says. "One night I'll run into them at Odeon. That's the thing—nothing is ever the end."

"Well, this is my *birthday*, and I hope we don't have to talk about things ending." Barbara is wearing her pink T-shirt, which seems to have shrunk in the wash. Her small breasts are visible beneath it. She has on white pedal pushers and has kicked off her black patent-leather sandals.

"Happy birthday," Sven says, and takes her hand.

I reach out and take Oliver's hand. The first time I met his family I cried. I slept on their fold-out sofa and drank champagne and watched *The Lady Vanishes* on TV, and during the night he crept downstairs to hold me, and I was crying. I had short hair then. I can remember his hand closing around it, crushing it. Now it hangs long and thin, and he moves it gently, pushing it aside. I can't remember the last time I cried. When I first met her, Barbara surprised me because she was so sharp-tongued. Now I have learned that it is their dull lives that make people begin to say cutting things.

I look over my shoulder at the beach at night—sand bleached white by the light of the moon, foamy waves silently washing ashore, a hollow sound from the wind all over, like the echo of a conch shell held against the ear. The roar in my head is all from pain. All day, the baby has been kicking and kicking, and now I know that the heaviness I felt earlier, the disquiet, must be labor. It's almost a full month early—labor coupled with danger. I keep my hands away from my stomach, as if it might quiet itself. Sven opens a bottle of club soda and it gushes into the tall glass pitcher that sits on the table between his chair and Barbara's. He begins to unscrew the cork in a bottle of white wine. Inside me, once, making my stomach pulse, the baby turns over. I concentrate, desperately, on the first thing I see. I focus on Sven's fingers and count them, as though my baby were born and now I have to look for perfection. There is every possibility that my baby will be loved and cared for and will grow up to be like any of these people. Another contraction, and I reach out for Oliver's hand but stop in time and stroke it, don't squeeze.

I am really at some out-of-the-way beach house, with a man I am not married to and people I do not love, in labor.

Sven squeezes a lemon into the pitcher. Smoky drops fall into the soda and wine. I smile, the first to hold out my glass. Pain is relative.

THE
CINDERELLA
WALTZ

Milo and Bradley are creatures of habit. For as long as I've known him, Milo has worn his moth-eaten blue scarf with the knot hanging so low on his chest that the scarf is useless. Bradley is addicted to coffee and carries a Thermos with him. Milo complains about the cold, and Bradley is always a little edgy. They come out from the city every Saturday—this is not habit but loyalty—to pick up Louise. Louise is even more unpredictable than most nine-year-olds; sometimes she waits for them on the front step, sometimes she hasn't even gotten out of bed when they arrive. One time she hid in a closet and wouldn't leave with them.

Today Louise has put together a shopping bag full of things she wants to take with her. She is taking my whisk and my blue pottery bowl, to make Sunday breakfast for Milo and Bradley; Beckett's *Happy Days*, which she has carried around for weeks, and which she looks through, smiling—but I'm not sure she's reading it; and a coleus growing out of a conch shell. Also, she has stuffed into one side of the bag the fancy

Victorian-style nightgown her grandmother gave her for Christmas, and into the other she has tucked her octascope. Milo keeps a couple of dresses, a nightgown, a toothbrush, and extra sneakers and boots at his apartment for her. He got tired of rounding up her stuff to pack for her to take home, so he has brought some things for her that can be left. It annoys him that she still packs bags, because then he has to go around making sure that she has found everything before she goes home. She seems to know how to manipulate him, and after the weekend is over she calls tearfully to say that she has left this or that, which means that he must get his car out of the garage and drive all the way out to the house to bring it to her. One time, he refused to take the hour-long drive, because she had only left a copy of Tolkien's *The Two Towers*. The following weekend was the time she hid in the closet.

"I'll water your plant if you leave it here," I say now.

"I can take it," she says.

"I didn't say you couldn't take it. I just thought it might be easier to leave it, because if the shell tips over the plant might get ruined."

"O.K.," she says. "Don't water it today, though. Water it Sunday afternoon."

I reach for the shopping bag.

"I'll put it back on my window sill," she says. She lifts the plant out and carries it as if it's made of Steuben glass. Bradley bought it for her last month, driving back to the city, when they stopped at a lawn sale. She and Bradley are both very choosy, and he likes that. He drinks French-roast coffee; she will debate with herself almost endlessly over whether to buy a coleus that is primarily pink or lavender or striped.

"Has Milo made any plans for this weekend?" I ask.

"He's having a couple of people over tonight, and I'm going to help them make crêpes for dinner. If they buy more bottles of that wine with the yellow flowers on the label, Bradley is going to soak the labels off for me."

"That's nice of him," I say. "He never minds taking a lot of time with things."

"He doesn't like to cook, though. Milo and I are going to cook. Bradley sets the table and fixes flowers in a bowl. He thinks it's frustrating to cook."

"Well," I say, "with cooking you have to have a good sense of timing. You have to coordinate everything. Bradley likes to work carefully and not be rushed."

I wonder how much she knows. Last week she told me about a conversation she'd had with her friend Sarah. Sarah was trying to persuade Louise to stay around on the weekends, but Louise said she always went to her father's. Then Sarah tried to get her to take her along, and Louise said that she couldn't. "You could take her if you wanted to," I said later. "Check with Milo and see if that isn't right. I don't think he'd mind having a friend of yours occasionally."

She shrugged. "Bradley doesn't like a lot of people around," she said.

"Bradley likes you, and if she's your friend I don't think he'd mind."

She looked at me with an expression I didn't recognize; perhaps she thought I was a little dumb, or perhaps she was just curious to see if I would go on. I didn't know how to go on. Like an adult, she gave a little shrug and changed the subject.

At ten o'clock Milo pulls into the driveway and honks his horn, which makes a noise like a bleating sheep. He knows the noise the horn makes is funny, and he means to amuse us. There was a time just after the divorce when he and Bradley would come here and get out of the car and stand around silently, waiting for her. She knew that she had to watch for them, because Milo wouldn't come to the door. We were both bitter then, but I got over it. I still don't think Milo would have come into the house again, though, if Bradley hadn't thought it was a good idea. The third time Milo came to pick her up after he'd left home, I went out to invite them in, but Milo said nothing. He was standing there with his arms at his sides like a wooden soldier, and his eyes were as dead to me as if they'd been painted on. It was Bradley whom I reasoned with. "Louise is over at Sarah's right now, and it'll make her feel more comfortable if we're all together when she comes in," I said to him, and Bradley turned to Milo and said, "Hey, that's right. Why don't we go in for a quick cup of coffee?" I looked into the back seat of the car and saw his red Thermos there; Louise had told me about it. Bradley meant that they should come in and sit down. He was giving me even more than I'd asked for.

It would be an understatement to say that I disliked Bradley at first. I was actually afraid of him, afraid even after I saw him, though he was slender, and more nervous than I, and spoke quietly. The second time I saw him, I persuaded myself that he was just a stereotype, but someone who certainly seemed harmless enough. By the third time, I had enough courage to suggest that they come into the house. It was embarrassing for all of us, sitting around the table—the same table where Milo and I had eaten our meals for the years we were married. Before he left, Milo had shouted at me that the house was a farce, that my playing the happy suburban housewife was a farce, that it was unconscionable of me to let things drag on, that I would probably kiss him and say, "How was your day, sweetheart?" and that he should bring home flowers and the evening paper. "Maybe I would!" I screamed back. "Maybe it would be nice to do that, even if we were pretending, instead of you coming home drunk and not caring what had happened to me or to Louise all day." He was holding on to the edge of the kitchen table, the way you'd hold on to the horse's reins in a runaway carriage. "I care about Louise," he said finally. That was the most horrible moment. Until then, until he said it that way, I had thought that he was going through something horrible—certainly something was terribly wrong—but that, in his way, he loved me after all. *"You don't love me?"* I had whispered at once. It took us both aback. It was an innocent and pathetic question, and it made him come and put his arms around me in the last hug he ever gave me. "I'm sorry for you," he said, "and I'm sorry for marrying you and causing this, but you know who I love. I told you who I love." "But you were kidding," I said. "You didn't mean it. You were kidding."

When Bradley sat at the table that first day, I tried to be polite and not look at him much. I had gotten it through my head that Milo was crazy, and I guess I was expecting Bradley to be a horrible parody—Craig Russell doing Marilyn Monroe. Bradley did not spoon sugar into Milo's coffee. He did not even sit near him. In fact, he pulled his chair a little away from us, and in spite of his uneasiness he found more things to start conversations about than Milo and I did. He told me about the ad agency where he worked; he is a designer there. He asked if he could go out on the porch to see the brook—Milo had told him about the stream in the back of our place that was as thin as a pencil but still gave us our own watercress. He went out on the porch and stayed there for at least five minutes, giving us a chance to talk. We didn't say one word until he came back. Louise came home from Sarah's house just as Bradley sat down at the table again, and she gave him a hug as well as us. I could see that she really liked him. I was amazed that I liked him, too. Bradley had won and I had lost, but he was as gentle and low-key as if none of it mattered. Later in the week, I called him and asked him to tell me if any free-lance jobs opened in his advertising agency.

(I do a little free-lance artwork, whenever I can arrange it.)
The week after that, he called and told me about another
agency, where they were looking for outside artists. Our calls
to each other are always brief and for a purpose, but lately
they're not just calls about business. Before Bradley left to
scout some picture locations in Mexico, he called to say that
Milo had told him that when the two of us were there years
ago I had seen one of those big circular bronze Aztec calen-
dars and I had always regretted not bringing it back. He
wanted to know if I would like him to buy a calendar if he
saw one like the one Milo had told him about.

Today, Milo is getting out of his car, his blue scarf flapping
against his chest. Louise, looking out the window, asks the
same thing I am wondering: "Where's Bradley?"

Milo comes in and shakes my hand, gives Louise a one-
armed hug.

"Bradley thinks he's coming down with a cold," Milo says.
"The dinner is still on, Louise. We'll do the dinner. We have
to stop at Gristede's when we get back to town, unless your
mother happens to have a tin of anchovies and two sticks of
unsalted butter."

"Let's go to Gristede's," Louise says. "I like to go there."

"Let me look in the kitchen," I say. The butter is salted, but
Milo says that will do, and he takes three sticks instead of
two. I have a brainstorm and cut the cellophane on a left-
over Christmas present from my aunt—a wicker plate that
holds nuts and foil-wrapped triangles of cheese—and, sure
enough: one tin of anchovies.

"We can go to the museum instead," Milo says to Louise.
"Wonderful."

But then, going out the door, carrying her bag, he changes
his mind. "We can go to America Hurrah, and if we see
something beautiful we can buy it," he says.

They go off in high spirits. Louise comes up to his waist,

almost, and I notice again that they have the same walk. Both of them stride forward with great purpose. Last week, Bradley told me that Milo had bought a weathervane in the shape of a horse, made around 1800, at America Hurrah, and stood it in the bedroom, and then was enraged when Bradley draped his socks over it to dry. Bradley is still learning what a perfectionist Milo is, and how little sense of humor he has. When we were first married, I used one of our pottery casserole dishes to put my jewelry in, and he nagged me until I took it out and put the dish back in the kitchen cabinet. I remember his saying that the dish looked silly on my dresser because it was obvious what it was and people would think we left our dishes lying around. It was one of the things that Milo wouldn't tolerate, because it was improper.

When Milo brings Louise back on Saturday night they are not in a good mood. The dinner was all right, Milo says, and Griffin and Amy and Mark were amazed at what a good hostess Louise had been, but Bradley hadn't been able to eat.

"Is he still coming down with a cold?" I ask. I was still a little shy about asking questions about Bradley.

Milo shrugs. "Louise made him take megadoses of vitamin C all weekend."

Louise says, "Bradley said that taking too much vitamin C was bad for your kidneys, though."

"It's a rotten climate," Milo says, sitting on the living-room sofa, scarf and coat still on. "The combination of cold and air pollution . . ."

Louise and I look at each other, and then back at Milo. For weeks now, he has been talking about moving to San Francisco, if he can find work there. (Milo is an architect.) This talk bores me, and it makes Louise nervous. I've asked him not to talk to her about it unless he's actually going to move, but he doesn't seem to be able to stop himself.

"O.K.," Milo says, looking at us both. "I'm not going to say anything about San Francisco."

"*California* is polluted," I say. I am unable to stop myself, either.

Milo heaves himself up from the sofa, ready for the drive back to New York. It is the same way he used to get off the sofa that last year he lived here. He would get up, dress for work, and not even go into the kitchen for breakfast—just sit, sometimes in his coat as he was sitting just now, and at the last minute he would push himself up and go out to the driveway, usually without a goodbye, and get in the car and drive off either very fast or very slowly. I liked it better when he made the tires spin in the gravel when he took off.

He stops at the doorway now, and turns to face me. "Did I take all your butter?" he says.

"No," I say. "There's another stick." I point into the kitchen.

"I could have guessed that's where it would be," he says, and smiles at me.

When Milo comes the next weekend, Bradley is still not with him. The night before, as I was putting Louise to bed, she said that she had a feeling he wouldn't be coming.

"I had that feeling a couple of days ago," I said. "Usually Bradley calls once during the week."

"He must still be sick," Louise said. She looked at me anxiously. "Do you think he is?"

"A cold isn't going to kill him," I said. "If he has a cold, he'll be O.K."

Her expression changed; she thought I was talking down to her. She lay back in bed. The last year Milo was with us, I used to tuck her in and tell her that everything was all right. What that meant was that there had not been a fight. Milo had sat listening to music on the phonograph, with a book or the newspaper in front of his face. He didn't pay very much attention to Louise, and he ignored me entirely. Instead of saying a prayer with her, the way I usually did, I would say to her that everything was all right. Then I would go downstairs and hope that Milo would say the same thing to me. What he finally did say one night was "You might as well find out from me as some other way."

"Hey, are you an old bag lady again this weekend?" Milo says now, stooping to kiss Louise's forehead.

"Because you take some things with you doesn't mean you're a bag lady," she says primly.

"Well," Milo says, "you start doing something innocently, and before you know it it can take you over."

He looks angry, and acts as though it's difficult for him to make conversation, even when the conversation is full of sarcasm and double-entendres.

"What do you say we get going?" he says to Louise.

In the shopping bag she is taking is her doll, which she has not played with for more than a year. I found it by accident when I went to tuck in a loaf of banana bread that I had baked. When I saw Baby Betsy, deep in the bag, I decided against putting the bread in.

"O.K.," Louise says to Milo. "Where's Bradley?"

"Sick," he says.

"Is he too sick to have me visit?"

"Good heavens, no. He'll be happier to see you than to see me."

"I'm rooting some of my coleus to give him," she says. "Maybe I'll give it to him like it is, in water, and he can plant it when it roots."

When she leaves the room, I go over to Milo. "Be nice to her," I say quietly.

"I'm nice to her," he says. "Why does everybody have to act like I'm going to grow fangs every time I turn around?"

"You were quite cutting when you came in."

"I was being self-deprecating." He sighs. "I don't really know why I come here and act this way," he says.

"What's the matter, Milo?"

But now he lets me know he's bored with the conversation. He walks over to the table and picks up a *Newsweek* and flips through it. Louise comes back with the coleus in a water glass.

"You know what you could do," I say. "Wet a napkin and put it around that cutting and then wrap it in foil, and put it in water when you get there. That way, you wouldn't have to hold a glass of water all the way to New York."

She shrugs. "This is O.K.," she says.

"Why don't you take your mother's suggestion," Milo says. "The water will slosh out of the glass."

"Not if you don't drive fast."

"It doesn't have anything to do with my driving fast. If we go over a bump in the road, you're going to get all wet."

"Then I can put on one of my dresses at your apartment."

"Am I being unreasonable?" Milo says to me.

"I started it," I say. "Let her take it in the glass."

"Would you, as a favor, do what your mother says?" he says to Louise.

Louise looks at the coleus, and at me.

"Hold the glass over the seat instead of over your lap, and you won't get wet," I say.

"Your first idea was the best," Milo says.

Louise gives him an exasperated look and puts the glass down on the floor, pulls on her poncho, picks up the glass again and says a sullen goodbye to me, and goes out the front door.

"Why is this my fault?" Milo says. "Have I done anything terrible? I—"

"Do something to cheer yourself up," I say, patting him on the back.

He looks as exasperated with me as Louise was with him. He nods his head yes, and goes out the door.

"Was everything all right this weekend?" I ask Louise.

"Milo was in a bad mood, and Bradley wasn't even there on Saturday," Louise says. "He came back today and took us to the Village for breakfast."

"What did you have?"

"I had sausage wrapped in little pancakes and fruit salad and a rum bun."

"Where was Bradley on Saturday?"

She shrugs. "I didn't ask him."

She almost always surprises me by being more grownup than I give her credit for. Does she suspect, as I do, that Bradley has found another lover?

"Milo was in a bad mood when you two left here Saturday," I say.

"I told him if he didn't want me to come next weekend, just to tell me." She looks perturbed, and I suddenly realize that she can sound exactly like Milo sometimes.

"You shouldn't have said that to him, Louise," I say. "You know he wants you. He's just worried about Bradley."

"So?" she says. "I'm probably going to flunk math."

"No, you're not, honey. You got a C-plus on the last assignment."

"It still doesn't make my grade average out to a C."

"You'll get a C. It's all right to get a C."

She doesn't believe me.

"Don't be a perfectionist, like Milo," I tell her. "Even if you got a D, you wouldn't fail."

Louise is brushing her hair—thin, shoulder-length, auburn hair. She is already so pretty and so smart in everything except math that I wonder what will become of her. When I was her age, I was plain and serious and I wanted to be a tree surgeon. I went with my father to the park and held a stethoscope—a real one—to the trunks of trees, listening to their silence. Children seem older now.

"What do you think's the matter with Bradley?" Louise says. She sounds worried.

"Maybe the two of them are unhappy with each other right now."

She misses my point. "Bradley's sad, and Milo's sad that he's unhappy."

I drop Louise off at Sarah's house for supper. Sarah's mother, Martine Cooper, looks like Shelley Winters, and I have never seen her without a glass of Galliano on ice in her hand. She has a strong candy smell. Her husband has left her, and she professes not to care. She has emptied her living room of furniture and put up ballet bars on the walls, and dances in a purple leotard to records by Cher and Mac Davis. I prefer to have Sarah come to our house, but her mother is adamant that everything must be, as she puts it, "fifty-fifty." When Sarah visited us a week ago and loved the chocolate pie I had made, I sent two pieces home with her. Tonight, when I left Sarah's house, her mother gave me a bowl of Jell-O fruit salad.

The phone is ringing when I come in the door. It is Bradley.

"Bradley," I say at once, "whatever's wrong, at least you don't have a neighbor who just gave you a bowl of maraschino cherries in green Jell-O with a Reddi-Wip flower squirted on top."

"Jesus," he says. "You don't need me to depress you, do you?"

"What's wrong?" I say.

He sighs into the phone. "Guess what?" he says.

"What?"

"I've lost my job."

It wasn't at all what I was expecting to hear. I was ready to hear that he was leaving Milo, and I had even thought that that would serve Milo right. Part of me still wanted him punished for what he did. I was so out of my mind when

Milo left me that I used to go over and drink Galliano with Martine Cooper. I even thought seriously about forming a ballet group with her. I would go to her house in the afternoon, and she would hold a tambourine in the air and I would hold my leg rigid and try to kick it.

"That's awful," I say to Bradley. "What happened?"

"They said it was nothing personal—they were laying off three people. Two other people are going to get the ax at the agency within the next six months. I was the first to go, and it was nothing personal. From twenty thousand bucks a year to nothing, and nothing personal, either."

"But your work is so good. Won't you be able to find something again?"

"Could I ask you a favor?" he says. "I'm calling from a phone booth. I'm not in the city. Could I come talk to you?"

"Sure," I say.

It seems perfectly logical that he should come alone to talk —perfectly logical until I actually see him coming up the walk. I can't entirely believe it. A year after my husband has left me, I am sitting with his lover—a man, a person I like quite well—and trying to cheer him up because he is out of work. ("Honey," my father would say, "listen to Daddy's heart with the stethoscope, or you can turn it toward you and listen to your own heart. You won't hear anything listening to a tree." Was my persistence willfulness, or belief in magic? Is it possible that I hugged Bradley at the door because I'm secretly glad he's down and out, the way I used to be? Or do I really want to make things better for him?)

He comes into the kitchen and thanks me for the coffee I am making, drapes his coat over the chair he always sits in.

"What am I going to do?" he asks.

"You shouldn't get so upset, Bradley," I say. "You know you're good. You won't have trouble finding another job."

"That's only half of it," he says. "Milo thinks I did this deliberately. He told me I was quitting on him. He's very angry at me. He fights with me, and then he gets mad that I don't enjoy eating dinner. My stomach's upset, and I can't eat anything."

"Maybe some juice would be better than coffee."

"If I didn't drink coffee, I'd collapse," he says.

I pour coffee into a mug for him, coffee into a mug for me.

"This is probably very awkward for you," he says. "That I come here and say all this about Milo."

"What does he mean about your quitting on him?"

"He said . . . he actually accused me of doing badly deliberately, so they'd fire me. I was so afraid to tell him the truth when I was fired that I pretended to be sick. Then I really *was* sick. He's never been angry at me this way. Is this always the way he acts? Does he get a notion in his head for no reason and then pick at a person because of it?"

I try to remember. "We didn't argue much," I say. "When he didn't want to live here, he made me look ridiculous for complaining when I knew something was wrong. He expects perfection, but what that means is that you do things his way."

"I *was*. I never wanted to sit around the apartment, the way he says I did. I even brought work home with me. He made me feel so bad all week that I went to a friend's apartment for the day on Saturday. Then he said I had walked out on the problem. He's a little paranoid. I was listening to the radio, and Carole King was singing 'It's Too Late,' and he came into the study and looked very upset, as though I had planned for the song to come on. I couldn't believe it."

"Whew," I say, shaking my head. "I don't envy you. You have to stand up to him. I didn't do that. I pretended the problem would go away."

"And now the problem sits across from you drinking coffee, and you're being nice to him."

"I know it. I was just thinking we look like two characters in some soap opera my friend Martine Cooper would watch."

He pushes his coffee cup away from him with a grimace.

"But anyway, I like you now," I say. "And you're exceptionally nice to Louise."

"I took her father," he says.

"Bradley—I hope you don't take offense, but it makes me nervous to talk about that."

"I don't take offense. But how can you be having coffee with me?"

"You invited yourself over so you could ask that?"

"Please," he says, holding up both hands. Then he runs his hands through his hair. "Don't make me feel illogical. He does that to me, you know. He doesn't understand it when everything doesn't fall right into line. If I like fixing up the place, keeping some flowers around, therefore I can't like being a working person, too, therefore I deliberately sabotage myself in my job." Bradley sips his coffee.

"I wish I could do something for him," he says in a different voice.

This is not what I expected, either. We have sounded like two wise adults, and then suddenly he has changed and sounds very tender. I realize the situation is still the same. It is two of them on one side and me on the other, even though Bradley is in my kitchen.

"Come and pick up Louise with me, Bradley," I say. "When you see Martine Cooper, you'll cheer up about your situation."

He looks up from his coffee. "You're forgetting what I'd look like to Martine Cooper," he says.

Milo is going to California. He has been offered a job with a new San Francisco architectural firm. I am not the first to know. His sister, Deanna, knows before I do, and mentions it when we're talking on the phone. "It's middle-age crisis," Deanna says sniffily. "Not that I need to tell you." Deanna would drop dead if she knew the way things are. She is scandalized every time a new display is put up in Bloomingdale's window. ("Those mannequins had eyes like an Egyptian princess, and *rags*. I swear to you, they had mops and brooms and ragged gauze dresses on, with whores' shoes—stiletto heels that prostitutes wear.")

I hang up from Deanna's call and tell Louise I'm going to drive to the gas station for cigarettes. I go there to call New York on their pay phone.

"Well, I only just knew," Milo says. "I found out for sure yesterday, and last night Deanna called and so I told her. It's not like I'm leaving tonight."

He sounds elated, in spite of being upset that I called. He's happy in the way he used to be on Christmas morning. I remember him once running into the living room in his underwear and tearing open the gifts we'd been sent by relatives. He was looking for the eight-slice toaster he was sure we'd get. We'd been given two-slice, four-slice, and six-slice toasters, but then we got no more. "Come out, my eight-slice beauty!" Milo crooned, and out came an electric clock, a blender, and an expensive electric pan.

"When are you leaving?" I ask him.

"I'm going out to look for a place to live next week."

"Are you going to tell Louise yourself this weekend?"

"Of course," he says.

"And what are you going to do about seeing Louise?"

"Why do you act as if I don't like Louise?" he says. "I will occasionally come back East, and I will arrange for her to fly to San Francisco on her vacations."

"It's going to break her heart."

"No it isn't. Why do you want to make me feel bad?"

"She's had so many things to adjust to. You don't have to go to San Francisco right now, Milo."

"It happens, if you care, that my own job here is in jeopardy. This is a real chance for me, with a young firm. They really want me. But anyway, all we need in this happy group is to have you bringing in a couple of hundred dollars a month with your graphic work and me destitute and Bradley so devastated by being fired that of course he can't even look for work."

"I'll bet he is looking for a job," I say.

"Yes. He read the want ads today and then fixed a crab quiche."

"Maybe that's the way you like things, Milo, and people respond to you. You forbade me to work when we had a baby. Do you say anything encouraging to him about finding a job, or do you just take it out on him that he was fired?"

There is a pause, and then he almost seems to lose his mind with impatience.

"I can hardly *believe*, when I am trying to find a logical solution to all our problems, that I am being subjected, by telephone, to an unflattering psychological analysis by my ex-wife." He says this all in a rush.

"All right, Milo. But don't you think that if you're leaving so soon you ought to call her, instead of waiting until Saturday?"

Milo sighs very deeply. "I have more sense than to have important conversations on the telephone," he says.

Milo calls on Friday and asks Louise whether it wouldn't be nice if both of us came in and spent the night Saturday and if we all went to brunch together Sunday. Louise is excited. I never go into town with her.

Louise and I pack a suitcase and put it in the car Saturday morning. A cutting of ivy for Bradley has taken root, and she has put it in a little green plastic pot for him. It's heartbreaking, and I hope that Milo notices and has a tough time dealing with it. I am relieved I'm going to be there when he tells her, and sad that I have to hear it at all.

In the city, I give the car to the garage attendant, who does not remember me. Milo and I lived in the apartment when we were first married, and moved when Louise was two years old. When we moved, Milo kept the apartment and sublet it—a sign that things were not going well, if I had been one to heed such a warning. What he said was that if we were ever rich enough we could have the house in Connecticut *and* the apartment in New York. When Milo moved out of the house, he went right back to the apartment. This will be the first time I have visited there in years.

Louise strides in in front of me, throwing her coat over the brass coatrack in the entranceway—almost too casual about being there. She's the hostess at Milo's, the way I am at our house.

He has painted the walls white. There are floor-length white curtains in the living room, where my silly flowered curtains used to hang. The walls are bare, the floor has been sanded, a stereo as huge as a computer stands against one wall of the living room, and there are four speakers.

"Look around," Milo says. "Show your mother around, Louise."

I am trying to remember if I have ever told Louise that I used to live in this apartment. I must have told her, at some point, but I can't remember it.

"Hello," Bradley says, coming out of the bedroom.

"Hi, Bradley," I say. "Have you got a drink?"

Bradley looks sad. "He's got champagne," he says, and looks nervously at Milo.

"No one *has* to drink champagne," Milo says. "There's the usual assortment of liquor."

"Yes," Bradley says. "What would you like?"

"Some bourbon, please."

"Bourbon." Bradley turns to go into the kitchen. He looks different; his hair is different—more wavy—and he is dressed as though it were summer, in straight-legged white pants and black leather thongs.

"I want Perrier water with strawberry juice," Louise says, tagging along after Bradley. I have never heard her ask for such a thing before. At home, she drinks too many Cokes. I am always trying to get her to drink fruit juice.

Bradley comes back with two drinks and hands me one. "Did you want anything?" he says to Milo.

"I'm going to open the champagne in a moment," Milo says. "How have you been this week, sweetheart?"

"O.K.," Louise says. She is holding a pale-pink, bubbly drink. She sips it like a cocktail.

Bradley looks very bad. He has circles under his eyes, and he is ill at ease. A red light begins to blink on the phone-answering device next to where Bradley sits on the sofa, and Milo gets out of his chair to pick up the phone.

"Do you really want to talk on the phone right now?" Bradley asks Milo quietly.

Milo looks at him. "No, not particularly," he says, sitting down again. After a moment, the red light goes out.

"I'm going to mist your bowl garden," Louise says to Bradley, and slides off the sofa and goes to the bedroom. "Hey, a little toadstool is growing in here!" she calls back. "Did you put it there, Bradley?"

"It grew from the soil mixture, I guess," Bradley calls back. "I don't know how it got there."

"Have you heard anything about a job?" I ask Bradley.

"I haven't been looking, really," he says. "You know."

Milo frowns at him. "Your choice, Bradley," he says. "I didn't ask you to follow me to California. You can stay here."

"No," Bradley says. "You've hardly made me feel welcome."

"Should we have some champagne—all four of us—and you can get back to your bourbons later?" Milo says cheerfully.

We don't answer him, but he gets up anyway and goes to

the kitchen. "Where have you hidden the tulip-shaped glasses, Bradley?" he calls out after a while.

"They should be in the cabinet on the far left," Bradley says.

"You're going with him?" I say to Bradley. "To San Francisco?"

He shrugs, and won't look at me. "I'm not quite sure I'm wanted," he says quietly.

The cork pops in the kitchen. I look at Bradley, but he won't look up. His new hairdo makes him look older. I remember that when Milo left me I went to the hairdresser the same week and had bangs cut. The next week, I went to a therapist who told me it was no good trying to hide from myself. The week after that, I did dance exercises with Martine Cooper, and the week after that the therapist told me not to dance if I wasn't interested in dancing.

"I'm not going to act like this is a funeral," Milo says, coming in with the glasses. "Louise, come in here and have champagne! We have something to have a toast about."

Louise comes into the living room suspiciously. She is so used to being refused even a sip of wine from my glass or her father's that she no longer even asks. "How come I'm in on this?" she asks.

"We're going to drink a toast to me," Milo says.

Three of the four glasses are clustered on the table in front of the sofa. Milo's glass is raised. Louise looks at me, to see what I'm going to say. Milo raises his glass even higher. Bradley reaches for a glass. Louise picks up a glass. I lean forward and take the last one.

"This is a toast to me," Milo says, "because I am going to be going to San Francisco."

It was not a very good or informative toast. Bradley and I sip from our glasses. Louise puts her glass down hard and bursts into tears, knocking the glass over. The champagne spills onto the cover of a big art book about the Unicorn Tapestries. She runs into the bedroom and slams the door.

Milo looks furious. "Everybody lets me know just what my insufficiencies are, don't they?" he says. "Nobody minds expressing himself. We have it all right out in the open."

"He's criticizing me," Bradley murmurs, his head still bowed. "It's because I was offered a job here in the city and I didn't automatically refuse it."

I turn to Milo. "Go say something to Louise, Milo," I say. "Do you think that's what somebody who isn't brokenhearted sounds like?"

He glares at me and stomps into the bedroom, and I can hear him talking to Louise reassuringly. "It doesn't mean you'll *never* see me," he says. "You can fly there, I'll come here. It's not going to be that different."

"You lied!" Louise screams. "You said we were going to brunch."

"We are. We are. I can't very well take us to brunch before Sunday, can I?"

"You didn't say you were going to San Francisco. What *is* San Francisco, anyway?"

"I just said so. I bought us a bottle of champagne. You can come out as soon as I get settled. You're going to like it there."

Louise is sobbing. She has told him the truth and she knows it's futile to go on.

By the next morning, Louise acts the way I acted—as if everything were just the same. She looks calm, but her face is small and pale. She looks very young. We walk into the restaurant and sit at the table Milo has reserved. Bradley pulls out a chair for me, and Milo pulls out a chair for Louise, locking his finger with hers for a second, raising her arm above her head, as if she were about to take a twirl.

She looks very nice, really. She has a ribbon in her hair. It is cold, and she should have worn a hat, but she wanted to wear the ribbon. Milo has good taste: the dress she is wearing, which he bought for her, is a hazy purple plaid, and it sets off her hair.

"Come with me. Don't be sad," Milo suddenly says to Louise, pulling her by the hand. "Come with me for a minute. Come across the street to the park for just a second, and we'll have some space to dance, and your mother and Bradley can have a nice quiet drink."

She gets up from the table and, looking long-suffering, backs into her coat, which he is holding for her, and the two of them go out. The waitress comes to the table, and Bradley orders three Bloody Marys and a Coke, and eggs Benedict for everyone. He asks the waitress to wait awhile before she brings the food. I have hardly slept at all, and having a drink is not going to clear my head. I have to think of things to say to Louise later, on the ride home.

"He takes so many *chances*," I say. "He pushes things so far with people. I don't want her to turn against him."

"No," he says.

"Why are you going, Bradley? You've seen the way he acts. You know that when you get out there he'll pull something on you. Take the job and stay here."

Bradley is fiddling with the edge of his napkin. I study him. I don't know who his friends are, how old he is, where he grew up, whether he believes in God, or what he usually drinks. I'm shocked that I know so little, and I reach out and touch him. He looks up.

"Don't go," I say quietly.

The waitress puts the glasses down quickly and leaves, embarrassed because she thinks she's interrupted a tender moment. Bradley pats my hand on his arm. Then he says the thing that has always been between us, the thing too painful for me to envision or think about.

"I love him," Bradley whispers.

We sit quietly until Milo and Louise come into the restaurant, swinging hands. She is pretending to be a young child, almost a baby, and I wonder for an instant if Milo and Bradley and I haven't been playing house, too—pretending to be adults.

"Daddy's going to give me a first-class ticket," Louise says. "When I go to California we're going to ride in a glass elevator to the top of the Fairman Hotel."

"The Fairmont," Milo says, smiling at her.

Before Louise was born, Milo used to put his ear to my stomach and say that if the baby turned out to be a girl he would put her into glass slippers instead of bootees. Now he is the prince once again. I see them in a glass elevator, not long from now, going up and up, with the people below getting smaller and smaller, until they disappear.

PLAYBACK

One of the most romantic evenings I ever spent was last
week, with Holly curled in my lap, her knees to the side, resting against the sloping arm of the wicker rocking chair. It
would have cut into her skin if I hadn't tucked my hand under
her bony knees. Her satin nightgown came to mid-calf when
she stood, but didn't cover her knees when she curled into
my lap. In the breeze, tiny curls blew against my cheek,
where it rested on top of her head. Ash used to say that her
fine, long hair reminded him of the way ribbon curled when
you held it stretched lightly across your thumb and ran a
pair of scissors along the top. The nightgown had been a
present from Ash: tiny pink flowers scattered here and there
among the narrow pleats, a nightgown from the 1930s. He
had bought it at her favorite store, Red Dog, where he had
bought her the mysterious homemade rug with a chorus line
of squirrels, eating what looked like shrimp. He had also
gotten her a satin jacket with "Angelo" written across the
back. He cut off the "o" and had a friend add embroidered

wings. On cool nights, she'd wear it over the old-fashioned nightgown.

The night I held her on my lap, Ash had called from a pay phone in a bar in Tennessee, to say that the rattlesnake killed in his friend Michael's garden was so big that the skin had stretched to cover Michael's fiddle case. Those were the kind of stories she wanted to hear: stories that justified her not going to Tennessee. She had a baby, Peter, who lived with her ex-husband in Boston, and a psychiatrist in Vermont: she did not want to interrupt her therapy. She had a pottery business, with her friends Andrea and Percy Green and Roger Billington, that was just starting to make a little money, and summer was the best time for selling it in the shop they had set up in Percy Green's big garage. I was visiting her for a month and a half. She knew I loved Vermont and thought I wouldn't go as far as Tennessee to visit. I think I would have. I think I would have done almost anything for her. I offered her my savings to fight her fat, villainous lawyer husband for Peter; in the winter, I drove to Vermont four weeks running to sit through group-therapy sessions, because everyone was supposed to bring someone from the family, and she had no family but her brother, in Nebraska, and an aunt in an old-age home.

I'm not the kind of woman who greets other women with little bird pecks on the cheek, and unlike Holly, I'm not used to embracing people; but when she came out to the porch, so sad from hearing Ash's voice, and shook her head and kissed me goodnight on the forehead, I put out my arms and she climbed into my lap. "He didn't talk long," she said. "He said he wrote me a letter that I haven't gotten yet." We must have rocked for hours, before the static on the kitchen radio got too much to put up with. Then some sort of embarrassment caught up with her: when she came back to the porch she was smiling an embarrassed smile. The angel jacket was zipped over her nightgown, and she said quietly: "Thanks,

Jane. Now I can go to sleep." The lacy angel wings disappeared into the kitchen. I heard her turn on the water and knew she was doing what I'd hoped my rocking would soothe her out of, taking the nightly combination that I was convinced was deadly: two vitamin B_6 pills, and half a pill each of Dalmane and Valium, taken one at a time, because in spite of all the medicine she had taken in her life, she still believed that she would choke to death when swallowing a pill. One thing we all liked about Ash was that he tried to talk her out of them. He tried to get her to take a long, tiring walk with him, or to smoke a joint. He'd pull her to the old carrousel mirror in the kitchen and make her look at her guilty expression as she swallowed the pills. Lamely, she told him that two vitamin B_6s couldn't hurt. Some nights he'd reason with her so that she only took half a Valium. If he ever rocked her on his lap, I don't know about it.

People often mistake us for sisters. It didn't happen at Smith, where people had watched us make friends, but later, when we went into New York to shop or to take dance classes. We were both lonely and self-sufficient—I was an only child, and her parents died when she was ten—and once we got over our jealousy because people were always comparing our looks, we realized that we were soul mates. I curled my hair to look like hers; she began to wear long, floating skirts like mine. When she got married I made the bouquet, and she threw it to me. The morning of the wedding I had wrapped thick satin ribbon around the layers of foil that held the stems together, knowing that she was marrying the wrong person, but for once too reticent to say what I thought. Fixing the flowers, I thought of the custom of binding women's feet in China: having any part of this was wrong.

She stayed married for nine years, all through her husband's time in the Army and in law school, years of living in a fourth-floor walk-up in New Haven, above a restaurant. They had a big, rusty car that she was always sanding and painting.

She said nothing about the dreary apartment but that the fan of stained glass above the front door was beautiful. When he became a lawyer, the house in the suburbs they moved to wasn't her taste, either, but she planted nicotiana plants that bloom at night—the most wonderful-smelling flowers I have ever known.

Peter was a breech birth, delivered, finally, by Caesarean. I sat in the waiting room with her husband, thinking: things aren't working out, and they won't even let us hear her crying. I had been spending a weekend in the country with my lover when Holly called to say she was going to the hospital. It was almost a month early—they were visiting friends in New York. I remember sitting in the waiting room, smelling of turpentine. Jason, the man I was in love with, had taken me to his house in East Hampton. A few hours before Holly called, I had been asleep in the sun, at the end of his dock, and because he thought it would be funny, because he couldn't resist, he had dipped into the bucket of gray paint—he was painting the dock—and stroked the wide brush full of cold, smooth paint over both knees as I slept. It didn't wash off in the water, and I had to use turpentine, wiping it again and again across my knees with his wife's torn blouse, more amused than I let on that he had done it, wondering how I could love a man who had a wife whose discarded blouses were from Saks. When the phone rang, a few hours before we were going to drive back to the city, Holly said: "I'm going to Lenox Hill. I'm saving myself some time." Then all at once Jason was dabbing at my knees with turpentine, telling me that I did too have time to dive off the dock, that it didn't matter if my hair was wet, that if I swam, I wouldn't have to shower. "Take it easy," he said. "You're not having the baby." No—time would pass, and then I wouldn't even have Jason. He'd reconcile with his wife, and her mysterious arthritis would disappear, and she'd be back playing the violin. But that day it seemed impossible. It was easy enough to sleep in the sun when back in the city I didn't even sleep late at night, in my dark apartment. Jason had been enough in love to pull pranks. In his house, I pulled on my jeans, no underwear underneath, borrowed a T-shirt from him, rushed out of the house never suspecting that it was one of the last times I'd ever see it. The very last time would be in winter, when I sat in the car and he went in to see that a pipe that had frozen had been repaired correctly. He was going back to his wife. I didn't want to see the presents I'd given him that were still inside: the moose cookie jar, the poster of a brigade of roaches: *"Con más poder de atrapar para matar bien muertas las cucarachas fuertes."* Percy Green's drawing of a foot with a hugely elongated big toe, captioned "Stretching the Mind."

The day Holly went into labor we had taken a fast ride back to the city, the top down on his big, white Ford, wet hair flapping against my head like dog's ears. No: I wasn't having this baby. The next spring, I would have an abortion. I would go to a restaurant with a surreally beautiful garden, and Jason would sit next to me, under the umbrella, before I went to the hospital. Pink flowers would fall into our hair, our laps, our food. I couldn't eat anything. I couldn't even tell him why. I dropped raw shrimp under the table, praying for the cat that didn't exist. Sipped a mimosa and spit the liquor back into the glass. My hand on top of his, his other hand sliding up my leg, under the big napkin—a ghastly foreshadowing of the white sheet they'd spread across me an hour later. "Eat," Jason said. "You have to eat something." Smiling. Touching. Hiding my food like a child, letting the pink flowers cover what they could.

Later that year, when Holly left her husband and moved to Vermont, she said to me: "Men are never going to be our salvation." We both believed it, enough to prick fingers and touch blood bubble to blood bubble, but of course children did that, not adults, and it was something men did, anyway. Then Holly met Ash, and for a while she was happy. It didn't last, though. I knew that there was trouble the day I went with Ash to pick berries from the scraggly blackberry bushes that grew around the crumbling foundation of what was once an old mansion. He was dropping them in his khaki cap, not caring that it would be stained forever.

"Why is Holly pulling away from me?" he said.

"Because of Peter," I told him. "Because her husband's going to win, and she knows she's losing Peter."

"Holly and I could have a baby. She sees him. Her ex-husband isn't trying to turn Peter against her, is he? I never noticed that."

"Ash," I said. "She doesn't have Peter."

He stopped picking berries. "You know what the two of you do? You condescend to me when you talk. I understand facts. Did it ever occur to either of you that there are other facts besides your facts?"

The sun was beating down on the berries, on his sad face, the stained fingers—it looked as though he had been involved in something violent, when all he had been doing was carefully picking berries. The violence was all inside his head. He was going to Tennessee, to give her time to think. Time to think about whether she could concentrate on him again, spend less time brooding about Peter, have another baby—the baby he wanted. He was staring down, dejected. A black ant ran through the berries. Many ants. He tried to flick them out, but they were quick, and went to the bottom. "It's so beautiful here in the summer, and she sits in the house—"

"Ash," I said to him. "What really matters to her is having Peter."

I always wondered if what I said made him decide for sure to go to Tennessee.

Her brother, Todd, came for the last two weeks in August. He had always been suspicious of the men his sister loved, and he was suspicious of Ash. "He's one of those smiling Southern boys you outgrow. They wear the same belts all their lives," he said. But he loved Holly, and he tried to give impartial advice.

"I know it's sick," Holly said to Todd, rocking with him on the back porch, "but our father's dead and I've made you into the permission-giver, and I guess what I'm hoping is that you'll tell me to go to Tennessee."

"You wouldn't leave Peter if I told you to."

"What if I made a success of myself, and I could fly back to Boston all the time?"

"It's not what you want to hear," he said, "but I remember when he was just learning to walk, and somebody took a picture of him with a flash, and he turned to you and he was blind. He was blind the way people get snowblind. I remember how the two of you felt your way toward each other— how you were both just arms and legs. You're his mother."

"And I go to a shrink in Montpelier and everybody thinks I'm very fragile, don't they?"

"Ash sat with me on this porch and told me he wanted at least three children. Kids aren't going to distract you from Peter. They're just going to remind you of him. Don't you remember when Georgia exploded that flash cube in his face and he turned around from the birthday cake like it had been a land mine? Vietnam. Fucking Vietnam."

He went into the house for iced tea, which he brought back to us on a heavy silver tray, one of those family heirlooms you can't imagine owning but can't imagine getting rid of. While he was gone, I said to Holly: "It's twelve years later, and almost every day, he gets the war into the conversation. He went to Nebraska to keep punishing himself."

When we finished drinking our tea, Todd and I decided to go swimming. Holly was a little angry at Todd, and she stayed behind to throw pots with Percy Green. Percy Green was stoned, so he didn't realize what he'd walked in on. "I pick up on something," he said. "That marvelous creative energy." He was wearing a Hawaiian shirt with men in gondolas rowing across his chest. His chest was large and well developed from lifting weights. His legs—and he was all leg, under the white shorts—were solid as trees. The only looseness in him anywhere was in his speech—a slight slur from being stoned. The necklace of tiny shells he had gotten in the Philippines, back in the days when he was a black belt in karate who repaired cameras for a living, dangled like a noose under one of the gondoliers' heads. He and Holly had been lovers once for a couple of weeks.

That afternoon Todd and I floated far from shore in the state park, in a rented rowboat. "She had a breech birth and a Caesarean and she's seeing a shrink twice a week and she still has a problem with drugs," he said. "Permission. Is she kidding? What could I stop her from doing, anyway?" The boat bobbed over a ripple of water. "Permission," he said. "Has she ever heard of the women's movement?"

When our boat drifted near the shoreline, I saw a tree branch curving into the lake—the split branch of a dogwood among pointed firs. Looking down into the water, I was sure that I could follow the slant of the shadow to the bottom, but I had dived into this water—I had mistaken eighteen or twenty feet for only six. The breeze was blowing, making the surface of the water ripple like patterns of lace.

"If she really needs my help," Todd said, "I could give her some advice on marketing pottery. When our aunt dies, she'll come into some inheritance money. I've been looking into debentures," he said.

Before I left for Vermont, I bought an answering machine. My friend Linda goes over to the apartment every four or five days to water the plants and listen to the tape, to see if there are any important messages. Last week she called and said that there was one she ought to play for me. She put the machine on playback and held the telephone to the microphone. It was Jason, the first message in so many months that I'd lost count: "Hello, machine. This is the voice you wanted to hear. It's calling to ask if you want to meet me for dinner. Or lunch. Or breakfast. I'm backing up, as you can tell. Doesn't this thing ever run out of tape? It's eleven o'clock Sunday morning, and I'm at the Empire Diner." A pause. Quietly: "I miss you."

"The aloe has white flies," Linda said. "I've never known an aloe to get white flies. I sprayed it with the thing from the kitchen sink, and when I go back next week, I'll zap it with bug spray."

On Monday, after Linda called, I walked down the driveway to shovel some of the gravel that had been delivered into the potholes that had deepened over the winter. I got the shovel from where it leaned against the tree, flicked caterpillars off the handle, and started digging into the pile of gravel, thinking that I shouldn't call Jason back. He didn't say he was leaving her. If I did something physical, I might not think about it. The mailman came, and I took the pile of letters. And there it was, on top: the letter from Ash, the one we all knew he'd write. Ash, with no phone, in Tennessee. Ash without Holly.

I walked to the high hedge of purple lantana—as impossible that lantana would thrive in Vermont as that an aloe would get white flies—and did one of the most awful things I've ever done. I read the letter. I slit the envelope carefully, with the long nail of my index finger, so I could patch it together and feign ignorance when Holly saw that the envelope was ripped. I was thinking of a lie before I even read it. I'd say that there might have been money in it (why would Ash send money?) and someone at the post office held it to the light and . . . No: I'd just put all the mail in the mailbox and let her get it, and look blank. The same expression I got on my face when Jason talked about himself and his wife doing the things of ordinary life. Jason had gone to get the Sunday paper. Hundreds of miles away, he had eaten French toast—that was what he always ordered at the Empire. I could hear the piano playing, see our reflections in the shiny black tabletops that gave us fun-house-mirror faces. A chic, funny place, no place Holly would ever sit with Ash. What he was asking her to do, in the letter, was to be with him. "They're probably poisoning you against me," he wrote, "but they don't know everything. They're in the country with you, but they're city people. They're the kind who cut before they're even sure the bite was from a snake. They'll try to soothe your wounds, but in the end they'll get you. I know that there isn't much for you here, but if you could come down for just a little while, the distance from that incestuous world might do you good. I don't think children are interchangeable, but there's time in life for more than one thing. I've just read a book—here's something your sophisticated friends would like —I was reading a book and I found out that because of the way space curves, there are stars that everybody thinks of as twin stars, but they're really the same one. Are you sure that I'm the naïve country boy Jane and your brother want you to think I am? Come down here, just for a week, and stand at the back door with me when the breeze is blowing and my arm is around you and look up at the sky. Then say yes or no."

A cardinal was in the road. A brightly colored, male cardinal. It stood there like a vulture—a vulture ready to feed on an animal that had been killed. But nothing was dead. The bird was small for a cardinal. No more a real omen than the little piece of paper you pull out of your fortune cookie that misspells something you should believe.

"Ash," I whispered. "How could you?"

I put all the mail in the mailbox but his letter. I ripped that to pieces as I crossed the road. The cardinal flew away. The bee that had been buzzing around me disappeared. The letter was ripped into pieces as tiny as confetti by the time I dropped them in the mud, by the stream, looking behind me for tiny white pieces I might have dropped, as guilty as a murderer whose knife drips blood. He didn't deserve her. He really didn't. That was no illusion; it was a dirty trick that if space curved, you thought that one star was two.

Todd's MG bumped slowly into the driveway. He held up something round and shiny. "Got this at a lawn sale," he said. "Can you believe it? Paella for a hundred, or we could take a bath in it. You know that Degas painting? The woman in the tub?"

I went in and poured some vodka over ice. I sat on the porch, shaking the glass. On the lawn, Todd was cleaning the gigantic pan with steel wool, washing away the dirt with a strong spray from the hose. I remembered making love to Jason at the end of the dock. Diving into the water. The long white hose that stretched from the back of the house to where the boat bobbed in the water—the East Hampton equivalent of the snake in the garden.

Simple, fortune-cookie fact: someone loved Holly more than anyone had ever loved me. Linda called again, four days later, and there was no second message from Jason. I hadn't really expected one.

Linda had sprayed the plant. The plant was sure to recover. She said she took it out of the sun for a few days, because the combination of light and chemicals might be too much.

Holly and I were mistaken for sisters, but she was more beautiful. Our long blond hair. Slender bodies. The way, in the city, people would smile at us with the same lack of embarrassment people have when they smile at twins. Oddities. Beautiful exceptions.

When I found out that I was pregnant, I had thought first about amniocentesis, because a first cousin had had a baby with a slight birth defect. My first impulse was to protect that baby in any way I could. At the end, I had just thought about what it would feel like to have my cervix pricked, the baby sucked out. That crazy romantic lunch—pink petals all over our laps, on the table—and I couldn't tell him. I had on a wrap-around skirt, and he slid his chair close to mine and was teasing, putting his hand underneath it, and I said to him, "I *am* eating, Jason," and "I love you—I can't eat." He wanted to go to my apartment. "I have an appointment," I said. "Tonight," he said. "I can't tonight," I said. "Another night. Some other night." He thought I was kidding. When he called, hours later, expecting to come over, I was lying in my bed, after the abortion, Linda sitting in a chair reading, watching, and I was trying not to sound woozy, in spite of the fact that they'd given me so many pills Linda almost had to carry me from the building to the cab. I had done it because I didn't have the nerve to test him—to find out if he loved me more than he loved his wife. Ash loved Holly, and that went a long way toward explaining why we looked so much alike, yet she was more beautiful. She walked like somebody who was loved. She didn't avoid looking into people's eyes for the same reason I did when she walked through the city. I thought how lucky she was—even though sometimes she could be frighteningly unhappy—the night I held her and rocked her in my lap. I knew for sure that I was right about her good luck a week later, when I stood at the window, about to pull the shades in my room to take a nap, and I looked out and saw Ash's old car, parked at the end of the treacherous driveway, and Ash, running toward the house, a huge torch of red gladiolas raised above his head.

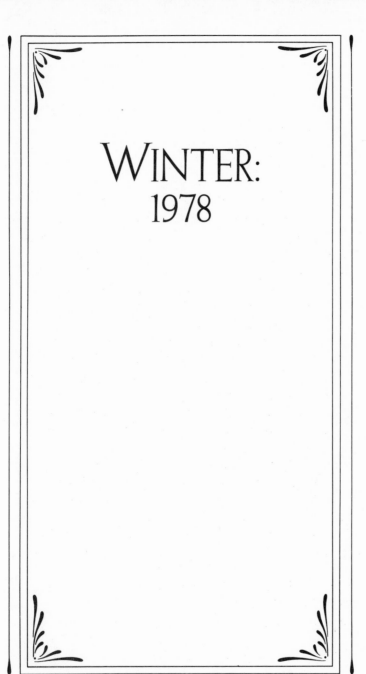

WINTER:
1978

The canvases were packed individually, in shipping cartons. Benton put them in the car and slammed the trunk shut.

"They'll be all right?" the man asked.

"They survived the baggage compartment of the 747, they'll do O.K. in the trunk," Benton said.

"I love his work," the man said to Nick.

"He's great," Nick said, and felt like an idiot.

Benton and Olivia had just arrived in L.A. Nick had gone to the airport to meet them. Olivia said she wasn't feeling well and insisted on getting a cab to the hotel, even though Nick offered to drive her and meet Benton at Allen Tompkins's house later.

The man who had also come to the airport to meet Benton was Tompkins's driver. Nick could never remember the man's name. Benton was in L.A. to show his paintings to Tompkins. Tompkins would buy everything he had brought. Benton was wary of Tompkins, and of his driver, so he had asked Nick to meet him at the airport and to go with him.

"How was your flight?" Nick said to Benton. All three of them were in the front seat of the Cadillac.

"It was O.K. We were half an hour late taking off, but I guess they made up the time in the air. The plane was only a few minutes late, wasn't it?"

"Allen and I are flying to Spain for Christmas," the driver said.

On the tape deck, Orson Welles was broadcasting *The War of the Worlds*. Cars seldom passed them; the man drove sixty-five, with the car on cruise control, nervously brushing hair out of his eyes. The last time Nick rode in this car, a Jack Benny show, complete with canned laughter, had been playing on the tape deck.

"An Arab bought the house next door, and he's having a new pool put in. It's in the shape of different flowers: one part of it's tulip-shaped, and the other part is a rose. I asked, and the pool man told me it was supposed to be a rose." The driver kneaded his left shoulder with his right hand. He was wearing a leather strap around his wrist with squares of hammered silver through the middle.

"Have you been to Marbella?" the driver said. "Beverly Hills is the pits. Only *he* would want to live in Beverly Hills."

They were on Allen Tompkins's street. "Hold it," the driver said to Benton and Nick, taking the car off cruise control but slowing only slightly as he pulled into the steep driveway. He hopped out and opened the door on their side of the car.

Benton hesitated a moment before reaching into the trunk. Glued to the underside of the trunk was a picture of Raquel Welch in a sequined gown. With her white teeth and tightly clothed, sequined body she looked like a mermaid in a nightmare.

Benton was in California because Allen Tompkins paid him triple what he could get for his paintings in New York. Benton had met Tompkins years ago, when he had been framing one of his paintings, staying on after his shift at the frame shop in New Haven where he worked was over. Tompkins had asked Benton how much the picture he was working on would cost when it was framed. "It's my painting, not for sale," Benton had told him. Very politely, Tompkins had asked if he had others. That night, Benton called Nick, drunk, raving that a man he had just met had given him a thousand dollars *cash*. He had gone out with Benton the next night, Benton laughing and running from store to store, to prove to himself that the money really bought things. Benton had bought a brown tweed coat and a pipe. That joke had only turned sour when Benton's wife, Elizabeth, commended him for selecting such nice things.

Now, seven years later, Benton was wearing jeans and a black velvet jacket, and they were sitting in Tompkins's library. It was cluttered with antique Spanish furniture, the curtains closed, the room illuminated by lamps with bases in the shape of upright fish that supported huge Plexiglas conch shell globes in their mouths. The lamps cast a lavender-pink light. Three Turkish prayer rugs were lined up across the center of the room—the only floor covering on the white-painted floorboards.

"Krypto and Baby Kal-El," Tompkins said, coming toward them with both hands outstretched. Benton smiled and shook both of Tompkins's hands. Then Nick shook his hand too, certain that any feeling of warmth came from Tompkins's just having shaken hands with Benton.

"I'm so excited," Tompkins said. He went to the long window behind where Benton and Nick sat on the sofa and pulled the string that drew the drapes apart. "Dusk falls on Gotham City," Tompkins said. He sat in the heavily carved chair beside the sofa. "All for me?" he said, raising his eyebrows at the crates. "If you like them," Benton said. The driver came into the library with a bottle of ouzo and a pitcher of orange juice on a tray. He put it on the small table midway between Benton and Tompkins.

"Sit down. Sit down and have a look," Tompkins said excitedly. The man sat on the floor by the crates, leaning against the sofa. Benton took a Swiss Army knife out of his pocket and began undoing the first crate.

"I'm using my special X-ray vision," Tompkins said, "and I love it already."

Tompkins got up and crouched by the open crate, fingers on the top of the frame, obviously enjoying every second of the suspense, before he pulled the picture out.

"Money and taste," the driver said to Nick.

"You could not remember the simplest song lyric," Tompkins said to his driver, slowly drawing out the painting. "Money and *time*," he sighed, pulling the canvas out of the crate. "Money and time," he said again, but this time it was halfhearted; he was interested in nothing but the picture he held in front of him. Benton was always amazed by that expression on Tompkins's face. It made Benton as happy as he had been years before when he and Elizabeth were still married, and it had been his morning routine to go into Jason's bedroom, gently shake him awake, and see his son's soft blue eyes slowly focus on his own.

It was three days after Benton had sold all his paintings to Tompkins, and Nick had gone to the hotel where Olivia and Benton were staying to try to persuade them to go to lunch.

The light came into the hotel room in a strange way. The curtains were hung from brass rings, and between the rings, because the curtains did not quite come to the top of the window, light leaked in. Benton and Olivia kept the curtains closed all day—what they saw of the daylight was a pale band across the paint.

Olivia was lounging on the bed in Benton's boxer shorts and a T-shirt imprinted with a picture of the hotel, and when Nick laughed at her she pointed to his own clothing: white cowboy boots with gold-painted eagles on the toes, white

jeans, a T-shirt with what looked like a TV test pattern on it.
Nick had almost forgotten that he had brought Olivia a
present. He took his hand out of his pocket and brought out
a toy pistol in the shape of a bulldog. He pulled the trigger
and the dog's mouth opened and the bulldog squeaked.

"Don't thank me," Nick said, putting it on the bedside
table with the other clutter. "A blinking red light means that
you have a message," he said. He picked up the phone and
dialed the hotel operator. "Nothing to it," Nick said, patting
Olivia's leg. "Red light blinks, you just pick up the phone
and get your message. If Uncle Nickie can do it, anybody
can."

He tickled Olivia's lips with an uneaten croissant from the
bedside table. He was holding it so she could bite the end.
She did. Nick dipped it in the butter, which had become
very soft, and held it to her mouth again. She puffed on her
joint and ignored him. He took a bite himself and put it back
on the plate. He went to the window and pulled back the
drapes, looking at the steep hill that rose in back of the hotel.

"I wish I lived in a hotel," he said. "Nice soft sheets, bathroom scrubbed every day, pick up the phone and get a
croissant."

"You can get all those things at home," Benton said, wrapping a towel around him as he came out of the bathroom. The
towel was too small. He gave up after several tugs and threw
it over the chair.

"The sheets I slept on last night illustrated the hunt of the
Unicorn. Poor bastard is not only fenced in, but I settled my
ass on him. Manuela does nothing in the bathroom but run
water in the tub and smoke Tiparillos. Maybe on the way
home I'll stop and pick up some croissants." Nick closed the
window. "Christmas decorations are already going up," he
said. He took a bottle of pills out of his pocket and put them
on the table. The label said: "Francis Blanco: 2 daily, as
directed."

"Any point in asking who Francis Blanco is?" Benton said.

"You're hovering like a mother over her chicks," Nick said. "Someday that bottle will grow wings and fly away, and then you'll wonder why you cared so much." Nick clasped his hands behind him. "Francis Blanco just overhauled my carburetor," he said. "You don't have to look far for anything."

In spite of the joke about being Uncle Nickie, Nick was Benton's age and four years younger than Olivia. Nick was twenty-nine, from a rich New England family, and he had come to California four years before and made a lot of money in the record industry. His introduction to the record industry had come from a former philosophy professor's daughter's supplier. In exchange for the unlisted numbers of two Sag Harbor dope dealers, Dex Whitmore had marched Nick into the office of a man in L.A. who hired him on the spot. Nick sent a post card of the moon rising over the freeways to the professor, thanking him for the introduction to his daughter, who had, in turn, introduced him to her yoga teacher, who was responsible for his gainful employment. Dex Whitmore would have liked the continuation of that little joke; back East, he had gone to the professor's house once a week to lead the professor's daughter in "yoga exercises." That is, they had gone to the attic and smoked dope and turned somersaults. Dex had been dead for nearly a year now, killed in a freak accident that had nothing to do with the fact that he sold drugs. He had been waiting at a dry cleaner's to drop off a jacket when a man butted in front of him. Dex objected. The man took out a pistol and put a bullet in his side, shooting through a bottle of champagne Dex had clasped under his arm. Later Dex's ex-wife filed a suit for more money from his estate, claiming that he had been carrying the bottle of champagne because he was on his way to reconcile with her.

Nick hadn't succeeded in getting Benton and Olivia to leave the hotel. He was hungry, so he parked his car and went into a bakery. The cupcakes looked better than the croissants, so he bought two of them and ate them sitting at the counter. It embarrassed him that Benton and Olivia couldn't stay at his house, but the year before, when they were in L.A., his dog had tried to bite Olivia. Ilena, the woman he lived with, also disliked Olivia, and he half thought that somehow she had communicated to the dog that he should lunge and growl.

He peeled the paper off of the second cupcake. One of the cupcakes had a little squirt of orange and red icing on top, piped out to look like maize. The other one had a crooked glob of pale brown, an attempt at a drumstick.

Nick was a friend of long standing, and used to most of Benton's eccentricities—including the fact that his idea of travel was to go somewhere and never leave the hotel. He and Benton had grown up in the same neighborhood. Benton had once supplied Nick with a fake I.D. for Christmas; Nick had turned Benton on to getting high with nutmeg. Each had talked Dorothy Birdley ("most studious") into sleeping with the other. Benton presented Nick as brilliant and sensitive; Nick told her, sitting underneath an early-flowering tree on the New Haven green, that Benton's parents beat him. In retrospect, she had probably slept with them because she was grateful anyone was interested in her: she had bottle-thick glasses and a long pointed nose, and she was very self-conscious about her appearance and defensive about being the smartest person in the high school.

It had been a real surprise for Nick when Benton began to think differently from him—when, home from college at Christmas, Benton had called to ask him if he wanted to go to the funeral parlor to pay his respects to Dorothy Birdley's father. He had never thought about facing Dorothy Birdley again, and Benton had made him feel ashamed for being reluctant. He drove and stayed in the car. Benton went in alone. Then they went to a bar in New Haven and talked about college. Benton liked it, and was going to transfer to the Fine Arts department; Nick hated the endless reading, didn't know what he wanted to study, and would never have had Benton's nerve to buck his father and change from studying business anyway. In other ways, though, Benton had become almost more prudent: "You go ahead," Benton said when the waitress came to see if they wanted another round. "I'll just have coffee." So Nick had sat there and gotten sloshed, and Benton had stayed sober enough to get them home. Then, when they graduated, Benton had surprised him again. He had gotten engaged to Elizabeth. In his letters to him that year, Benton had expressed amusement at how up-tight Elizabeth was, and Nick had been under the impression that Benton was loosening up, that Elizabeth was just a pretty girl Benton saw from time to time. When Benton married her, things started to turn around. Nick, that year, stumbled into a high-paying job in New York; his relationship with his father was better, after they had a falling-out and his father called to apologize. Benton's father, on the other hand, left home; the job Benton thought he'd landed with a gallery fell through, and he went to work as a clerk in a framing store. In December, six months after he married Elizabeth, she was pregnant. Then it was Nick who did the driving and Benton who drank. Coming out of a bar together, the night Benton told Nick that Elizabeth was pregnant, Benton had been so argumentative that Nick was afraid he had been trying to start a fight with him.

"I end up on the bottom, and you end up on the top, after your father tried to talk your mother into shipping you out to his brother's in Montana in high school, you drove him so crazy. Now he's advising you about what stock to buy."

"What are you talking about?" Nick had said.

"I told you that. Your mother told my mother."

"You never told me," Nick said.

"I did," Benton said, rolling down the window and pitching his cigarette.

"It must have been Idaho," Nick said. "My uncle lives in Idaho."

They rode in silence. "I'm not so lucky," Nick said, suddenly depressed. "I might have Ilena's car, but she's in Honolulu tonight."

"What's she doing there?"

"She's with a tea merchant."

"What's she doing with a tea merchant?"

"Wearing orchids and going to pig barbecues. How do I know?"

"Honolulu," Benton said. "I don't have the money to get to Atlantic City."

"What's there?"

"I don't have the money to eat caramel corn and see a horse jump off a pier."

"Have you talked to her about an abortion?" Nick said.

"Sure. Like trying to convince her the moon's a yo-yo."

He rolled down his window again. Wind rushed into the car and blew the ashes around. Nick saw the moon, burning white, out the side window of the car.

"I don't have the money for a kid," Benton said. "I don't have the money for popcorn."

To illustrate his point, he took his wallet out of his back pocket and dropped it out the window. "Son of a bitch, I don't believe it," Nick said. They were riding on the inside lane, fast, and there was plenty of traffic behind them. What seemed to be a quarter of a mile beyond where Benton had thrown his wallet, Nick bumped off the highway, emergency lights flashing. The car was nosed down so steeply on the hill rolling beneath the emergency lane (which he had overshot) that the door flew open when he cracked it to get out. Nick climbed out of the car, cursing Benton. He got a flashlight out of the trunk and started to run back, remembering having seen some sort of sign on the opposite side of the road just where Benton had thrown his wallet. It was bitter cold, and he was running with a flashlight, praying a cop wouldn't come along. Miraculously, he found the wallet in the road and darted for it when traffic stopped. He ran down the median, back to the car, wallet in his pocket, beam from the flashlight bobbing up and down. "God damn it," he panted, pulling the car door open.

The light came on. For a few seconds no cars passed. Everything on their side of the highway was still. Nick's heart felt like it was beating in his back. Benton had fallen up against the door and was slumped there, breathing through his mouth. Nick pulled the wallet out of his pocket and put it on the seat. As he dropped it, it flopped open. Nick was looking at a picture of Elizabeth, smiling her madonna smile.

He drove back to the hotel to get Olivia and Benton for dinner. The lobby looked like a church. There were no lights on, except for dim spotlights over the pictures. Nobody was in the lobby. He went over to the piano and played a song. A man came down the steps into the room, applauding quietly when he finished.

"Quite nice," the man said. "Are you a musician?"

"No," Nick said.

"You staying here, then?"

"Some friends are."

"Strange place. What floor's your friend on?"

"Fourth," Nick said.

"Not him, then," the man said. "I'm on the third, and some man cries all night."

He sat down and opened the newspaper. There was not enough light in the lobby to read by. Nick played "The Sweetheart Tree," forgot how it went halfway through, got up and went into the phone booth. It was narrow and high, and when he closed the wood door he felt like he was in a confessional.

"Father, I have sinned," he whispered. "I have supplied

already strung-out friends with Seconal, and I have been un-
friendly to an Englishman who was probably only lonesome."

He dialed his house. Ilena picked it up.

"Reconsider," he said. "Come to dinner. We're going to
Mr. Chow's. You love Chow's."

"I've got nothing to say to her," Ilena said.

"Come on," he said. "Go with us."

"She's always stoned."

"Go with us," he said.

Ilena sighed. "How was work?"

"Work was great. Exciting. Rewarding. All that I always
hope work will be. The road manager for Barometric Pressure
called to yell about there not being any chicken tacos in the
band's dressing room. Wanted to know whether I did or did
not send a telegram to New York."

"Well," she said. "Now I've asked about work. Only fair
that you ask me about the doctor."

"I forgot," he said. "How did it go?"

"The bastard cauterized my cervix without telling me he
was going to do it."

"God. That must have hurt."

"I see why people go around stoned. I just don't want to
eat dinner with them."

"Okay, Ilena. Did you walk Fathom?"

"Manuela just had him out. I threw the Frisbee for him half
the afternoon."

"That's nice of you."

"I can hardly stand up straight."

"I'm sorry."

"I'll see you later," Ilena said.

He went out of the phone booth and walked up the stairs.
Pretty women never liked other pretty women. He rang the
buzzer outside Benton and Olivia's room.

Benton opened the door in such a panic that Nick smiled,
thinking he was clowning because Nick had told him earlier

that he was too lethargic. It only took a few seconds to figure out it wasn't a joke. Benton had on a white shirt hanging outside his jeans and a tie hanging over his shoulder. Olivia had on a dress and was sitting, still as a mummy, hands in her lap, in a chair with its back to the desk.

"You know that call? The phone call from Ena? You know what the message was? My brother's dead. You know what the hotel told Ena days ago? That I'd checked out. She called back, and today they told her I was here. Wesley is dead."

"Oh, Christ," Nick said.

"He and a friend were on Lake Champlain. They drowned. In November, they were out in a boat on Lake Champlain. Today was the funeral. Why the hell did they tell her I'd checked out? It doesn't matter anymore why they told her that." Benton turned to Olivia. "Get up," he said. "Pack."

"There's no point in my going," she said, her voice almost a whisper. "I'll fly to New York with you and go to the apartment."

"Elizabeth would hate not to see you," Benton said. "She likes to see you and clutch Jason from the hawk."

"Elizabeth is at your mother's?" Nick said.

"Elizabeth misses no opportunity to ingratiate herself with my family. They're not at my mother's. They're at his house, in Weston, for some reason."

"I thought he lived on Park Avenue."

"He moved to Connecticut." Benton slammed his suitcase shut. "For God's sake, I've made plane reservations. Will you pack your suitcase?"

"I'll drive you to the airport," Nick said.

"God damn it," Benton said, "I don't mean to be ungracious, but I realize that, Nick." Benton was packing Olivia's suitcase. He looked at the bedside table and sighed and held the suitcase underneath it and swept everything in. He put a sign about the continental breakfast the hotel served back on the table.

"I really love you," Olivia said, "and when something awful happens, you treat me like shit."

Olivia got up and Nick put his arm around her shoulder and steered her toward the door. Benton came behind them, carrying both suitcases.

"You were lucky you could get a plane this close to Thanksgiving," Nick said.

"I guess I was. Forgot it was Thanksgiving."

"Maybe people don't go home for Thanksgiving anymore," Nick said.

Nick was remembering what Thanksgiving used to be like, and the good feeling he got as a child when the holidays came and it snowed. One Christmas his parents had given him an archery set, and he had talked his father into setting it up outside in the snow. His father had been drunk and had taken a fruit cake from the kitchen counter and put the round, flat cake on top of his head like a hat, and stood to the side of the target, tipping his fruitcake hat, yelling to Nick to shoot it off his head while his mother rapped on the window, gesturing them inside.

"I hope you enjoyed your stay," the woman behind the desk said to Benton.

"Fine," Benton said.

"How you doing?" Dennis Hopper said.

"Fine," the woman behind the desk said. She reached around Benton and handed Dennis Hopper his mail.

The security guard was sitting on a chair drinking a Coke. He was staring at them. Nick hoped that by the time he got them to the airport Olivia would have stopped crying.

"Want to come East and liven up the wake?" Benton said to Nick.

"They don't want to see me," Olivia said. "Why can't I go back to the apartment?"

"You're who I live with. My brother just died. We're going to be with my family."

"I wish I could go," Nick said. "I wish I could act like everybody else in my office—phone in and say I'm having an anxiety attack."

"Come with us," Olivia said, squeezing his hand. "Please."

"I can't just get on a plane," he said.

"If there's a seat," she said.

"I don't know," Nick said. "Are you serious?"

"I'm serious," Benton said. "Olivia's probably as serious as she gets on Valium."

"That was nasty," she said. "I'm not stoned."

"I don't know," Nick said. Olivia looked at him. "About the plane, I mean," he said.

"She misunderstands things when she's stoned," Benton said.

They got into Nick's car and he pulled out onto the narrow, curving road behind the hotel. "I'll call Ilena," Nick said. "Are we going to miss the plane if I go back into the hotel?"

"We've got time," Benton said. "Go on."

He left the car running and went back into the hotel. The security guard was making funny whiny noises and shuffling across the floor, and the girl behind the desk was laughing. She saw him looking at them and called out: "It's an imitation of one of the rabbits in *Watership Down*."

The security guard, amused at his own routine, crossed his eyes and wiggled his nose.

The house in Weston was huge. It was a ten-room house on four acres, the back lawn bordered by massive fir trees, and in front of them thick vines growing large, oblong pumpkins. Around the yard were sunflowers, frost-struck, bent almost in half. Nick squatted to stare at one of their black faces.

He had seen the sunflowers curving in the moonlight when they arrived the night before and Benton's mother, Ena, lit the yard with floodlights; the flowers were just outside the aura of light, and he had squinted before he was able to make out what they were. It was morning now, and he was examining one. He ran his fingers across its rough face.

The reality of Wesley's death hadn't really hit him until he got to the house, walked across the lawn, and went inside. Then, although he hadn't seen Wesley for years, and had never been to the house, Nick felt that Ena didn't belong there, and that Wesley was very far away.

Ena had been waiting for them, and the house had been burning with light—hard to see from the highway, she had told Benton on the phone—but inside there was a horrible pall over everything, in spite of the brightness. He had not been able to get to sleep, and when he had slept, he had dreamed about the gigantic, bent sunflowers. Wesley was dead.

The movie they had shown on the plane, which they stared at but did not listen to, had a scene in it of a car chase through San Francisco, with Orientals smiling in the back seat of a speeding car and waving little American flags. It did not seem possible that such a thing could be happening if Wesley was really dead.

Ena was at the house because she thought that assembling there was a tribute to Wesley—no matter that in the six months he'd lived there he never invited the family to his house, and that the things they saw there now made Wesley more of an enigma And they had already begun to take his things. They obviously felt guilty or embarrassed about it, because when the three of them came in the night before, people began to confess: Elizabeth had taken Wesley's Rapidograph, for Jason; for herself she had taken a dome-shaped paperweight, a souvenir of Texas with a longhorn cow facing down a cowboy with a lasso underwater, in a tableau that would fill with snow when the dome was shaken; Uncle Cal had taken a picture of Ena as a schoolgirl, in a heart-shaped frame. Ena had taken a keyring with three keys on it from Wesley's night table. She did not know what locks the keys fit, because she had tried them on everything in the house with no luck, but they were small antique keys and she wanted to get a chain for them and wear them as a necklace. Wesley was dead, drowned in Lake Champlain, two life vests floating near where the boat capsized, no explanation.

Benton came out of the house. It was a cold morning, and it was early; Nick did not feel too cold because he had found a jacket on a hook by the back door—Wesley's, no doubt—and put it on. Benton, in the black velvet jacket, hugged his arms in front of him.

"I just realized that I dragged you here from California," Benton said. "What are you doing out here?"

"I couldn't sleep. I came out to look around."

"What did you find?"

"Pumpkins still growing in his garden."

At the back of the lawn, past a tangle of leafless berry bushes, was a fallen-down chicken coop. The roof barely cleared their heads. There was a cement floor, and most of the walls were still standing, but they were caving in, or missing boards.

"Long time since this was in operation," Benton said.

"Imagine Wesley out in the country," Nick said.

Most of the back wall was missing from the coop. When they came to the end, Nick jumped down, about five feet, to the ground, and Benton jumped behind him. The woods were covered with damp leaves, thickly layered.

"Although the shape that coop was in, I guess he was hardly the gentleman farmer," Benton said. "What do you think about the way Ena's acting?"

"Ena's edgy."

"She is," Benton said. He pushed a branch out of his face; it was so brittle that it snapped. He used the piece of broken branch to poke at other branches. "I went into Jason's bedroom and thought about kidnapping him. I didn't even have the heart to wake him up to say hello."

"What time was it when you came out?"

"Seven. Seven-thirty."

They saw a white house to their left, just outside the woods, and turned back for Wesley's house. Wind chimes were clinking from a tree beside the chicken coop—long green tubes hitting together.

Nick hadn't seen the chimes when he walked back to the chicken coop earlier. They reminded him of the strange graveyard he and Wesley and Benton had gone through when they were in college and Wesley was a senior in high school, on a trip they took to see a friend who had moved to Charlemont, Massachusetts. It was Christmastime, after a snow, and Benton and Nick had been wearing high rubber boots. Wesley, as usual, had on his sneakers. They had sighted the snowy graveyard, and it had been somebody's idea to walk through it. Wesley had been the first one out of the car, and he had also been the first to sight the broomstick slanted into the ground like a flagpole, with wind chimes hanging from the top of it. It was next to one of the tombstones. There was a deep path leading to it—someone had put it there earlier in the day. It looked crazy—a touch from Mardi Gras, nothing you would expect to see standing in a graveyard. The ground was frozen beneath the snow—the person had dug hard to put the broomstick in, and the chimes tinkled and clanked together in the wind. Wesley had photographed that, and also a tombstone with a larger-than-life dog stretched on top— a Borzoi, perhaps, or some odd cross—and the dog appeared to be looking toward a tree that cast a shadow. There was snow mounded on the dog's head and back, and the tree branches it looked toward were weighted with snow.

"You know that picture Wesley took in the graveyard?" Nick said.

"The dog? The one you told him would make a fine Christmas card?"

Nick nodded yes. "You know what fascinates me about photographs? Did you ever notice the captions? Photographer gets a shot of a dwarf running out of a burning hotel and it's labeled 'New York: 1968.' Or there's a picture of two hump-backed girls on the back of a pony, and it says 'Central Park: 1966.' "

"I remember those, too," Benton said. "I wonder why he never showed them? Nobody else in this family is modest. Even Elizabeth tacks her drawings up alongside Jason's." Benton kicked some moss off his shoe. "It irritated the hell out of him that I'd put my camera on a tripod and wait for the right shot. Remember how he used to carry on about how phony that was?" Benton had stopped to look at some mint, sticking out between the rubble. "He idolized you," Benton said.

"He's dead and I work at Boulevard Records and handle complaints about chicken that doesn't show up," Nick said. "He didn't idolize me."

They were coming closer to the house, and the tinkling of the chimes was faint. They were walking by the pumpkin vines that wove across the ground in front of the tall black-green trees.

Nick was thinking of another one of Wesley's photographs —one he had taken when he and Benton were still in college. The three of them had been in a booth in a restaurant in New Haven, on a Sunday, and Wesley had said, "Don't move." They were waiting for their order, and Nick's hands were resting on the New York *Times*. The picture was pale gray and Nick had been absolutely astonished to see what Wesley had made his hands look like. One hand seemed to be clasping the other as though it was a strange hand. Both hands had been eerily beautiful, the newspaper out of focus beneath them—hands, suspended, with one cradling, or sheltering, the other. When Wesley showed him the photograph he had been so surprised that he couldn't speak. Finally, having had time to think, he said something close to what he meant, but not exactly what he wanted to ask. "How

did you get that softness?" he had asked Wesley, and Wesley
had hesitated. Then he had said: "I developed it in Acufine."

They went quietly into the house and stood by the heat
grate in the kitchen. Nick took down a pan hanging from a
nail in the beam over the stove and filled it with water for
coffee. Then he sat on the kitchen table. The only real detail
they knew of Wesley's death was that the life vests had been
floating near the boat. Ena had told them about it the night
before. The life vests had stopped in time for Nick. She did
not say anything about the color, but Nick knew as she talked
that they were bright orange, and the water was gray and
deep. One floated beside the boat, one farther off. He had to
catch his breath when the image formed. He was as shocked
as if he had been there when they recovered the body.

Benton was finding cups, putting the filter in the coffee
pot. Benton turned off the burner. The bubbles grew smaller.
Steam rose from the pan.

"We're both thinking the same thing, aren't we?" Benton
said. "Capsized boat, life vests floating free, middle of winter."

" 'Lake Champlain: 1978,' " Nick said.

Ena was knitting. The afghan covered her lap and legs and
spilled onto the floor, a wide flame pattern of brown and tan
and green.

"You look like a cowboy, Nickie," she said. "Why do
young men want to look like cowboys now?"

"Leave him alone," Elizabeth said.

"I didn't mean to criticize. I just wanted to know."

"What am I supposed to dress like?" Nick said.

"My husband wore three-piece suits, and ties even on Saturday, and after thirty-five years of marriage he left me to
marry his mistress, by whom he had a five-year-old son."

"Forget it," Uncle Cal said. He was leaning against the

fireplace, tapping his empty pipe against the wood, looking at Ena through yellow-tinted aviator glasses. "Spilled milk," he said. "My brother's a fool, and pretty soon he's going to be an old fool. Then see how she likes him when he dribbles his martini."

"You never got along with him before he left me," Ena said. "You can't feign objectivity."

"Don't talk about it in front of Jason," Elizabeth said.

Jason and Benton had just come inside. Benton had been holding a flashlight while Jason picked the mint Benton and Nick had discovered earlier.

"Pick off the leaves that the frost got, and then we'll tie the stalks with rubber bands and hang them upside down to dry," Benton said.

It had gotten colder outside. The cold had come in with them and spread like a cloud to the living room, where it stayed for a minute until the heat began to absorb it.

"Why do they have to be upside down?"

"So the leaves can't speak and criticize us for picking them."

"You don't hear all that stuff about plants having feelings anymore," Uncle Cal said. "That was a big item, wasn't it? Tomato plants curling their leaves when the guy who'd burned them the day before stuck a book of matches in their face the next day." He lit his pipe.

Squeals from the kitchen as Benton held Jason upside down. "Can you talk upside down?" Benton said. "Talk to Daddy."

Jason was yelling and laughing.

"Put him right side up," Elizabeth said, going and standing in the doorway that separated the kitchen from the living room.

Benton stood Jason back on his feet.

"Aw, Lizzie," Benton said.

"Who's Lizzie?" Jason said.

"She is. Lizzie is a nickname for Elizabeth."

"No one has ever called me Lizzie in my life," Elizabeth said.

Uncle Cal was putting logs in the fireplace. Above the mantel was a poster of the Lone Ranger and Tonto on horseback. Cloudy sky. Mountains behind them. The Lone Ranger was positioned directly in front of a tall cactus, so that it appeared the cactus was rising out of his hat.

"Lizzie is also the nickname for a lizard," Benton said.

"It's nice you're so clever," Elizabeth said to Benton.

"Lizzie loves me," Benton said. He put his thumb to his lip and flipped it forward, blowing her a kiss.

"Beautiful, beautiful," Uncle Cal said. He was admiring the fire, with strong yellow flames crackling out of the logs. Ena had explained to them that there was only wood for one fire, and she had decided to save it until the family could be together. It seemed impossible for everyone to be in the same room at the same time, though, so finally she had told Cal to lay the fire. Benton and Jason were in the kitchen; Olivia was upstairs taking a bath. She was humming loudly.

"I'm going to stay here a while," Ena said. "No one should feel that they have to stay with me."

"I'm staying," Uncle Cal said.

"I've already called Hanley Paulson, and he's delivering more firewood tonight. I can always count on Hanley. I think Wesley would have liked him, and the other people around here. Wesley didn't move here just to take care of me."

"Is there something wrong with you?" Uncle Cal said.

"No. Nothing is wrong with me. He wanted to be closer to me because sometimes I get lonesome."

"Don't tell me you ran down some sob story that made Wesley feel guilty for living in the city," Benton said, coming to the doorway.

"Some people," Ena said, staring at him with eyes hot from the fire, "think about the needs of others without having to be told."

"Christ," Benton said in disgust. "Is that what you did to Wesley?"

"I love it," Uncle Cal said. "I wish I'd never blocked up my fireplace."

"Take down the paneling," Elizabeth said.

"And I wish I'd never painted my living room green," Uncle Cal said.

Nick was playing solitaire. Elizabeth was sitting and looking bored, shifting her eyes from the fireplace to the empty doorway to the kitchen. When things were silent in there too long, she got up to investigate. Benton was holding Jason on his shoulders, and Jason was fastening the bunches of mint to the wooden ceiling beams with tacks.

"Come to kiss us?" Benton said to Elizabeth. "Legend has it that when you stand under mistletoe—or mint—you have to be kissed."

She looked at Jason, grinning as he sat high above them, one bunch of mint left in his hand. She went over to Jason and kissed his hand.

"Kiss Daddy," he said.

Benton was standing with his eyes closed, lips puckered in exaggeration, bending forward.

Elizabeth walked out of the room.

"Kiss him," Jason hollered, and kicked his feet, in damp brown socks, against Benton's chest.

"Kiss him," Jason called again.

Elizabeth sighed and went upstairs, leaving Benton to deal with the situation he'd created. Nick put an ace on top of a deuce and had no more cards to play. He went to the kitchen and poured a shot glass full of bourbon.

"Would anyone else like a drink?" Nick said, coming back into the living room.

"I swore off," Uncle Cal said, tapping his chest.

"Give me whatever you're drinking," Ena said to Nick.

Everyone was ignoring Jason, crying in the kitchen, and Benton, whispering to him.

Nick went into the kitchen to get Ena a drink, and Jason broke away from Benton and tried to kick Nick. When Nick drew away in time, Jason made fists and stood there, crying.

"I'm your friend," Nick said. He put half a shot of bourbon in a glass and filled it with water. He dropped in an ice cube.

"I go to bed at ten," Uncle Cal said.

"Why *can't* I?" Jason screamed in the kitchen.

"Because she's a naked lady. Decency forbids," Benton said. "It will take me one minute to tell her she's been in there long enough."

Olivia was singing very loudly.

"I want to come with you," Jason said.

Benton walked out of the kitchen and went to get Olivia out of her bath. She was doing her Judy Collins imitation, loudly, which she only did when she was stoned. Obviously, she had taken a joint into the bathroom.

Uncle Cal followed Benton up the stairs. It was nine-thirty.

"Early to bed, clears up the head," Uncle Cal said. He was sleeping in Ena's room, on a Futon mattress he had brought with him that he tried to get everyone to try out. Jason liked it best. He used it as a trampoline.

"I don't think Hanley is coming tonight," Ena said. She had gotten herself another drink. The fire was ash. She got out of the chair and turned up the thermostat, and instead of coming back to the living room, she began to climb the stairs, calling to Uncle Cal that he should do yoga exercises in the morning instead of at night, because if his back went out, she wouldn't know whom to call in the middle of the night.

The next evening Nick talked to Ilena. Manuela picked up the phone and started telling him about his messages. He cut her off. Then she told him about what had been delivered that day—as she described it, it was a milk-chocolate top of a woman's body. She and Ilena had stood it up on the kitchen table, and the table was far enough away from the window that the sun wouldn't melt it. Manuela told him not to worry. She read him the message on the card that was enclosed. It was from Mr. Bornstein, a man he vaguely remembered from some party in Beverly Hills. Mr. Bornstein was with Fat Productions. He had another company called Fat Chance.

Ilena got on the phone. "Hi, Nick," she said.

"It's winter here," he said. "You should see it."

"I wasn't invited," she said.

"You hate Olivia," he said. "Anyway—it's not the time to bring somebody new into the house when Wesley just died."

"I wouldn't have come," Ilena said. "I just felt like sulking."

"So what's up?" he said. "You there sulking?"

"My cervix hurts. And somebody stole our hose. Unless you did something with the hose."

"The garden hose? What would I do with it?"

"That's what I thought. So somebody must have stolen it."

"What would they want with it?" he said.

"Strangle a Puerto Rican, maybe."

"How's the dog?" he said.

"He missed you and wouldn't eat, so Manuela poached a chicken for him. The chicken made him forget his grief."

"Good," he said.

"When are you coming back?"

"Pretty soon. Tomorrow or the next day, I guess. I was hoping it would snow."

"That creepy man keeps calling. The one Benton sells his stuff to. He's having a costume party, and he called yesterday to say that somebody was still needed to dress as Commissioner Gordon. Then he called this morning to say that somebody named Turaj was going as Gordon, but he still needed to find somebody to be the mother of Kal-El. Tell me there's not going to be a lot of coke at that party."

"Yeah," Nick said. "I guess that's where the snow is."

"He's so creepy. He gives me the creepy-crawls. I hope he doesn't call here anymore."

"Just tell him that I can't do it."

"That chocolate body in the other room gives me the creeps too."

"Other than that," he said, "is everything all right there?"

"Manuela wanted a raise, so I gave her one."

"Does that mean she's going to clean the bathroom?"

"I told her you didn't like her smoking cigars. She said she wouldn't anymore."

"Great. Sounds like everything will be perfect when I get back."

"What would you know about perfection? I'm perfect, and you don't appreciate me. I don't even have an eroded cervix anymore."

"I hope you feel better soon, Ilena."

"Thanks," she said. "See you when I see you. I might go to Ojai with Perry Dwyer and his sister this weekend."

"Have a good time in Ojai," he said.

They said goodbye and he hung up the kitchen phone. Elizabeth was leaning against the stove, staring at him. He waited for her to say something, but she didn't. She went to the window and looked at Jason and Benton, playing tag in the circle of light in the back yard.

"He must be doing well," she said. "He's been paying child support."

"He's got quite a reputation on the West Coast."

"Do you know the man he sells the paintings to?"

"I saw him again when Benton was in L.A."

"Is he crazy, or does Benton exaggerate?"

"Crazy," Nick said.

Nick stood beside her and watched Benton chugging along, pretending to be running as fast as he could to catch Jason, then moving in comic slow motion.

"That's like the picture," Elizabeth said.

"What is?"

"That."

She was pointing to his hands, folded on the window sill. He felt a tingling in his fingers, as if his hands were about to move.

"Benton told me that picture always embarrassed you," she said. "You know—everybody in this family is embarrassed by beautiful things. That's why Benton never shows Ena or Cal his paintings. Even Benton's given in to it: he made fun of me for putting one of my watercolors up on the bulletin board alongside Jason's. You've probably hung around all these people so long that you've fallen into the pattern."

"I'm not embarrassed by it. It was just a picture he took one day when I was sitting in some diner."

"You look like a holy person when you clasp your hands."

She looked out the window again.

"What did you want to say to me when I was on the phone, Elizabeth?"

"Nothing," she said. "I was being envious. I was thinking how nice it is that he has a friend who'll fly from one coast to the other to pal around with him." She coughed. "And I've always been a little jealous of you—that people study you, photograph you—and they don't pay attention to me." She put her nose against the window. "Saying that Lizzie was a nickname for a lizard," she said.

Benton did not go to Westport with them because Jason acted up. Jason said that Benton had promised that the two of them could play tag. He was about to cry, and Benton had been trying since the day before to get back into Jason's good graces.

After Nick had opened the door on the driver's side of Elizabeth's car, he realized that he had made a silly, macho move. She was sober, and he had been drunk since before he called Ilena. He should have let her drive the car.

Elizabeth was shivering, her scarf over her mouth, staring straight ahead. He couldn't think of anything to say. It had been her idea to get out of the house and go get a drink, and he was surprised that he had agreed. Finally she said something. "Turn right," she said.

He turned, and was on a narrow road he wished she were navigating. "Hard to believe we're an hour outside New York," she said. "It's nice, when it isn't pitch black. This road reminds me of a road that winds in back of my grandmother's house in Pennsylvania."

She reached over and pushed down a lever. The heat came on.

"What kills me is that she knows Hanley Paulson charges outrageous prices for firewood, and she still won't consider having anyone else deliver it because Hanley is an old-timer, and she's so charmed by people who hang on."

She adjusted the heater to low. This time Nick remembered to look at the road, and not at what she was doing. He was trying to remember if he had just been told that his dog was, or was not, eating. A small animal ran in front of the car and made it to the other side. "Again," she said, and pointed for him to turn right.

They went to a bar with a lot of cars parked outside. A man was inside, sitting on a stool, collecting money. "Zenith String Band," he said, although neither of them had asked.

They sat side-by-side behind a small round table. One of the people on stage had broken a string, and another member of the band had stopped playing to pretend to beat him over the head with his fiddle. They ordered bourbon. A curly-haired girl handed another guitar up onto the stage, and everyone was playing together again.

"I hated it that he turned everybody against me," she said. "He was so angry that I wouldn't have an abortion, and look at the way he loves Jason. You'd think he'd be glad I didn't listen to him, but he's still making jokes, and I'm still the villain."

She was speaking quite loudly. The people at the next table were looking at them and pretending not to. He knew he should do something to pass it off, so he gave them a little smile, but he was drunk and the smile spread too far over his face; what he was giving them was an evil smirk.

"What a family. Cal with his mansion on Long Island, never liking what the decorator does, having some goddam vegetarian decorator who paints the walls the color of carrots and turnips. He gives better Christmas presents to his decorator than he does to Jason. Poor Cal, out in East Hampton, and poor Ena, who's staying in Wesley's house when he's dead because he wouldn't have her there when he was alive. The only person in the family worth anything was Wesley."

They sat in silence, drinking, until the set was over. It was slowly starting to sink in that he was not in California—that lantana would not be growing outside when they went out, that it would be dark and cold. He usually said that he loved California, but when he was back East he felt much better. He began to wish for snow again. When the musicians climbed down from the stage he asked for the check. He left money on the table, wondering if he was crazy to suspect that the people at the next table were going to take the money. Since no one ran out of the bar after them in all the time it took to start Elizabeth's car in the cold, he decided that it was paranoia.

He thought that he remembered the way back and was glad

that he did. Elizabeth's eyes were closed. He put on the heater.
Elizabeth put it off.

"It's cold," he said.

"Better ways to keep warm."

He was looking at the speedometer, to make sure he was
driving fast enough. It felt like he was floating. He accelerated
a little, watched the needle climb. Drunken driving.

"Pull over," Elizabeth said, hand over her mouth, other
hand on his wrist. He did, quickly, expecting her to be sick.

Wind blew in the car as she jumped out and ran through
the leaves unsteadily, over to a stone wall. He looked away as
she bent over.

She came back to the car carrying a cat.

"I got myself something nice," she said, shivering.

"It's somebody's cat," he said.

"He might be your friend, but he's a real bastard. Telling
Jason that lizards are called Lizzie."

"Get even with Benton," he said. "Don't get even with me."

She looked at him, and he knew exactly where Jason got
his perturbed expression, the look that crossed his face when
his mother told him that Uncle Cal's mattress was not a toy.

"That's what they're all doing," she said. "They're all at
Wesley's house getting even. Olivia singing in the tub to pretend that everything's cool, Cal being nice to Ena because his
last EKG readout scared him and he wants to be sure she'll
nurse him. Benton playing Daddy. That one really kills me."

The cat hopped into the back seat. He looked at it. Its eyes
were glowing.

"What I like about animals is that they're not pretentious,"
she said.

"You've taken somebody's cat," he said.

She was pathetic and ridiculous, but neither of those things
explained why the affection he felt for her was winning out
over annoyance. He couldn't remember if she had proposi-

tioned him, or if he had just imagined it. He put his head against the window. It seemed like a situation he would have found himself in in college. It was a routine from years ago. He took her hand.

"This is silly," he said.

He did not know her license-plate number, so he put down *?—#! on the registration form. Then, realizing what he had done, he blacked that out and wrote in a series of imaginary numbers.

The motel was on Route 58, just off the Merritt Parkway. He was careful to notice where he was, because he thought that when he went out to the parking lot, she might simply have driven away. He gave the woman his credit card, got it back, slipped the room key across the counter until it fell off the edge into his hand instead of trying to pick it up with his fingers, and went out to the parking lot. She was in the car, holding the cat. He knocked on her window. She got out of the car. The cat, in her arms, looked all around.

"I know where there's an all-night diner," she said drunkenly.

"You seem to know your way around very well."

"I used to come see Wesley," she said.

She said it matter-of-factly, climbing the stairs in back of him, and at first he didn't get it. "And I know for a fact that he didn't intend to use all the servicemen Ena used, and that when he had wood delivered it wasn't going to be the famous Hanley Paulson who brought it," she said, as he put the key in the lock and opened the door. "He might have left New York to nursemaid Ena, but he was only going so far. He was a nice person, and people took advantage of him."

He held her. He put his arms around her back and hugged her. This was Benton's ex-wife, Wesley's lover, standing in front of him in a black sweater and black silk underpants, and instead of its seeming odd to him, it only made him feel left out that he was the only one who had no connection with her.

"Who was the man who drowned with him?" she said, as if Nick would know. "Nobody he cared about, because I never heard of him. I didn't even know he was Wesley's friend."

The cat was watching them. It was sitting in a green plastic chair, and when he looked at the cat, the cat began to lick its paw. Elizabeth drew away from him to see why he had stopped stroking her back.

"Would you like to forget about it and go to the diner?" she said.

"I was thinking about the cat," he said. "We ought to return the cat."

"If you want to return the cat, you go return the cat."

"We can do it later," he said.

Later, he got hopelessly lost looking for the road where they had gotten the cat. He thought that he had found just the place, but when he got out of the car he saw that there was no stone wall. He carried the cat back to the car and consulted Elizabeth. She had no idea where they were. Finally he had to backtrack all the way to the bar and find the road from there that they had been on earlier. He got out of the car, carrying the cat. He dropped it on the stone wall. It didn't move.

"It wants to go with us," Elizabeth called out the window.

"How do you know?" he said. He felt foolish for asking, for assuming that she might know.

"Bring it back," she said.

The cat sat and stared. He picked it up again and walked back to the car with it. It jumped out of his arms, into the back seat.

"What he says to Jason is very clever," Elizabeth said, as he started the car. "I'd be amused, if Jason weren't my son."

When he found out that she and Wesley had been lovers, it had been clear to him that she was sleeping with him to exorcise Wesley's ghost, or to get even with him for dying; now he wondered if she had told him to go to the motel to get even with Benton, too.

"If you want Benton to know about what happened tonight, you're going to have to tell him yourself. I'm not telling him," he said.

Her face was not at all the face in the picture of Benton's wallet from years ago. Her eyes were shut as if she were asleep, but her face was not composed.

"I didn't mean to insult you," he said. "I'm sorry."

"I'm used to it," she said. She rummaged in her purse and pulled her brush out and began brushing her hair. "If the family had known about Wesley and me, they'd write that off as retaliation, too. They love easy answers."

They were on the road that led to the house, passing houses that stood close to the road. There was nothing in California that corresponded to the lights burning in big old New England houses at night. It made him want to live in this part of the world again, to be able to drive and see miles of dark fields. The apple orchards, the low rock walls, the graveyards. A lot of people went through them, and it did not mean that they were preoccupied with death. The car filled with light when a car with its high beams on came toward them. For a few seconds he saw his hands on either side of the wheel and thought, sadly, that what Wesley had seen about them had never come true.

"At the risk of being misunderstood as looking for sympathy, there's one other thing I want to tell you about Benton," Elizabeth said. "He used to put his camera on his tripod and take pictures of Jason when he was an infant—roll after roll. He'd stand by his crib and take pictures of Jason when he was sleeping. I remember asking him why he was taking so

many pictures when Jason's expression wasn't changing, and
you know what he said? He said that he was photographing
light."

Déjà vu: Ena with the afghan, Uncle Cal circling figures on
the stock page, knocking his empty pipe against the old wooden
chest in front of the sofa with the regular motion of a metro-
nome, Elizabeth reading a book, her feet tucked primly beneath her, coffee steaming on the table by her chair.

"Went out and got drunk," Uncle Cal said in greeting. "I
couldn't." He tapped his shirt pocket. It made a crinkling
noise. Pipe cleaners stuck out of the pocket, next to a pack of
cigarettes.

Elizabeth was reading *A Tale of Two Cities*. She continued
to read as if he hadn't come into the room. The cat was curled
by the side of the chair.

"Hanley Paulson isn't coming," Elizabeth said.

"We can go to lunch and leave him a note and the check,"
Uncle Cal said.

"That would be just fine," Ena said. "He's not a common
delivery person—he's a friend of long standing."

"Maybe someone told him Wesley was dead, and he isn't
coming."

"I called him," Ena said. "Not Wesley."

"Wesley wouldn't have paid seventy-five dollars for half a
cord of wood," Elizabeth said.

"Everyone is perfectly free to go out," Ena said.

Nick went into the kitchen. He saw Benton and Jason and
Olivia, all red-cheeked, with puffs of air coming out of their
mouths. They were playing some sort of game in which they
came very close to Olivia and ducked at the last second, so
she couldn't reach out and touch them. The sky was gray-
white, and it looked like snow. Olivia was loosening the scarf
around her neck and lighting one of her hand-rolled narrow

cigarettes. Either that, or she had stopped caring and was smoking a joint. He watched her puff. A regular cigarette. Olivia's jeans were rolled to the knee, and the bright red socks she wore reminded him of the large red stocking his uncle had hung by the mantel for him when he was young. "Let's see Santa fill that," his uncle had laughed, as the toe of the stocking grazed the hearth. In the morning, his usual stocking was in the toe of the large stocking, and his father was glaring at his uncle. His father did not even like his brother—how could he have wanted to send him to live with him?

Uncle Cal came into the kitchen and took cheese out of the refrigerator.

"I'm going to grill some French bread with cheese on top," he said. "Will anyone share my lunch?"

"Give me whatever you're having," Ena said.

"No, thank you," Elizabeth said.

"Not good for me, but I love it," Uncle Cal said to Nick. "You?"

"Sure," Nick said.

"You watch it so it doesn't get too brown," Uncle Cal said, smoothing Brie over the two halves of bread. "I'm going out for a second to clear my lungs."

Nick looked out the window. Uncle Cal was bending forward, cupping his hands, lighting a cigarette. He had only taken one puff when a car pulled into the driveway.

"Is that Hanley's truck?" Ena called.

"It's just a car," Nick said.

"I hope it isn't someone coming to express sympathy unannounced," Ena said. She was still wearing her pajamas, and a quilted Chinese coat.

Nick watched as a boy got out of the car and Benton went to talk to him. Benton and the boy talked for a while, and then Benton left him standing there, Jason circling his car with one arm down, one arm high, buzzing like a plane. Benton pushed open the kitchen door.

"Where do you want the wood stacked?" he called.

"Is that Hanley Paulson?" Ena asked, getting up.

"It's his son. He wants to know where to put the wood."

"Oh, dear," Ena said, pulling off her jacket and going to the closet for her winter coat. "Outside the kitchen door where it will be sheltered, don't you think?"

Benton closed the kitchen door.

"Where's Hanley?" Ena said, hurrying past Nick. Still in her slippers, she went onto the lawn. "Are you Hanley's son?" Nick heard her say. "Please come in."

The boy walked into the kitchen behind Ena. He had a square face, made squarer by dirty blond bangs, cut straight across. He stood in the kitchen, hands plunged in his pockets, looking at Ena.

"Where would you like the wood, ma'am?" he said.

"Oh," she said, "well, Hanley always stacks it at my house under the overhang by the kitchen door. We can do the same thing here, don't you think?"

"It's ten dollars extra for stacking," the boy said.

When the boy left the kitchen, Ena went out behind him. Nick watched her standing outside the door as the boy went to his car and backed it over the lawn. He opened the back hatch and began to load the wood out.

"This is very dry wood?" Ena said.

"This is what he gave me to deliver," the boy said.

Jason put his arms up for a ride, and Benton plopped him on his shoulders. Jason's dirty shoes had made streaks down the front of Benton's jacket. Uncle Cal put his arm through Olivia's, and the two of them began to walk toward the back of the property. Nick watched Ena as she looked first toward Uncle Cal and Olivia, then to Benton and Jason, charging a squirrel, Benton hunching forward like a bull.

"Everyone has forgotten about lunch," Ena said, coming back into the kitchen. She broke off a piece of the cooked bread and took a bite. She put it on the counter and poured herself a drink, then went back into the living room with the piece of bread and the glass of bourbon and sat in her chair, across from Elizabeth.

"Hanley Paulson would have come in for coffee," Ena said. "I don't know that I would have wanted that young man in for coffee."

Nick tore off a piece of bread and went into the living room. Ena was knitting. Elizabeth was reading. He thought that he might as well get the plane that night for California. He got up to answer the phone, hoping it was Ilena, but Elizabeth got up more quickly than he, and she went into the dining room and picked it up. She spoke quietly, and he could only catch a few words of what she said. Since Ena could hear no better than he could, he did not think she was crying because the phone calls expressing sympathy about Wesley's death made her remember. He felt certain that she was weeping because of the way things had worked out with Hanley Paulson's son. It was the first time he had ever seen Ena cry. She kept her head bent and sniffed a little. Elizabeth was on the phone a long while, and after a few deep sniffs Ena finally raised her head.

"How do your parents like Scottsdale, Nickie?" she said.

"They like it," he said. "They always wanted to get away from these cold winters."

"The winter is bad," Ena said, "but the people have great character. At least they used to have great character." She began to knit again. "I can't imagine why Cal would leave that fabulous house in Essex for that monstrosity in East Hampton. You always liked it here, didn't you, Nickie?"

"I was hoping it would snow," he said. "But I guess with just my cowboy suit, I'm not really prepared for it."

Uncle Cal came into the living room and asked Ena if he

should tip Hanley Paulson's son. Ena told him that she didn't see why, but Nick could tell from Uncle Cal's expression that he intended to do it anyway.

"He wants to know if it's all right to take a few of the pumpkins," Uncle Cal said. Before Ena answered, he said: "Of course I told him to help himself."

"We're going to play baseball," Jason shouted, running into the living room. "And I'm first at bat, and you're first base, and Nick can pitch."

Olivia came in and sat down, still in her coat, shivering.

"You don't mind, do you?" Uncle Cal said to Ena. "He's just taking a few pumpkins we don't have any use for."

"Come on," Jason said, tugging Nick's arm. "Please."

"Leave him alone if he doesn't want to do what you want him to do, Jason," Elizabeth said. She had just come back into the room.

"Who was that on the phone?" Ena said. She took a drink of bourbon. Nick noticed that she had put a sprig of mint in the glass.

"That person named Richard. He read something from a book called *An Exaltation of Larks*." Elizabeth shook her head. "He's the one you call The Poet, isn't he, Cal? Wasn't the man who called two days ago and read that long poem by Donne named Richard?"

"It's not a practice I've ever heard of," Ena said. "I think it was the same man."

"Come on," Jason whined to Elizabeth. "Aren't you going to come out and play baseball?"

"I wasn't invited."

"You're so touchy," he said. "You're invited. Come on."

Nick and Elizabeth got their coats and walked out the back door into the cold. Benton had found a chewed-up baseball bat in the back of the garage, and a yellow tennis ball. As they got into position to play, Hanley Paulson's son passed through the game area, carrying an armful of pumpkins. The back hatch of his car was open, and there were already about a dozen pumpkins inside. He closed the hatch and started the car and bumped down the driveway, raising his fist and shaking it from side to side when Uncle Cal waved goodbye.

Looking at his watch, Nick wondered if it could be possible that the boy had stacked all the wood and gathered the pumpkins in only half an hour. It was amazing what could be accomplished in half an hour.

The night before Nick left for L.A., there was a big dinner. Ena cooked it, saying that it was to make up for the Thanksgiving dinner she hadn't felt like fixing. Everyone said that this dinner was very good and that on Thanksgiving no one had been hungry.

"I would have made a pumpkin pie, but the pumpkins disappeared," Ena said, looking across the table at Uncle Cal.

"What do you mean?" he said. "The kid took two or three pumpkins. There must be a dozen left out there."

"He took all the pumpkins," Ena said.

"You're being ridiculous," Uncle Cal said. "Where's the flashlight? I'll go out and get you a pumpkin."

Uncle Cal and Ena were both drunk. She had not wanted to make a pie, and he did not want to go outside in the cold to shine a flashlight into the pumpkin patch.

"I was mistaken," Ena said finally. "I thought you had given him all the pumpkins."

"He got them himself," Uncle Cal said. "I didn't give him anything. I let him round them up." He cut into his roast beef. "He was just a kid," he said.

"Olivia hasn't touched her roast beef," Ena said.

"You talk about me as though I'm not here," Olivia said.

"What does she mean?" Ena said.

"I mean that you don't address me directly. You talk *about* me, as though I'm not here."

"I realize that you are here," Ena said.

"I'm enjoying this roast beef," Uncle Cal said. "If Morris could see me now, he'd die. Morris is my decorator. Doesn't eat meat. Talks about it all the time, though, so that you'd think there were plates of meat all over *reminding* him about how much *meat* there was in the world."

"Your decorator," Olivia said.

"Yes?" Uncle Cal said.

"Don't be pissy," Benton said.

"I don't think anybody even remembers why we're here. It seems to me that this is just another family gathering where everybody lolls around by the fireplace and drinks." Olivia took a sip of her wine. Nick winced, because he had seen her taking Valium in the kitchen before dinner.

"That's uncivilized," Ena said.

"*This* is uncivilized," Olivia said.

Nick had expected one of them—probably Olivia—to begin crying. But it was Jason who began to cry, and who ran from the table.

Elizabeth had left the table to go after Jason, and Benton had followed her upstairs without saying anything else to Olivia.

"You said what you thought," Uncle Cal said to Olivia. "Nothing wrong with that."

Olivia got up and stalked away from the table.

"She did what she felt like doing," Uncle Cal said to Ena. "Nothing wrong with that."

"Oh, nothing's wrong with anything, is it?" Ena said to Cal.

"My heart," he said. "You should see that last EKG. Looked like an ant's-eye view of the Himalayas, where there should have been a pretty straight line. Of course you have a straight line, straight as a piece of string, you're dead. It should have been bumpy, I mean—but not like it was."

"Then what are you doing yoga for?" Ena said. "You'll kill yourself twisting into all those stupid positions."

"Probably going to be dead anyway," Uncle Cal said, tapping his pocket.

"Stop being morose," Ena said.

"Might stop being anything," Cal said.

"Stop worrying about your *health*," Ena said. "It's what's in the cards. Wesley was a young man, and he drowned."

"That was an accident," Uncle Cal said. "An accident."

"It wasn't any accident," Olivia hollered from the living room.

"It *was*," Elizabeth said. She had come downstairs again, and she looked like she was about to murder somebody.

"Elizabeth—" Nick said.

Elizabeth sat down and smoothed her skirt and smiled to show that she was all right, calm and all right. Then she began to cry.

Nick got up and put his arm around her, sitting on his heels and crouching by her chair. He said her name again, but it didn't do any good. It hadn't done any good the night before, either, in the motel room.

Upstairs, Jason was pretending to be a baby. Benton had gotten him into his pajamas and had taken the sheet from the bed and was holding Jason, sheet thrown around him like a huge poncho, facing the window. Jason was afraid, and he was trying to pretend that it was animals he was afraid of. He wanted to know if there were bears in the woods. "Not around here," Benton said. Fox, then? Maybe—"but they don't attack people. Maybe none around here, anyway." Jason wanted to know where all the animals came from.

"You know where they came from. You know about evolution."

"I don't know," Jason said. "Tell me."

"Tell you the whole history of evolution? You think I went to school yesterday?"

"Tell me something," Jason said.

Benton told him this fact of evolution: that one day dinosaurs shook off their scales and sucked in their breath until they became much smaller. This caused the dinosaurs' brains to pop through their skulls. The brains were called antlers, and the dinosaurs deer. That was why deer had such sad eyes, Benton told Jason—because they were once something else.

GRAVITY

My favorite jacket was bought at L. L. Bean. It got from
Maine to Atlanta, where an ex-boyfriend of mine found it at
a thrift shop and bought it for my birthday. It was a little tight
for him, but he was wearing it when he saw me. He said that
if I had not complimented him on the jacket he would just
have kept it. In the pocket I found an amyl nitrite and a Hershey's Kiss. The candy was put there deliberately.

In the eight years I've had it, I've lost all the buttons but
the top one—the one I never button because nobody closes the
button under the collar. Four buttons are gone, but I can
only remember how the next-to-last one disappeared: I saw
it dangling but thought it would hold. Later, crouched on the
floor, I said, "It stands to reason that since I haven't moved
off this barstool, it has to be on the floor *right here*," drunkenly staring at the floor beneath my barstool at the Café
Central.

Nick, the man I'm walking with now, couldn't possibly
fit into the jacket. He wishes that I didn't fit into it, either.
He hates the jacket. When I told him I was thinking about

buying a winter scarf, he suggested that rattails might go with the jacket nicely. He keeps stopping at store windows, offering to buy me a sweater, a coat. Nothing doing.

"I'm going crazy," Nick says to me, "and you're depressed because you've lost your buttons." We keep walking. He pokes me in the side. "Buttons might as well be marbles," he says.

"Did you ever play marbles?"

"Play marbles?" he says. "Don't you just look at them?"

"I don't think so. I think there's a game you can play with them."

"I had cigar boxes full of marbles when I was a kid. Isn't that great? I had marbles and stamps and coins and *Playboy* cutouts."

"All at the same time?"

"What do you mean?"

"The stamps didn't come before the *Playboy* pictures?"

"Same time. I used the magnifying glass with the pictures instead of the stamps."

The left side of my jacket overlaps the right, and my arms are crossed tightly in front of me, holding it closed. Nick notices and says, "It's not very cold," putting an arm around my shoulders.

He's right. It isn't. Last Friday afternoon, the doctor told me I was going to have to go to the hospital on Wednesday, the day after tomorrow, to have a test to find out if some blockage in a Fallopian tube has been causing the pain in my left side, and I'm a coward. I have never believed anything in *The Bell Jar* except Esther Greenwood's paranoid idea that when you're unconscious you feel pain and later you forget that you felt it.

He's taken his arm away. I keep tight hold on my jacket with one hand and put my other hand around his wrist so he'll take his hand out of his pocket.

"Give me the hand," I say. We walk along like that.

The other buttons fell off without seeming to be loose. They came off last winter. That was when I first fell in love with Nick, and other things seemed very unimportant. I thought then that during the summer I'd sew on new buttons. It's October now, and cold. We're walking up Fifth Avenue, just a few blocks away from the hospital where I'll have the test. When he realizes it, he'll turn down a side street.

"You're not going to die," he says.

"I know," I say, "and it would be silly to be worried about anything short of dying, wouldn't it?"

"Don't take it out on me," he says, and steers me onto Ninety-sixth Street.

There are no stars this evening, so Nick is talking about the stars. He asks if I've ever imagined the thoughts of the first astronomer turning the powerful telescope on Saturn and seeing not only the planet but rings—smoky loops. He stops to light a cigarette.

The chrysanthemums planted down the middle of Park Avenue are just a blur in the dark. I think of de Heem's flowers: move close to one of his paintings and you see a snail curled on the wood, and tiny insects coating the leaves. It happens sometimes when you bring flowers in from the garden—a snail that looks and feels like pus, climbing a stem.

Last Friday, Nick said, "You're not going to die." He got out of bed and moved me away from the vase of flowers. It was the day I had gone to the doctor, and then we went away to visit Justin for the weekend. (Ten years ago, when Nick started living with Barbara, Justin was their next-door neighbor on West Sixteenth Street.) Everything was lovely, the way it always is at Justin's house in the country. There was a vase of phlox and daisies in the bedroom, and when I went

to smell the flowers I saw the snail and said that it looked
like pus. I wasn't even repelled by it—just sorry it was there,
curious enough to finger it.

"Justin's not going to know what you're crying about. Justin
doesn't deserve this," Nick whispered.

When touched, the snail did not contract. Neither did it
keep moving.

Fact: her name is Barbara. She is the Boulder Dam. She is
small and beautiful, and she has a hold on him even though
they never married, because she was there first. She is the
Boulder Dam.

Last year we had Christmas at Justin's. Justin wants to think
of us as a family—Nick and Justin and me. His real family
is one aunt, in New Zealand. When he was a child she made
thick cookies for him that never baked through. Justin's ideas
are more romantic than mine. He thinks that Nick should
forget Barbara and move, with me, into the house that is for
sale next door. Justin, in his thermal slippers and knee-high
striped socks under his white pajamas, in the kitchen brew-
ing Sleepytime tea, saying to me, "Name me one thing more
pathetic than a fag with a cold."

Barbara called, and we tried to ignore it. Justin and I ate
cold oranges after the Christmas dinner. Justin poured champagne. Nick talked to Barbara on the phone. Justin blew
out the candles, and the two of us were sitting in the dark,
with Nick standing at the phone and looking over his shoulder into the suddenly darkened corner, frowning in confusion.

Standing in the kitchen later that night, Nick had said,
"Justin, tell her the truth. Tell her you get depressed on
Christmas and that's why you get drunk. Tell her it's not
because of one short phone call from a woman you never
liked."

Justin was making tea again, to sober up. His hand was
over the burner, going an inch lower, half an inch more . . .

"Play chicken with him," he whispered to me. "Don't you be the one who gets burned."

A lady walks past us, wearing a blue hat with feathers that look as if they might be arrows shot into the brim by crazy Indians. She smiles sweetly. "The snakes are crawling out of Hell," she says.

In a bar, on Lexington, Nick says, "Tell me why you love me so much." Without a pause, he says, "Don't make analogies."

When he is at a loss—when he is lost—he is partly lost in her. It's as though he were walking deeper and deeper into a forest, and I risked his stopping to smell some enchanted flower or his finding a pond and being drawn to it like Narcissus. From what he has told me about Barbara, I know that she is deep and cool.

Lying on the cold white paper on the doctor's examining table, I tried to concentrate not on what he was doing but on a screw holding one of the four corners of the flat, white ceiling light.

As a child, I got lost in the woods once. I had a dandelion with me, and I used it, hopelessly, like a flashlight, the yellow center my imaginary beam. My parents, who might have saved me, were drunk at a back-yard party as I kept walking the wrong way, away from the houses I might have seen. I walked slower and slower, being afraid.

Nick makes a lot of that. He thinks I am lost in my life. "All right," I say as he nudges me to walk faster. *"Everything's symbolic."*

"How can you put me down when you make similes about everything?"

"I do not," I say. "The way you talk makes me want to put out my knuckles to be beaten. You're as critical as a teacher."

. . .

The walk is over. He's even done what I wanted: walked the thirty blocks to her apartment, instead of taking a cab, and if she's anxious and looking out the window, he's walked right up to the door with me, and she'll see it all—even the kiss.

It amazes him that at the same time variations of what happens to Barbara happen to me. She had her hair cut the same day I got mine trimmed. When I went to the dentist and he told me my gums were receding slightly, I hoped she'd outdo me by growing fangs. Instead, when my side started to hurt she got much worse pains. Now she's slowly getting better, back at the apartment after a spinal-fusion operation, and he's staying with her again.

Autumn, 1979. On the walk we saw one couple kissing, three people walking dogs, one couple arguing, and a cab-driver parked in front of a drugstore, changing from a denim jacket to black leather. He pulled on a leather cap, threw the jacket into the back seat, and drove away, making a U-turn on Park Avenue, headed downtown. One man looked at me as if he'd just found me standing behind the counter of a kissing booth, and one woman gave Nick such a come-on look that it made him laugh before she was even out of ear-shot.

"I can't stand it," Nick says.

He doesn't mean the craziness of New York.

He opens the outside door with his key, after the kiss, and for a minute we're squeezed together in the space between locked doors. I've called it jail. A coffin. Two astronauts, strapped in on their way to the moon. I've stood there and felt, more than once, the lightness of a person who isn't being kept in place by gravity, but my weightlessness has been from sadness and fear.

Barbara is upstairs, waiting, and Nick doesn't know what to say. I don't. Finally, to break the silence, he pulls me to him.

He tells me that when I asked for his hand earlier, I called it "the hand."

His right hand is extended, fingers on the bone between my breasts. I look down for a second, the way a surgeon must have a moment of doubt, or even a moment of confidence, looking at the translucent, skin-tight rubber glove: his hand and not his hand, about to do something important or not important at all.

"*Anybody* else would have said 'your hand,'" Nick says. "When you said it that way, it made it sound as if my hand was disembodied." He strokes my jacket. "You've got your security blanket. Let me keep all the parts together. On the outside, at least."

Disembodied, that hand would be a symbol from Magritte: a castle on a rock, floating over the ocean; a green apple without a tree.

Alone, I'd know it anywhere.

SUNSHINE
AND
SHADOW

The woods Jake and Laura Ann were walking in were a few miles from his aunt's house, in a remote corner of Pennsylvania. His aunt was in Key Biscayne for the winter. The night before, they had trained the car headlights on the stump where she kept a jar with the house key hidden inside. Leaving New York had been a sudden whim; all day he had been thinking about the farm, and when he had mentioned it late at night to Laura Ann she had sprung out of bed and begun dressing, half seriously, half mocking. This was a just punishment for so much fretfulness. He had already complained that he wanted a garage that didn't cheat him. That he wished the damned cleaner would smile less and lose his clothes less often. And snow falling on a Friday night— what was the point, when alternate-side-of-the-street parking couldn't be suspended?

"Come on," she had said. "We act like old people. Let's go to Pennsylvania. It'll be beautiful in the morning with the sun on the snow." It was as predictable as her amazed smile: when she took up things he had halfheartedly instigated, he

would then go along with them, gradually convincing himself that he was doing her a favor. He found himself standing
as she pulled her baggy jeans over the thermal long johns she
slept in and searched through the sweaters in their closet. She
took out the blue turtleneck. Then she stood in front of the
mirror, parting her hair, sticking in a shiny, star-shaped clip
to keep it out of her face. The first time he had brought her
to his aunt's house, ten years before, their last spring vacation
from college, she had been such a city slicker that walking
through the woods she had asked what the red and aqua
tubes were that she saw scattered in the bushes, not knowing
they were shotgun shells.

In the morning they walked through the woods, jeans
tucked into their rubber fishing boots. In front of them,
heaped in the junkyard they had cut through as a shortcut,
were broken pieces of a carrousel: saddles without stirrups
and huge horse heads with frosty eyes and broken teeth. As
she raised the camera to focus, he noticed her diamond
wedding band sparkling. The brim of her hat was pulled low;
it was a real John Wesley Hardin hat, a favorite left over
from the sixties.

"Bracket it," he said.

She moved the camera away from her eye. "Did I ever tell
you about bracketing?" she said.

"I read it in a book, I suppose."

She inched up on the horse heads, as if they might move.
She crouched in the snow. It was quiet; the click disturbed
the woods like a shot.

He loved her amazed smile—the way he could announce
some unexpected piece of information and arouse her curi-
osity. She couldn't believe that he would know a thing like
that—retain a term that didn't even apply to something he
did. . . . When he met her she had been the eager, bright
student of literature, whose professor embarrassed her when

she gave an interpretation of a book in a class and he asked whether she would also climb a ladder by using the spaces between rungs.

They had brought water with them from the city, because his aunt had turned off the water before she left for the winter. It had been a long, tiring day. He drank a glass of cold water, savoring it like brandy, and he stood looking out the living-room window, into the back field. It was Saturday night and she was reading old magazines, pacing around the house, sitting close to the Franklin stove. She walked away from him at the window, and he was ten feet or so away from her, but he felt the distance, that something missing he couldn't put his finger on. He decided it was fatigue: they were both tired from walking so far in the snow. They were listening to one of his aunt's collection of great old records that his aunt did not realize were great. A scratchy "Pennies From Heaven" was playing, and in his mind he played saxophone in the background, his fingers tapping out the notes on the cold windowpane. When he moved his head nose-close to the window he could see the cement driveway, full of cracks and gullies, the part of the driveway where his mother had run a hose into the car and killed herself with carbon monoxide. The spring before, he had noticed that the driveway was now so overgrown that a wild rosebush had sent up dozens of runners.

He saw Laura Ann's reflection in the window, and though he couldn't see the details of her face, he knew them so well that they were as vivid imagined as seen: those large doe eyes, full of wonder. Now there was nothing to indicate that she didn't forgive him for his having had an affair with her friend except those eyes, sad even above a smile. He pressed his forehead to the window and looked at the black, star-covered sky. When he was a child, a friend had told him that the stars were sky stones. It probably explained a lot that he had never gotten any misinformation about sex—only about the stars.

The quilt on top of the blanket was called Sunshine and Shadow. It had been on this bed as long as he could remember, but it was only lately, in the city, when quilts became fashionable, that he had found out the name of the pattern. It was a quilt begun by his grandmother and finished by his mother and his aunt. He had stared at it when he was a child: squares of differing sizes, alternately light and dark—a diamond pattern radiating from the smallest gray square in the center. He had hypnotized himself into dizziness studying the pattern and come to no conclusions, the way he had stared at inanimate objects years ago when he was tripping. Whatever revelations he had were long gone; he couldn't paraphrase them, so he didn't know how to talk about them. He could remember things he had thought about, but he couldn't remember his conclusions. Or, if he could, they no longer seemed to have any context.

Laura Ann was lying next to him in bed, breathing quietly, deep in sleep. The light was coming up. The star-shaped barrette had almost worked its way loose; her long, curly hair was spread around her on the pillow like a Vargas girl's in *Playboy*, but instead of being picture-pretty, her face was puffy from sleep. He kissed the tip of a curl and wondered if he loved her. On a trip to Pennsylvania a year ago, they had built a snowman, and while he chipped away, trying to make it anatomically correct below its snow belly, she had worked equally hard to pile on breasts. Somewhere in the woods, behind the junkyard, until it melted, there had been a hermaphroditic snowman.

He put his cheek against her hair, trying to think about all the strange, funny times he had had with Laura Ann, trying to forget his ex-lover. Awake, Laura Ann was often as quiet about things as she was now, in sleep, but not deliberately secretive. She had begun a course in photography during her lunch hour. He had seen the little gray plastic film container on a table and asked about it. She was going to study photography, she had said simply. Just another thing she had considered, and acted on, without ever mentioning it. His anger had been childish, saying that photography made everything into potential art, that there were easy shots sure to succeed. "You're not the first one to come up with that," she had said.

What she had not said was that knowing odd facts could be an equally cheap trick: why Bill Monroe fired Richard Greene; who made the first chocolate-chip cookie; the way to get dried wax off of candlesticks. He had always remembered odd facts, trying to outshine his brother, Derek, who operated in a fog and always came out in the clear. He rolled over and remembered advice from his shrink: Don't fall asleep thinking bad thoughts about yourself. He remembered apologizing to Laura Ann for condemning photography by showing an interest in her recent prints, and the irregular black borders around them. "You chisel out the negative holder," she had said, holding her first finger an inch above the thumb so that he could see the imaginary negative holder. "You print it exactly the way it was shot. Then there's no way you can cheat."

Before he had gone to California the previous spring, he had tried to clear his head about what he wanted. When Derek called from Los Angeles and threw around phrases like "in the money" or "out of the money," discussing closing transactions and sure ways to beat the system, all he could think of was that silliness in *Bonnie and Clyde* when Bonnie and Clyde go to the movies and watch Ginger Rogers and the chorus singing "We're in the Money" in *Gold Diggers of 1933*. Now his brother was in California with a teenage girlfriend, driving a silver Porsche and practically living on undercooked pasta. He visited him and was amazed at his brother's life—that Derek and Liz sat on the sofa and bent over a small, square pin with a picture of Elvis Costello on it and snorted coke off of Elvis's face the way millions of middle-class people sat down for an evening cocktail.

He came back to New York with huaraches from Olvera Street and ten pints of the best-tasting strawberries he had ever eaten. He remembered standing on the other side of the X-ray machine at the airport, watching the fuzzy stacks of strawberries pass through. Thinking about The Situation, he had drunk too much wine and smoked too much with his brother, and he had fixated on one little aspect of Mary or Laura Ann: Laura Ann's hair versus Mary's wide-set eyes. Taking an overview? Laura Ann, naked, long and smooth-skinned; Mary, her sexy adolescent thinness, her flat breasts. Mary had given him an ultimatum: Decide or forget it. Laura Ann, who didn't know he was having an affair then, had given him a soft leather traveling bag.

When he returned that summer, the city looked grim. Few places to see the sky, buildings crowding each other. He looked out the window of the cab and saw a sharp-nosed gargoyle above the door of a building; he saw bums curled with their backs to buildings, sleeping expressionlessly, as if they had just shared some intimacy with the sidewalk. He thought about calling Mary, but didn't. She had an answering machine, and he didn't want to risk hearing Mary's voice that was not Mary's voice.

His last thought before he went to sleep now made him smile: as he had passed a man walking his golden retriever, the man had said to the dog, "I don't believe you, Morty. You pissed on the one sign of life in that treebox."

Laura Ann knew Mary. Those tearful late-night phone calls she had made months ago weren't to some mystery lover, as he had at first suspected, but to Mary. And then the phone calls stopped and she began to be nice to him again. "You pretend to be so casual," she said. "It's a good cover-up, but I know what's underneath. I know how you spend hours with your calculator meticulously going over your bank statement. I know that you'll even read a bad book to the end. I know how you make love."

The last time he saw Mary, she was sitting at a table inside the Empire Diner when he was walking by. She didn't see him. On his way back from his cash machine, he walked into the Empire. They were squirting Windex on the table where Mary and her friends had been. He went to the phone at the end of the counter and said what he'd wanted to say for a long time. "If I love anybody, I love you, Laura Ann. Admit that you've never forgiven me. I don't want to come back and walk into that strain again."

"You wouldn't come back if you didn't want to," she said.

The woman at the piano bobbed her shoulders as she played "Fascinatin' Rhythm." A man in a gorilla suit walked in and began talking to one of the waiters, gesturing with his paw. A chauffeur, arms crossed, waited outside by a long white Cadillac.

"You love me," she said. Then, in a near whisper: "The way I cheat and chip dried food off the plates when I'm setting the table. The way I rub your shoulders. My perfume."

"Your voice," he said.

"I'm exhausted." She sighed. "Don't take it personally if I've gone to sleep when you come home."

The counterman was talking in a huddle with a waitress. "I *told* him that we don't take reservations. 'You show up, that's when we take your name,' I said to him. 'You come back with four other people, we'll give you the back table.' I was just doing my job."

Jake searched through his wallet and took out a business card. He dialed another number.

"This is Doctor Garfield," Garfield's voice said. "I'm not

available at this time. Please leave your message at the tone, or call me at my home in an emergency." Garfield gave his home number, and there was a beep. Listening to the silence that followed, Jake thought: Alexander Graham Bell would never have believed that it would come to this.

Walking back to the apartment, he thought about what he had always been sure he loved: the fields in Pennsylvania, acres of them, stretching away from his aunt's farm, so flat and green. And the porch swing, missing the middle board, that he sat on to watch sunsets. The tangled mounds of peas that he tied around thick stakes in the garden, trying to keep them growing upward. The summer his uncle ripped the honeysuckle off the porch and poured poison on the ground— the stub where the vine had begun. The porch, where the honeysuckle used to crisscross the screen, the floor transformed into complicated patterns of lace when the sunlight shone through the leaves. And the time he begged to be dressed in the neighbor's bee-keeping suit, the big spaceman helmet with netting over the front covering his head and face, and then the unexpected, horrible dread he had felt as bees swarmed around him and crawled on the suit. He had stayed rooted to the spot, paying no attention to the neighbor, who shouted from his tractor in the not-too-far distance that it was all right—there wasn't any way he could hurt the bees. It was a million times worse than being zipped into the stiff yellow rain slicker and sent off to school. In the field, he had been petrified. Finally, the neighbor's voice had reached him and he knew he had to move, and he *did* move, trying hopelessly to shrug away the bees. Then he managed to turn his back on the hives, and eventually, as he walked, they disappeared behind him. He was at that point of life where he realized he wasn't supposed to cry anymore, but he was on the verge of tears when he sat eating toast in the neighbor's kitchen, toast soggy with butter and spread with thick, dark honey, hardly able to swallow because his throat was so constricted. Later, watching television, looking at the way astronauts floated toward each other to connect in space, he would think about the way he must have looked. There had been one acid trip, one of the last, when he had felt that same heavy disembodiment—that he was grounded, and he had to move, but it was impossible, and if he had taken off, he would have drifted not far from the ground, at a peculiar tilt, like the old man walking through air in the Chagall painting. This realization —and this present life of confusion—was a long way from his thoughts, when he had rocked in a swing missing a board, on the front porch of a house in Pennsylvania.

She was, as she had said she would be, in bed. She didn't open her eyes, although he thought that she had heard him walk in. If she had, this particular night, those steady green eyes might have had the power Kryptonite had on Superman. He was always struggling to think that he didn't need her. That love didn't mean need. That crazy conflict acid produced, of having your senses touched sharply, yet knowing you were powerless to respond. Even before acid, that sudden, strength-sucking anxiety—the fear, standing in front of the big white boxes of bees swarming in and out.

What strength it took just to lie there, eyelids lightly closed, nothing to suggest that the way she looked, curled on the bed, was a position difficult to maintain. He knew that if he asked her in the morning, she would look at him with exasperation and say that she had been asleep.

He sat at the foot of the bed. She had not pulled the shade. The streetlight, streaming light through the curtains, blotched her body—luminous shapes that were almost a triangle, almost a circle. If she had opened her eyes and seen him sitting there, smiling fondly, whatever he told her about being unsure of whether they should stay together would be discounted. Her version of it would be that he thought about her so much and stared so often because he was in love. It would be like the story the neighbor told his aunt and uncle all summer: how he had loved those bees, how he had been mesmerized by them. And how, being a gentle boy, he had not wanted to make a move if it might possibly hurt them.

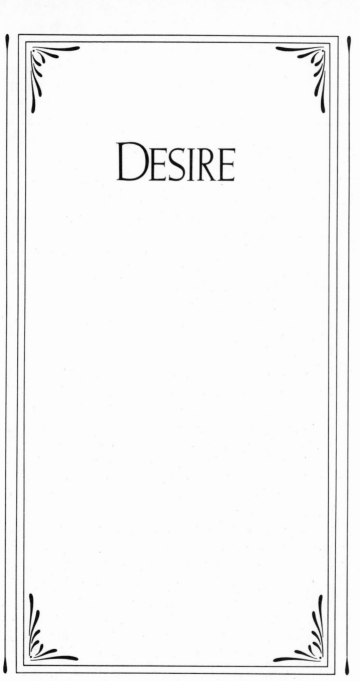

DESIRE

Bryce was sitting at the kitchen table in his father's house, cutting out a picture of Times Square. It was a picture from a coloring book, but Bryce wasn't interested in coloring; he just wanted to cut out pictures so he could see what they looked like outside the book. This drawing was of people crossing the street between the Sheraton-Astor and F. W. Woolworth. There were also other buildings, but these were the ones the people seemed to be moving between. The picture was round; it was supposed to look as if it had been drawn on a bottle cap. Bryce had a hard time getting the scissors around the edge of the cap, because they were blunt-tipped. At home, at his mother's house in Vermont, he had real scissors and he was allowed to taste anything, including alcohol, and his half sister Maddy was a lot more fun than Bill Monteforte, who lived next door to his father here in Pennsylvania and who never had time to play. But he had missed his father, and he had been the one who called to invite himself to this house for his spring vacation.

His father, B.B., was standing in the doorway now, complaining because Bryce was so quiet and so glum. "It took quite a few polite letters to your mother to get her to let loose of you for a week," B.B. said. "You get here and you go into a slump. It would be a real problem if you had to do anything important, like go up to bat with the bases loaded and two outs."

"Mom's new neighbor is the father of a guy that plays for the Redskins," Bryce said.

The scissors slipped. Since he'd ruined it, Bryce now cut on the diagonal, severing half the people in Times Square from the other half. He looked out the window and saw a squirrel stealing seed from the bird feeder. The gray birds were so tiny anyway, it didn't look as if they needed anything to eat.

"Are we going to that auction tonight, or what?" Bryce said.

"Maybe. It depends on whether Rona gets over her headache."

B.B. sprinkled little blue and white crystals of dishwasher soap into the machine and closed it. He pushed two buttons and listened carefully.

"Remember now," he said, "I don't want you getting excited at the auction if you see something you want. You put your hand up, and that's a *bid*. You have to really, really want something and then ask me before you put your hand up. You can't shoot your hand up. Imagine that you're a soldier down in the trenches and there's a war going on."

"I don't even care about the dumb auction," Bryce said.

"What if there was a Turkish prayer rug you wanted and it had the most beautiful muted colors you'd ever seen in your life?" B.B. sat down in the chair across from Bryce. The back of the chair was in the shape of an upside-down triangle. The seat was a right-side-up triangle. The triangles were covered with aqua plastic. B.B. shifted on the chair. Bryce could see that he wanted an answer.

"Or we'll play Let's Pretend," B.B. said. "Let's pretend a lion is coming at you and there's a tree with a cheetah in it and up ahead of you it's just low dry grass. Would you climb the tree, or start running?"

"Neither," Bryce said.

"Come on. You've either got to run or *something*. There's known dangers and unknown dangers. What would you do?"

"People can't tell what they'd do in a situation like that," Bryce said.

"No?"

"What's a cheetah?" Bryce said. "Are you sure they get in trees?"

B.B. frowned. He had a drink in his hand. He pushed the ice cube to the bottom and they both watched it bob up. Bryce leaned over and reached into the drink and gave it a push, too.

"No licking that finger," B.B. said.

Bryce wiped a wet streak across the red down vest he wore in the house.

"Is that my boy? 'Don't lick your finger,' he takes the finger and wipes it on his clothes. Now he can try to remember what he learned in school from the *Book of Knowledge* about cheetahs."

"What *Book of Knowledge?*"

His father got up and kissed the top of his head. The radio went on upstairs, and then water began to run in the tub up there.

"She must be getting ready for action," B.B. said. "Why does she have to take a bath the minute I turn on the dishwasher? The dishwasher's been acting crazy." B.B. sighed. "Keep those hands on the table," he said. "It's good practice for the auction."

Bryce moved the two half circles of Times Square so that they overlapped. He folded his hands over them and watched the squirrel scare a bird away from the feeder. The sky was the color of ash, with little bursts of white where the sun had been.

"I'm the same as dead," Rona said.

"You're not the same as dead," B.B. said. "You've put five pounds back on. You lost twenty pounds in that hospital, and you didn't weigh enough to start with. You wouldn't eat anything they brought you. You took an intravenous needle out of your arm. I can tell you, you were nuts, and I didn't have much fun talking to that doctor who looked like Tonto who operated on you and thought you needed a shrink. It's water over the dam. Get in the bath."

Rona was holding on to the sink. She started to laugh. She had on tiny green-and-white striped underpants. Her long white nightgown was hung around her neck, the way athletes drape towels around themselves in locker rooms.

"What's funny?" he said.

"You said, 'It's water over the—' Oh, you know what you said. I'm running water in the tub, and—"

"Yeah," B.B. said, closing the toilet seat and sitting down. He picked up a Batman comic and flipped through. It was wet from moisture. He hated the feel of it.

The radio was on the top of the toilet tank, and now the Andrews Sisters were singing "Hold Tight." Their voices were as smooth as toffee. He wanted to pull them apart, to hear distinct voices through the perfect harmony.

He watched her get into the bath. There was a worm of a scar, dull red, to the left of her jutting hipbone, where they had removed her appendix. One doctor had thought it was an ectopic pregnancy. Another was sure it was a ruptured ovary. A third doctor—her surgeon—insisted it was her appendix, and they got it just in time. The tip had ruptured.

Rona slid low in the bathtub. "If you can't trust your body not to go wrong, what can you trust?" she said.

"Everybody gets sick," he said. "It's not your body trying to do you in. The mind's only one place: in your head. Look, didn't Lyndon Johnson have an appendectomy? Remember how upset people were that he pulled up his shirt to show the scar?"

"They were upset because he pulled his dog's ears," she said.

She had a bath toy he had bought for her. It was a fish with a happy smile. You wound it with a key and then it raced around the tub spouting water through its mouth.

He could hear Bryce talking quietly downstairs. Another call to Maddy, no doubt. When the boy was in Vermont, he was on the phone all the time, telling B.B. how much he missed him; when he was here in Pennsylvania, he missed his family in Vermont. The phone bill was going to be astronomical. Bryce kept calling Maddy, and Rona's mother kept calling from New York; Rona never wanted to take the calls because she always ended up in an argument if she wasn't prepared with something to talk about, so she made B.B. say she was asleep, or in the tub, or that a soufflé was in the last stages. Then she'd call her mother back, when she'd gathered her thoughts.

"Would you like to go to that auction tonight?" he said to Rona.

"An auction? What for?"

"I don't know. There's nothing on TV and the kid's never been to an auction."

"The kid's never smoked grass," she said, soaping her arm.

"Neither do you anymore. Why would you bring that up?"

"You can look at his rosy cheeks and sad-clown eyes and know he never has."

"Right," he said, throwing the comic book back on the tile. "*Right.* My kid's not a pothead. *I was talking about going to an auction.* Would you also like to tell me that elephants don't fly?"

She laughed and slipped lower in the tub, until the water reached her chin. With her hair pinned to the top of her head and the foam of bubbles covering her neck, she looked like a lady in Edwardian times. The fish was in a frenzy, cutting through the suds. She moved a shoulder to accommodate it, shifted her knees, tipped her head back.

"There were flying elephants in those books that used to be all over the house when he visited," she said. "I'm so glad he's eight now. All those *crazy* books."

"You were stoned all the time," he said. "Everything looked funny to you." Though he hadn't gotten stoned with her, sometimes things had seemed peculiar to him, too. There was the night his friends Shelby and Charles had given a dramatic reading of a book of Bryce's called *Bertram and the Ticklish Rhinoceros.* Rona's mother had sent her a loofah for Christmas that year. It was before you saw loofahs all over the place. Vaguely, he could remember six people crammed into the bathroom, cheering as the floating loofah expanded in water.

"What do you say about the auction?" he said. "Can you keep your hands still? That's what I told him was essential—hands in lap."

"Come here," she said, "I'll show you what I can do with my hands."

The auction was in a barn heated with two wood stoves—one in front, one in back. There were also a few electric heaters up and down the aisles. When B.B. and Rona and Bryce came in the back door of the barn, a man in a black-and-red lumberman's jacket closed it behind them, blowing cigar smoke in their faces. A woman and a man and two teenagers were arguing about a big cardboard box. Apparently one of the boys had put it too close to the small heater. The other boy was defending him, and the man, whose face was bright red, looked as if he was about to strike the woman. Someone else kicked the box away while they argued. B.B. looked in. There were six or eight puppies inside, mostly black, squirming.

"Dad, are they in the auction?" Bryce said.

"I can't stand the smoke," Rona said. "I'll wait for you in the car."

"Don't be stupid. You'll freeze," B.B. said. He reached out and touched the tips of her hair. She had on a red angora hat, pulled over her forehead, which made her look extremely pretty but also about ten years old. A child's hat and no make-up. The tips of her hair were still wet from the bathwater. Touching her hair, he was sorry that he had walked out of the bathroom when she said that about her hands.

They got three seats together near the back.

"Dad, I can't see," Bryce said.

"The damn Andrews Sisters," B.B. said. "I can't get their spooky voices out of my head."

Bryce got up. B.B. saw, for the first time, that the metal folding chair his son had been sitting in had "PAM LOVES DAVID FOREVER AND FOR ALL TIME" written on it with Magic Marker. He took off his scarf and folded it over the writing. He looked over his shoulder, sure that Bryce would be at the stand where they sold hot dogs and soft drinks. He wasn't; he was still inspecting the puppies. One of the boys said something to him, and his son answered. B.B. got up immediately and went over to join them. Bryce was reaching into his pocket.

"What are you doing?" B.B. said.

"Picking up a puppy," Bryce said. He said it as he lifted the animal. The dog turned and rooted its snout in Bryce's armpit, its eyes closed. With his free hand, Bryce handed the boy some money.

"What are you *doing*?" B.B. said.

"Dime a feel," the boy said. Then, in a different tone, he said, "Week or so, they start eating food."

"I never heard of anything like that," B.B. said. The loofah popped up in his mind, expanded. Their drunken incredulity. The time, as a boy, he had watched a neighbor drown a litter of kittens in a washtub. He must have been younger than Bryce when that happened. And the burial: B.B. and the neighbor's son and another boy who was an exchange student had attended the funeral for the drowned kittens. The man's wife came out of the house, with the mother cat in one arm, and reached in her pocket and took out little American flags on toothpicks and handed them to each of the boys and then went back in the house. Her husband had dug a hole and was shoveling dirt back in. First he had put the kittens in a shoebox coffin, which he placed carefully in the hole he had dug near an abelia bush. Then he shoveled the dirt back in. B.B. couldn't remember the name of the man's son now, or the Oriental exchange student's name. The flags were what they used to give you in your sundae at the ice-cream parlor next to the bank.

"You can hold him through the auction for a quarter," the boy said to Bryce.

"You have to give the dog back," B.B. said to his son.

Bryce looked as if he was about to cry. If he insisted on having one of the dogs, B.B. had no idea what he would do. It was what Robin, his ex-wife, deserved, but she'd probably take the dog to the pound.

"Put it down," he whispered, as quietly as he could. The room was so noisy now that he doubted that the teenage boy could hear him. He thought he had a good chance of Bryce's leaving the puppy if there was no third party involved.

To his surprise, Bryce handed over the puppy, and the teenager lowered it into the box. A little girl about three or four had come to the rim of the box and was looking down.

"I bet you don't have a dime, do you, cutie?" the boy said to the girl.

B.B. reached in his pocket and took out a dollar bill, folded it, and put it on the cement floor in front of where the boy crouched. He took Bryce's hand, and they walked to their seats without looking back.

"It's just a bunch of junk," Rona said. "Can we leave if it doesn't get interesting?"

They bought a lamp at the auction. It had a nice base, and as soon as they found another lampshade it would be just right for the bedside table. Now it had a cardboard shade on it, imprinted with a cracked, fading bouquet.

"What's the matter with you?" Rona said. They were back in their bedroom.

"Actually," B.B. said, holding on to the window ledge, "I feel very out of control."

"What does that mean?"

She put *From Julia Child's Kitchen* on the night table, picked up her comb, and grabbed a clump of her hair. She combed through the snaggled ends, slowly.

"Do you think he has a good time here?" he said.

"Sure. He asked to come, didn't he? You could look at his face and see that he enjoyed the auction."

"Maybe he just does what he's told."

"What's the matter with you?" she said. "Come over here."

He sat on the bed. He had stripped down to his under-shorts, and there were goose bumps all over his body. A bird was making a noise outside, screaming as if it were being killed. It stopped abruptly. The goose bumps slowly went away. Whenever he turned up the thermostat he always knew he was going to be sorry along about 5 A.M., when it got too hot in the room but he was too tired to get up and go turn it down. She said that was why they got headaches. He reached across her now for the Excedrin. He put the bottle back on top of the cookbook and gagged down two of them.

"What's he doing?" he said to her. "I don't hear him."

"If you made him go to bed, the way other fathers do, you'd know he was in bed. Then you'd just have to wonder if he was reading under the covers with a flashlight or—"

"Don't say it," he said.

"I wasn't going to say that."

"What were you going to say?"

"I was going to say that he might have taken more Godivas out of the box my mother sent me. I've eaten two. He's eaten a whole row."

"He left a mint and a cream in that row. I ate them," B.B. said.

He got up and pulled on a thermal shirt. He looked out the window and saw tree branches blowing. *The Old Farmer's Almanac* predicted snow at the end of the week. He hoped it didn't snow then; it would make it difficult taking Bryce back to Vermont. There were two miles of unplowed road leading to Robin's house.

He went downstairs. The oval table Bryce sat at was where the dining room curved out. Window seats were built around it. When they rented the house, it was the one piece of furniture left in it that neither of them disliked, so they had kept it. Bryce was sitting in an oak chair, and his forehead was on his arm. In front of him was the coloring book and a box of crayons and a glass vase with different-colored felt-tip pens stuck in it, falling this way and that, the way a bunch of flowers would. There was a pile of white paper. The scissors. B.B. assumed, until he was within a few feet of him, that Bryce was asleep. Then Bryce lifted his head.

"What are you doing?" B.B. said.

"I took the dishes out of the dishwasher and it worked," Bryce said. "I put them on the counter."

"That was very nice of you. It looks like my craziness about the dishwasher has impressed every member of my family."

"What was it that happened before?" Bryce said.

Bryce had circles under his eyes. B.B. had read once that that was a sign of kidney disease. If you bruised easily, leukemia. Or, of course, you could just take a wrong step and break a leg. The dishwasher had backed up, and all the filthy water had come pouring out in the morning when B.B. opened the door—dirtier water than the food-smeared dishes would account for.

"It was a mess," B.B. said vaguely. "Is that a picture?"

It was part picture, part letter, B.B. realized when Bryce clamped his hands over his printing in the middle.

"You don't have to show me."

"How come?" Bryce said.

"I don't read other people's mail."

"You did in Burlington," Bryce said.

"Bryce—that was when your mother cut out on us. That was a letter for her sister. She'd set it up with her to come stay with us, but her sister's as much a space cadet as Robin. Your mother was gone two days. The police were looking for her. What was I supposed to do when I found the letter?"

Robin's letter to her sister said that she did not love B.B. Also, that she did not love Bryce, because he looked like his father. The way she expressed it was: "Let spitting images spit together." She had gone off with the cook at the natural-food restaurant. The note to her sister—whom she had apparently called as well—was written on the back of one of the restaurant's flyers, announcing the menu for the week the cook ran away. Tears streaming down his cheeks, he had stood in the spare bedroom—whatever had made him go in there?—and read the names of desserts: "Tofu-Peach Whip!" "Granola Raspberry Pie!" "Macadamia Bars!"

"It's make-believe anyway," his son said, and wadded up

the piece of paper. B.B. saw a big sunflower turn in on itself.
A fir tree go under.

"Oh," he said, reaching out impulsively. He smoothed out
the paper, making it as flat as he could. The ripply tree sprang
up almost straight. Crinkled birds flew through the sky. B.B.
read:

When I'm B.B.'s age I can be with you allways.
We can live in a house like the Vt. house only not in Vt. no sno.
We can get married and have a dog.

"Who is this to?" B.B. said, frowning at the piece of paper.
"Maddy," Bryce said.

B.B. was conscious, for the first time, how cold the floorboards were underneath his feet. The air was cold, too. Last
winter he had weather-stripped the windows, and this winter
he hadn't. Now he put a finger against a pane of glass in
the dining-room window. It could have been an ice cube, his
finger numbed so quickly.

"Maddy is your stepsister," B.B. said. "You're never going
to be able to marry Maddy."

His son stared at him.

"You understand?" B.B. said.

Bryce pushed his chair back. "Maddy's not ever going to
have her hair cut again," he said. He was crying. "She's going
to be Madeline and I'm going to live with only her and have
a hundred dogs."

B.B. reached out to dry his son's tears, or at least to touch
them, but Bryce sprang up. She was wrong: Robin was so
wrong. Bryce was the image of her, not him—the image of
Robin saying, "Leave me alone."

He went upstairs. Rather, he went to the stairs and started
to climb, thinking of Rona lying in bed in the bedroom, and
somewhere not halfway to the top, adrenaline surged through

his body. Things began to go out of focus, then to pulsate. He reached for the railing just in time to steady himself. In a few seconds the first awful feeling passed, and he continued to climb, pretending, as he had all his life, that this rush was the same as desire.

HAPPY

"Your brother called," I say to my husband on the telephone. "He called to find out if he left his jumpsuit here. As though another weekend guest might have left a jumpsuit."

"As it happens, he did. I mailed it to him. He should have gotten it days ago."

"You never said anything about it. I told him . . ."

"I didn't say anything because I know you find great *significance* in what he leaves behind."

"Pictures of the two of you with your mother, and you were such unhappy little boys . . ."

"Anything you want me to bring home?" he says.

"I think I'd like some roses. Ones the color of peaches."

He clears his throat. All winter, he has little coughs and colds and irritations. The irritations are irritating. At night, he hemms over *Forbes* and I read Blake, in silence.

"I meant that could be found in Grand Central," he says. "An éclair."

"All right," he says. He sighs.

· · ·

"One banana, two banana, three banana, four . . ."

"I think you have the wrong number," I say.

"*Fifteen years*, and you still don't know my voice on the phone."

"Oh," I say. "Hi, Andy."

Andy let his secretary use his apartment during her lunch hour to have an affair with the Xerox repairman. Andy was on a diet, drinking pre-digested protein, and he had thrown everything out in his kitchen, so he wouldn't be tempted. He was allowed banana extract to flavor his formula. The secretary and the repairman got hungry and rummaged through the kitchen cabinets, and all they could find was a gallon jug of banana extract.

"I got the Coors account," Andy says. "I'm having a wall of my office painted yellow and silver."

The dog and I go to the dump. The dump permit is displayed on the back window: a drawing of a pile of rubbish, with a number underneath. The dog breathes against the back window and the sticker gets bright with moisture. The dog likes the rear-view mirror and the back window equally well, and since his riding with his nose to the rear-view mirror is a clear danger, I have put three shoe boxes between the front seats as a barrier. One of the boxes has shoes inside that never fit right.

Bob Dylan is singing on the tape deck: "May God bless and keep you always, May your wishes all come true . . ."

"Back her up!" the dump man hollers. Smoke rises behind him, from something smoldering out of a pyramid into flatness. The man who runs the dump fans the smoke away, gesturing with the other hand to show me the position he wants my car to be in. The dog barks madly, baring his teeth.

"Come on, she'll get up that little incline," the dump man hollers.

The wheels whir. The dog is going crazy. When the car stops, I open my door, call "Thank you!" and tiptoe through the mush. I take the plastic bag filled with garbage and another pair of shoes that didn't work out and throw it feebly, aiming for the top of the heap. It misses by a mile, but the dump man has lost interest. Only the dog cares. He is wildly agitated.

"Please," I say to the dog when I get in the car.

"May you always be courageous," Dylan sings.

It is a bright fall day; the way the sun shines makes the edges of things radiate. When we get home, I put the dog on his lead and open the door, go into the mud room, walk into the house. When I'm away for a weekend or longer, things always look the way I expect they will when I come back. When I'm gone on a short errand, the ashtray seems to have moved forward a few inches, the plants look a little sickly, the second hand on the clock seems to be going very fast . . . I don't remember the clock having a second hand.

The third phone call of the day. "Will you trust me?" a voice says. "I need to know how to get to your house from the Whitebird Diner. My directions say go left at the fork for two miles, but I did, and I didn't pass an elementary school. I think I should have gone right at the fork. A lot of people mix up left and right; it's a form of dyslexia." Heavy breathing. "Whew," the voice says. Then: "Trust me. I can't tell you what's going on because it's a surprise."

When I don't say anything, the voice says: "Trust me. I wouldn't be some nut out in the middle of nowhere, asking whether I go right or left at the fork."

I go to the medicine cabinet and take out a brandy snifter of pills. My husband's bottle of Excedrin looks pristine. My brandy snifter is cut glass, and belonged to my grandfather. It's easy to tell my pills apart because they're all different

colors: yellow Valium, blue Valium, green Donnatal. I never
have to take those unless I go a whole week without eating
Kellogg's All-Bran.

A bear is ringing the front doorbell. There are no shades on
the front windows, and the bear can see that I see it. I shake
my head no, as if someone has come to sell me a raffle ticket.
Could this be a bear wanting to sell me something? It does
not seem to have anything with it. I shake my head no again,
trying to look pleasant. I back up. The bear has left its car
with the hazard light flashing, and two tires barely off Black
Rock Turnpike. The bear points its paws, claws up, praying.
It stands there.

I put a chain on the door and open it. The bear spreads
its arms wide. It is a brown bear, with fur that looks like
whatever material it is they make bathroom rugs out of. The
bear sings, consulting a notebook it has pulled out from somewhere in its side:

> Happy birthday to you
> I know it's not the day
> This song's being sung early
> In case you run away
>
> Twenty-nine was good
> But thirty's better yet
> Face the day with a big smile
> There's nothing to regret
>
> I wish that I could be there
> But it's a question of money
> A bear's appropriate instead
> To say you're still my honey

The bear steps back, grandly, quite pleased with itself. It
has pink rubber lips.

"From your sister," the bear says. I see the lips behind the lips. "I could really use some water," the bear says. "I came from New York. There isn't any singing message service out here. As it is, I guess this was cheaper than your sister flying in from the coast, but I didn't come cheap."

I step aside. "Perrier or tap water?" I say.

"Just regular water," the bear says.

In the kitchen, the bear removes its head and puts it on the kitchen table. The head collapses slowly, like a popover cooling. The bear has a long drink of water.

"You don't look thirty," the bear says.

The bear seems to be in its early twenties.

"Thank you," the bear says. "I hope that didn't spoil the illusion."

"Not at all," I say. "It's fine. Do you know how to get back?"

"I took the train," the bear says. "I overshot you on purpose—got my aunt's car from New Haven. I'm going back there to have dinner with her, then it doesn't take any more smarts than getting on the train to get back to the city. Thank you."

"Could I have the piece of paper?" I say.

The bear reaches in its side, through a flap. It takes out a notebook marked "American Lit. from 1850." It rips a page out and hands it to me.

I tack it on the bulletin board. The oil bill is there, as yet unpaid. My gynecologist's card, telling me that I have a 10 A.M. appointment the next day.

"Well, you don't look thirty," the bear says.

"Not only that, but be glad you were never a rabbit. I think I'm pregnant."

"Is that good news?" the bear says.

"I guess so. I wasn't trying not to get pregnant."

I hold open the front door, and the bear walks out to the porch.

"Who are you?" I say.

"Ned Brown," the bear says. "Fitting, huh? Brown? I used to work for an escort service, but I guess you know what that turned into." The bear adjusts its head. "I'm part-time at Princeton," it says. "Well," it says.

"Thank you very much," I say, and close the door.

I call the gynecologist's office, to find out if Valium has an adverse effect on the fetus.

"Mister Doctor's the one to talk to about prescription medicine," the nurse says. "Your number?"

Those photographs in *Life*, taken inside the womb. It has ears at one week, or something. If they put in a needle to do amniocentesis, it moves to the side. The horror story about the abortionist putting his finger inside, and feeling the finger grabbed. I think that it is four weeks old. It probably has an opinion on Bob Dylan, pro or con.

I have some vermouth over ice. Stand out in the back yard, wearing one of my husband's big woolly jackets. His clothes are so much more comfortable than mine. The dog has dragged down the clothesline and is biting up and down the cord. He noses, bites, ignores me. His involvement is quite erotic.

There is a pale moon in the sky. Early in the day for that. I see what they mean about the moon having a face—the eyes, at least.

From the other side of the trees, I hear the roar of the neighbors' TV. They are both deaf and have a Betamax with their favorite *Hollywood Squares* programs recorded. My husband pulled a prank and put a cassette of *Alien* in one of the boxes. He said that he found the cassette on the street. He excused himself from dinner to do it. He threw away a cassette of *Hollywood Squares* when we got home. It seemed wasteful, but I couldn't think what else to do with it, either.

Some squash are still lying on the ground. I smash one and scatter the seeds. I lose my balance when I'm bent over. That's a sign of pregnancy, I've heard: being off-kilter. I'll buy flat shoes.

"Do you know who I really love?" I say to the dog.

He turns his head. When spoken to, he always pays attention for a polite amount of time.

"I love you, and you're my dog," I say, bending to pat him.

He sniffs the squash seeds on my hand, noses my fingers but doesn't lick them.

I go in the house and get him a Hershey bar.

"What do you think about everything?" I say to the dog.

He stops eating the clothesline and devours the candy. He beats his tail. Next I'll let him off the lead, right? Wrong. I scratch behind his ears and go into the house and look for the book I keep phone numbers in. A card falls out. I see that I have missed a dentist's appointment. Another card: a man who tried to pick me up at the market.

I dial my sister. The housekeeper answers.

"Madame Villery," I say. "Her sister."

"Who?" she says, with her heavy Spanish accent.

"Which part?"

"Pardon me?"

"Madame Villery, or her sister?" I say.

"Her sister!" the housekeeper says. "One moment!"

"Madame!" I hear her calling. My sister's poor excuse for a dog, a little white yapper, starts in.

"Hello," my sister says.

"That was *some* surprise."

"What did he do?" my sister says. "Tell me about it."

It takes me back to when we were teenagers. My sister is three years younger than I am. For years, she said "Tell me about it."

"The bear rang my doorbell," I say, leaving out the part about the phone call from the diner.

"Oh, God," she says. "What were you doing? Tell me the truth."

For years she asked me to tell her the truth.

"I wasn't doing anything."

"Oh, you were—what? Just cleaning or something?"

Years in which I let her imagination work.

"Yes," I say, softening my voice.

"And then the bear was just standing there? What did you think?"

"I was amazed."

I never gave her too much. Probably not enough. She married a Frenchman that I found, and find, imperious. I probably could have told her there was no mystery there.

"Listen," I say, "it was great. How are you. How's life in L.A.?"

"They're not to be equated," she says. "I'm fine, the pool is sick. It has cracked pool."

"The cement? On the bottom or—"

"Don't you love it?" she whispers. "She says, 'It has cracked pool.'"

"Am I ever going to see you?"

"He put me on a budget. I don't have the money to fly back right now. You're not on any budget. You could come out here."

"You know," I say. "Things."

"Are you holding out on me?" she says.

"What would I hold out?"

"Are you really depressed about being thirty? People get so upset—"

"It's O.K.," I say, making my voice lighter. "Hey," I say. *"Thank* you."

She blows a kiss into the phone. "Wait a minute," she says. "Remember when we played grown-up? We thought they were *twenty*! And the pillows under our nightgowns to make us pregnant? How I got pregnant after you put your finger in my stream of urine?"

"Are you?" I say, suddenly curious.

"No," she says, and doesn't ask if I am.

We blow each other a kiss. I hang up and go outside. The day is graying over. There's no difference between the way the air looks and the non-color of my drink. I pour it on the grass. The dog gets up and sniffs it, walks away, resumes his chewing of the clothesline.

I've taken out one of the lawn chairs and am sitting in it, facing the driveway, waiting for my husband. When the car turns into the drive, I take the clothesline and toss it around the side of the house, so he won't see. The dog doesn't know what to do: be angry, or bark his usual excited greeting.

"And now," my husband says, one arm extended, car door still open, "heeeere's hubby." He thinks Ed McMahon is hilarious. He watches only the first minute of the *Tonight* show, to see Ed. He reaches behind him and takes out a cone of flowers. Inside are roses, not exactly peach-colored, but orange. Two dozen? And a white bag, smudged with something that looks like dirt; that must be the chocolate frosting of my éclair seeping through. I throw my arms around my husband. Our hipbones touch. Nothing about my body has started to change. For a second, I wonder if it might be a tumor—if that might be why I missed my period.

"Say it," he whispers, the hand holding the flowers against my left ear, the hand with the bag covering my right.

Isn't this the stereotype of the maniac in the asylum— hands clamped to both ears to . . . what? Shut out voices? Hear them more clearly? The drink has made me woozy, and all I hear is a hum. He moves his hands up and down, rubbing the sides of my head.

"Say it," he's whispering through the constant roar. "Say 'I have a nice life.'"

WAITING

"It's beautiful," the woman says. "How did you come by this?" She wiggles her finger in the mousehole. It's a genuine mousehole: sometime in the eighteenth century a mouse gnawed its way into the cupboard, through the two inside shelves, and out the bottom.

"We bought it from an antique dealer in Virginia," I say.

"Where in Virginia?"

"Ruckersville. Outside of Charlottesville."

"That's beautiful country," she says. "I know where Ruckersville is. I had an uncle who lived in Keswick."

"Keswick was nice," I say. "The farms."

"Oh," she says. "The tax writeoffs, you mean? Those mansions with the sheep grazing out front?"

She is touching the wood, stroking lightly in case there might be a splinter. Even after so much time, everything might not have been worn down to smoothness. She lowers her eyes. "Would you take eight hundred?" she says.

"I'd like to sell it for a thousand," I say. "I paid thirteen hundred, ten years ago."

"It's beautiful," she says. "I suppose I should try to tell you it has some faults, but I've never seen one like it. Very nice. My husband wouldn't like my spending more than six hundred to begin with, but I can see that it's worth eight." She is resting her index finger on the latch. "Could I bring my husband to see it tonight?"

"All right."

"You're moving?" she says.

"Eventually," I say.

"That would be something to load around." She shakes her head. "Are you going back South?"

"I doubt it," I say.

"You probably think I'm kidding about coming back with my husband," she says suddenly. She lowers her eyes again. "Are other people interested?"

"There's just been one other call. Somebody who wanted to come out Saturday." I smile. "I guess I should pretend there's great interest."

"I'll take it," the woman says. "For a thousand. You probably could sell it for more and I could probably resell it for more. I'll tell my husband that."

She picks up her embroidered shoulder bag from the floor by the corner cabinet. She sits at the oak table by the octagonal window and rummages for her checkbook.

"I was thinking, What if I left it home? But I didn't." She takes out a checkbook in a red plastic cover. "My uncle in Keswick was one of those gentleman farmers," she says. "He lived until he was eighty-six, and enjoyed his life. He did everything in moderation, but the key was that he did *everything*." She looks appraisingly at her signature. "Some movie actress just bought a farm across from the Cobham store," she says. "A girl. I never saw her in the movies. Do you know who I'm talking about?"

"Well, Art Garfunkel used to have a place out there," I say.

"Maybe she bought his place." The woman pushes the check to the center of the table, tilts the vase full of phlox, and puts the corner of the check underneath. "Well," she says. "Thank you. We'll come with my brother's truck to get it on the weekend. What about Saturday?"

"That's fine," I say.

"You're going to have some move," she says, looking around at the other furniture. "I haven't moved in thirty years, and I wouldn't want to."

The dog walks through the room.

"What a well-mannered dog," she says.

"That's Hugo. Hugo's moved quite a few times in thirteen years. Virginia. D.C. Boston. Here."

"Poor old Hugo," she says.

Hugo, in the living room now, thumps down and sighs.

"Thank you," she says, putting out her hand. I reach out to shake it, but our hands don't meet and she clasps her hand around my wrist. "Saturday afternoon. Maybe Saturday evening. Should I be specific?"

"Any time is all right."

"Can I turn around on your grass or no?"

"Sure. Did you see the tire marks? I do it all the time."

"Well," she says. "People who back into traffic. I don't know. I honk at them all the time."

I go to the screen door and wave. She is driving a yellow Mercedes, an old one that's been repainted, with a license that says "RAVE-1." The car stalls. She re-starts it and waves. I wave again.

When she's gone, I go out the back door and walk down the driveway. A single daisy is growing out of the foot-wide crack in the concrete. Somebody has thrown a beer can into the driveway. I pick it up and marvel at how light it is. I get the mail from the box across the street and look at it as cars pass by. One of the stream of cars honks a warning to me, although I am not moving, except for flipping through the mail. There is a CL&P bill, a couple of pieces of junk mail, a post card from Henry in Los Angeles, and a letter from my husband in—he's made it to California. Berkeley, California, mailed four days ago. Years ago, when I visited a friend in Berkeley we went to a little park and some people wandered in walking two dogs and a goat. An African pygmy goat. The woman said it was housebroken to urinate outside and as for the other she just picked up the pellets.

I go inside and watch the moving red band on the digital clock in the kitchen. Behind the clock is an old coffee tin decorated with a picture of a woman and a man in a romantic embrace; his arms are nearly rusted away, her hair is chipped, but a perfectly painted wreath of coffee beans rises in an arc above them. Probably I should have advertised the coffee tin, too, but I like to hear the metal top creak when I lift it in the morning to take the jar of coffee out. But if not the coffee tin, I should probably have put the tin breadbox up for sale.

John and I liked looking for antiques. He liked the ones almost beyond repair—the kind that you would have to buy twenty dollars' worth of books to understand how to restore. When we used to go looking, antiques were much less expensive than they are now. We bought them at a time when we had the patience to sit all day on folding chairs under a canopy at an auction. We were organized; we would come and inspect the things the day before. Then we would get there early the next day and wait. Most of the auctioneers in that part of Virginia were very good. One, named Wicked Richard, used to lace his fingers together and crack his knuckles as he called the lots. His real name was Wisted. When he did classier auctions and there was a pamphlet, his name was listed as Wisted. At most of the regular auctions, though, he introduced himself as Wicked Richard.

I cut a section of cheese and take some crackers out of a container. I put them on a plate and carry them into the dining room, feeling a little sad about parting with the big corner cupboard. Suddenly it seems older and bigger—a very large thing to be giving up.

The phone rings. A woman wants to know the size of the refrigerator that I have advertised. I tell her.

"Is it white?" she says.

The ad said it was white.

"Yes," I tell her.

"This is your refrigerator?" she says.

"One of them," I say. "I'm moving."

"Oh," she says. "You shouldn't tell people that. People read these ads to figure out who's moving and might not be around, so they can rob them. There were a lot of robberies in your neighborhood last summer."

The refrigerator is too small for her. We hang up.

The phone rings again, and I let it ring. I sit down and look at the corner cupboard. I put a piece of cheese on top of a cracker and eat it. I get up and go into the living room and offer a piece of cheese to Hugo. He sniffs and takes it lightly from my fingers. Earlier today, in the morning, I ran him in Putnam Park. I could hardly keep up with him, as usual. Thirteen isn't so old, for a dog. He scared the ducks and sent them running into the water. He growled at a beagle a man was walking, and tugged on his leash until he choked. He pulled almost as hard as he could a few summers ago. The air made his fur fluffy. Now he is happy, slowly licking his mouth, getting ready to take his afternoon nap.

John wanted to take Hugo across country, but in the end we decided that, as much as Hugo would enjoy terrorizing so many dogs along the way, it was going to be a hot July and it was better if he stayed home. We discussed this reasonably. No frenzy—nothing like the way we had been swept in at some auctions to bid on things that we didn't want, just because so many other people were mad for them. A reasonable discussion about Hugo, even if it was at the last minute: Hugo, in the car, already sticking his head out the window to bark goodbye. "It's too hot for him," I said. I was standing outside in my nightgown. "It's almost July. He'll be a hassle for you if campgrounds won't take him or if you have to park in the sun." So Hugo stood beside me, barking his high-pitched goodbye, as John backed out of the driveway. He forgot: his big battery lantern and his can opener. He remembered: his tent, the cooler filled with ice (he couldn't decide when he left whether he was going to stock up on beer or Coke), a camera, a suitcase, a fiddle, and a banjo. He forgot his driver's license, too. I never understood why he didn't keep it in his wallet, but it always seemed to get taken out for some reason and then be lost. Yesterday I found it leaning up against a bottle in the medicine cabinet.

Bobby calls. He fools me with his imitation of a man with an English accent who wants to know if I also have an avocado-colored refrigerator for sale. When I say I don't, he asks if I know somebody who paints refrigerators.

"Of course not," I tell him.

"That's the most decisive thing I've heard you say in five years," Bobby says in his real voice. "How's it going, Sally?"

"Jesus," I say. "If you'd answered this phone all morning, you wouldn't think that was funny. Where are you?"

"New York. Where do you think I am? It's my lunch hour. Going to Le Relais to get tanked up. A little *le pain et le beurre*, put down a few Scotches."

"Le Relais," I say. "Hmm."

"Don't make a bad eye on me," he says, going into his Muhammad Ali imitation. "Step on my foot and I kick you to the moon. Glad-hand me and I shake you like a loon." Bobby clears his throat. "I got the company twenty big ones today," he says. "Twenty Gs."

"Congratulations. Have a good lunch. Come out for dinner, if you feel like the drive."

"I don't have any gas and I can't face the train." He coughs

again. "I gave up cigarettes," he says. "Why am I coughing?"
He moves away from the phone to cough loudly.

"Are you smoking grass in the office?" I say.

"Not this time," he gasps. "I'm goddam dying of something." A pause. "What did you do yesterday?"

"I was in town. You'd laugh at what I did."

"You went to the fireworks."

"Yeah, that's right. I wouldn't hesitate to tell you that part."

"What'd you do?" he says.

"I met Andy and Tom at the Plaza and drank champagne. They didn't. I did. Then we went to the fireworks."

"Sally at the *Plaza*?" He laughs. "What were they doing in town?"

"Tom was there on business. Andy came to see the fireworks."

"It rained, didn't it?"

"Only a little. It was O.K. They were pretty."

"The fireworks," Bobby says. "I didn't make the fireworks."

"You're going to miss lunch, Bobby," I say.

"God," he says. "I am. Bye."

I pull a record out from under the big library table, where they're kept on the wide maghogany board that connects the legs. By coincidence, the record I pull out is the Miles Davis Sextet's *Jazz at the Plaza*. At the Palm Court on the Fourth of July, a violinist played "Play Gypsies, Dance Gypsies" and "Oklahoma!" I try to remember what else and can't.

"What do you say, Hugo?" I say to the dog. "Another piece of cheese, or would you rather go on with your siesta?"

He knows the word "cheese." He knows it as well as his name. I love the way his eyes light up and he perks his ears for certain words. Bobby tells me that you can speak gibberish to people, ninety per cent of the people, as long as you throw in a little catchword now and then, and it's the same when I talk to Hugo: "Cheese." "Tag." "Out."

No reaction. Hugo is lying where he always does, on his right side, near the stereo. His nose is only a fraction of an inch away from the plant in a basket beneath the window. The branches of the plant sweep the floor. He seems very still.

"Cheese?" I whisper. "Hugo?" It is as loud as I can speak.

No reaction. I start to take a step closer, but stop myself. I put down the record and stare at him. Nothing changes. I walk out into the back yard. The sun is shining directly down from overhead, striking the dark-blue doors of the garage, washing out the color to the palest tint of blue. The peach tree by the garage, with one dead branch. The wind chimes tinkling in the peach tree. A bird hopping by the iris underneath the tree. Mosquitoes or gnats, a puff of them in the air, clustered in front of me. I sink down into the grass. I pick a blade, split it slowly with my fingernail. I count the times I breathe in and out. When I open my eyes, the sun is shining hard on the blue doors.

After a while—maybe ten minutes, maybe twenty—a truck pulls into the driveway. The man who usually delivers packages to the house hops out of the United Parcel truck. He is a nice man, about twenty-five, with long hair tucked behind his ears, and kind eyes.

Hugo did not bark when the truck pulled into the drive.

"Hi," he says. "What a beautiful day. Here you go."

He holds out a clipboard and a pen.

"Forty-two," he says, pointing to the tiny numbered block in which I am to sign my name. A mailing envelope is under his arm.

"Another book," he says. He hands me the package.

I reach up for it. There is a blue label with my name and address typed on it.

He locks his hands behind his back and raises his arms, bowing. "Did you notice that?" he says, straightening out of

the yoga stretch, pointing to the envelope. "What's the joke?"
he says.

The return address says "John F. Kennedy."

"Oh," I say. "A friend in publishing." I look up at him. I
realize that that hasn't explained it. "We were talking on the
phone last week. He was—People are still talking about where
they were when he was shot, and I've known my friend for
almost ten years and we'd never talked about it before."

The UPS man is wiping sweat off his forehead with a
handkerchief. He stuffs the handkerchief into his pocket.

"He wasn't making fun," I say. "He admired Kennedy."

The UPS man crouches, runs his fingers across the grass.
He looks in the direction of the garage. He looks at me. "Are
you all right?" he says.

"Well—" I say.

He is still watching me.

"Well," I say, trying to catch my breath. "Let's see what
this is."

I pull up the flap, being careful not to get cut by the
staples. A large paperback called *If Mountains Die*. Color
photographs. The sky above the Pueblo River gorge in the
book is very blue. I show the UPS man.

"Were you all right when I pulled in?" he says. "You were
sitting sort of funny."

I still am. I realize that my arms are crossed over my chest
and I am leaning forward. I uncross my arms and lean back
on my elbows. "Fine," I say. "Thank you."

Another car pulls into the driveway, comes around the
truck, and stops on the lawn. Ray's car. Ray gets out, smiles,
leans back in through the open window to turn off the tape
that's still playing. Ray is my best friend. Also my husband's
best friend.

"What are you doing here?" I say to Ray.

"Hi," the UPS man says to Ray. "I've got to get going.
Well." He looks at me. "See you," he says.

"See you," I say. "Thanks."

"What am I doing here?" Ray says. He taps his watch. "Lunchtime. I'm on a business lunch. Big deal. Important negotiations. Want to drive down to the Redding Market and buy a couple of sandwiches, or have you already eaten?"

"You drove all the way out here for lunch?"

"Big business lunch. Difficult client. Takes time to bring some clients around. Coaxing. Takes hours." Ray shrugs.

"Don't they care?"

Ray sticks out his tongue and makes a noise, sits beside me and puts his arm around my shoulder and shakes me lightly toward him and away from him a couple of times. "Look at that sunshine," he says. "Finally. I thought the rain would never stop." He hugs my shoulder and takes his arm away. "It depresses me, too," he says. "I don't like what I sound like when I keep saying that nobody cares." Ray sighs. He reaches for a cigarette. "Nobody cares," he says. "Two-hour lunch. Four. Five."

We sit silently. He picks up the book, leafs through. "Pretty," he says. "You eat already?"

I look behind me at the screen door. Hugo is not here. No sound, either, when the car came up the driveway and the truck left.

"Yes," I say. "But there's some cheese in the house. All the usual things. Or you could go to the market."

"Maybe I will," he says. "Want anything?"

"Ray," I say, reaching my hand up. "Don't go to the market."

"What?" he says. He sits on his heels and takes my hand. He looks into my face.

"Why don't you—There's cheese in the house," I say.

He looks puzzled. Then he sees the stack of mail on the grass underneath our hands. "Oh," he says. "Letter from John." He picks it up, sees that it hasn't been opened. "O.K.," he says. "Then I'm perplexed again. Just that he wrote you?

That he's already in Berkeley? Well, he had a bad winter. We all had a bad winter. It's going to be all right. He hasn't called? You don't know if he hooked up with that band?"

I shake my head no.

"I tried to call you yesterday," he says. "You weren't home."

"I went into New York."

"And?"

"I went out for drinks with some friends. We went to the fireworks."

"So did I," Ray says. "Where were you?"

"Seventy-sixth Street."

"I was at Ninety-eighth. I knew it was crazy to think I might run into you at the fireworks."

A cardinal flies into the peach tree.

"I did run into Bobby last week," he says. "Of course, it's not really running into him at one o'clock at Le Relais."

"How was Bobby?"

"You haven't heard from him, either?"

"He called today, but he didn't say how he was. I guess I didn't ask."

"He was O.K. He looked good. You can hardly see the scar above his eyebrow where they took the stitches. I imagine in a few weeks when it fades you won't notice it at all."

"You think he's done with dining in Harlem?"

"Doubt it. It could have happened anywhere, you know. People get mugged all over the place."

I hear the phone ringing and don't get up. Ray squeezes my shoulder again. "Well," he says. "I'm going to bring some food out here."

"If there's anything in there that isn't the way it ought to be, just take care of it, will you?"

"What?" he says.

"I mean—If there's anything wrong, just fix it."

He smiles. "Don't tell me. You painted a room what you thought was a nice pastel color and it came out electric pink.

Or the chairs—you didn't have them reupholstered again, did you?" Ray comes back to where I'm sitting. "Oh, God," he says. "I was thinking the other night about how you'd had that horrible chintz you bought on Madison Avenue put onto the chairs and when John and I got back here you were afraid to let him into the house. God—that awful striped material. Remember John standing in back of the chair and putting his chin over the back and screaming, 'I'm innocent!' Remember him doing that?" Ray's eyes are about to water, the way they watered because he laughed so hard the day John did that. "That was about a year ago this month," he says.

I nod yes.

"Well," Ray says. "Everything's going to be all right, and I don't say that just because I want to believe in one nice thing. Bobby thinks the same thing. We agree about this. I keep talking about this, don't I? I keep coming out to the house, like you've cracked up or something. You don't want to keep hearing my sermons." Ray opens the screen door. "Anybody can take a trip," he says.

I stare at him.

"I'm getting lunch," he says. He is holding the door open with his foot. He moves his foot and goes into the house. The door slams behind him.

"Hey!" he calls out. "Want iced tea or something?"

The phone begins to ring.

"Want me to get it?" he says.

"No. Let it ring."

"Let it ring?" he hollers.

The cardinal flies out of the peach tree and onto the sweeping branch of a tall fir tree that borders the lawn—so many trees so close together that you can't see the house on the other side. The bird becomes a speck of red and disappears.

"Hey, pretty lady!" Ray calls. "Where's your mutt?"

Over the noise of the telephone, I can hear him knocking around in the kitchen. The stuck drawer opening.

"You *honestly* want me not to answer the phone?" he calls.

I look back at the house. Ray, balancing a tray, opens the door with one hand, and Hugo is beside him—not rushing out, the way he usually does to get through the door, but padding slowly, shaking himself out of sleep. He comes over and lies down next to me, blinking because his eyes are not yet accustomed to the sunlight.

Ray sits down with his plate of crackers and cheese and a beer. He looks at the tears streaming down my cheeks and shoves over close to me. He takes a big drink and puts the beer on the grass. He pushes the tray next to the beer can.

"Hey," Ray says. "Everything's cool, O.K.? No right and no wrong. People do what they do. A neutral observer, and friend to all. Same easy advice from Ray all around. Our discretion assured." He pushes my hair gently off my wet cheeks. "It's O.K.," he says softly, turning and cupping his hands over my forehead. "Just tell me what you've done."

AFLOAT

Annie brings a hand-delivered letter to her father. They stand together on the deck that extends far over the grassy lawn that slopes to the lake, and he reads and she looks off at the water. When she was a little girl she would stand on the metal table pushed to the front of the deck and read the letters aloud to her father. If he sat, she sat. Later, she read them over his shoulder. Now she is sixteen, and she gives him the letter and stares at the trees or the water or the boat bobbing at the end of the dock. It has probably never occurred to her that she does not have to be there when he reads them.

Dear Jerome,
    Last week the bottom fell out of the birdhouse you hung in the tree the summer Annie was three. Or something gnawed at it and the bottom came out. I don't know. I put the wood under one of the big clay pots full of pansies, just to keep it for old times' sake. (I've given up the fountain pen for a felt-tip. I'm really not a romantic.) I send to you for a month our daughter. She still wears

bangs, to cover that little nick in her forehead from the time she fell out of the swing. The swing survived until last summer when —or maybe I told you in last year's letter—Marcy Smith came by with her "friend" Hamilton, and they were so taken by it that I gave it to them, leaving the ropes dangling. I mean that I gave them the old green swing seat, with the decals of roses even uglier than the scraggly ones we grew. Tell her to pull her bangs back and show the world her beautiful widow's peak. She now drinks spritzers. For the first two weeks she's gone I'll be in Ogunquit with Zack. He is younger than you, but no one will ever duplicate the effect of your slow smile. Have a good summer together. I will be thinking of you at unexpected times (unexpected to me, of course).

> Love,
> Anita

He hands the letter on to me, and then pours club soda and Chablis into a tall glass for Annie and fills his own glass with wine alone. He hesitates while I read, and I know he's wondering whether the letter will disturb me—whether I'll want club soda or wine. "Soda," I say. Jerome and Anita have been divorced for ten years.

In these first few days of Annie's visit, things aren't going very well. My friends think that it's just about everybody's summer story. Rachel's summers are spent with her ex-husband, and with his daughter by his second marriage, the daughter's boyfriend, and the boyfriend's best friend. The golden retriever isn't there this summer, because last summer he drowned. No one knows how. Jean is letting her optometrist, with whom she once had an affair, stay in her house in the Hamptons on weekends. She stays in town, because she is in love with a chef. Hazel's the exception. She teaches summer school, and when it ends she and her husband and their son go to Block Island for two weeks, to the house they always rent. Her husband has his job back, after a year in A.A. I study her life and wonder how it works. Of the three best friends I have, she blushes the most easily, is the worst dressed, is the least politically informed, and prefers AM rock stations to FM classical music. Our common denominator is that none of us was married in a church and all of us worried about the results of the blood test we had before we could get a marriage license. But there are so many differences. Say their names to me and what comes to mind is that Rachel cried when she heard Dylan's *Self Portrait* album, because, to her, that meant that everything was over; Jean fought off a man in a supermarket parking lot who was intent on raping her, and still has nightmares about the arugula she was going to the store to get; Hazel can recite Yeats's "The Circus Animals' Desertion" and bring tears to your eyes.

Sitting on the deck, I try to explain to Annie that there *should* be solidarity between women, but that when you look for a common bond you're really looking for a common denominator, and you can't do that with women. Annie puts down *My Mother/My Self* and looks out at the water.

Jerome and I, wondering when she will ever want to swim, go about our days as usual. She's gone biking with him, so there's no hostility. She has always sat at the foot of the bed while Jerome was showering at night and talked nonsense with me while she twisted the ends of her hair, and she still does. At her age, it isn't important that she's not in love, and she was once before anyway. When she pours for herself, it's sixty-forty white wine and club soda. Annie—the baby pushed in a swing. The bottom fell out of the birdhouse. Anita really knows how to hit below the belt.

Jerome is sulky at the end of the week, floating in the Whaler.

"Do you ever think that Anita's thinking of you?" I ask.

"Telepathy, you mean?" he says. He has a good tan. A scab by his elbow. Somehow, he's hurt himself. His wet hair is drying in curly strands. He hasn't had a haircut since we came to the summer house.

"No. Do you ever wonder if she just might be thinking about you?"

"I don't think about her," he says.

"You read the letter Annie brings you every year."

"I'm curious."

"Just curious for that one brief minute?"

Yes, he nods. "Notice that I'm always the one that opens the junk mail, too," he says.

According to Jerome, he and Anita gradually drifted apart. Or, at times when he blames himself, he says it's because he was still a child when he married her. He married her the week of his twentieth birthday. He says that his childhood wounds still weren't healed; Anita was Mama, she was the person he always felt he had to prove himself to—the stuff any psychiatrist will run down for you, he says now, trailing his hand in the water. "It's like there was a time in your life when you believed in paste," he says. "Think how embarrassed you'd be to go buy paste today. Now it's rubber cement. Or at least Elmer's glue. When I was young I just didn't know things."

I never had any doubt when things ended with my first husband. We knew things were wrong; we were going to a counselor and either biting our tongues or arguing because we'd loosened them with too much alcohol, trying to pretend that it didn't matter that I couldn't have a baby. One weekend Dan and I went to Saratoga, early in the spring, to visit friends. It was all a little too sun-dappled. Too *House Beautiful*, the way the sun, in the early morning, shone through the lace curtains and paled the walls to polka dots of light. The redwood picnic table on the stone-covered patio was as bright in the sunlight as if it had been waxed. We were drinking iced tea, all four of us out in the yard early in the morning, amazed at what a perfect day it was, how fast the garden was growing, how huge the heads of the peonies were. Then some people stopped by, with their little girl—people new to

Saratoga, who really had no friends there yet. The little girl was named Alison, and she took a liking to Dan—came up to him without hesitation, the way a puppy that's been chastised will instantly choose someone in the room to cower by, or a bee will zero in on one member of a group. She came innocently, the way a child would come, fascinated by . . . by his curly hair? The way the sunlight reflected off the rims of his glasses? The wedding ring on his hand as he rested his arm on the picnic table? And then, as the rest of us talked, there was a squealing game, with the child suddenly climbing from the ground to his lap, some whispering, some laughing, and then the child, held around her middle, raised above his head, parallel to the ground. The game went on and on, with cries of "Again!" and "Higher!" until the child was shrill and Dan complained of numb arms, and for a second I looked away from the conversation the rest of us were having and I saw her raised above him, smiling down, and Dan both frowning and amused—that little smile at the edge of his lips—and the child's mouth, wide with delight, her long blond hair flopped forward. He was keeping her raised off the ground, and she was hoping that it would never end, and in that second I knew that for Dan and me it was over.

We took a big bunch of pink peonies back to the city with us, stuck in a glass jar with water in the bottom that I held wedged between my feet. I had on a skirt, and the flowers flopped as we went over the bumpy road and the sensation I felt was amazing: it wasn't a tickle, but a pain. When he stopped for gas I went into the bathroom and cried and washed my face and dried it on one of those brown paper towels that smell more strongly than any perfume. I combed my hair. When I was sure I looked fine I came back to the car and sat down, putting one foot on each side of the jar. He started to drive out of the gas station, and then he just drifted to a stop. It was still sunny. Late afternoon. We sat there with the sun heating us and other cars pulling around our car, and

he said, "You are impossible. You are so emotional. After a
perfect day, what have you been crying about?" Then there
were tears, and since I said nothing, eventually he started to
drive: out into the merging lane, then onto the highway,
speeding all the way back to New York in silence. It was
already over. The only other thing I remember about that day
is that down by Thirty-fourth Street we saw the same man
who had been there the week before, selling roses guaranteed
to smell sweet and to be everlasting. There he was, in the
same place, his roses on a stand behind him.

We swim, and gradually work our way back to the gunwale
of the Whaler: six hands, white-knuckled, holding the rim.
I slide along, hand over hand, then move so that my body
touches Jerome's from behind. With my arms around his
chest, I kiss his neck. He turns and smiles and kisses me.
Then I kick away and go to where Annie is holding on to the
boat, her cheek on her hands, staring at her father. I swim up
to her, push her wet bangs to one side, and kiss her forehead.
She looks aggravated, and turns her head away. Just as quickly,
she turns it back. "Am I interrupting you two getting it on
out here?" she says.

"I kissed both of you," I say, between them again, feeling
the weightlessness of my legs dangling as I hold on.

She continues to stare at me. "Girls kissing girls is so
dumb," she says. "It's like the world's full of stupid hostesses
who graduated from Sweet Briar."

Jerome looks at her silently for a long time.

"I guess your mother's not very demonstrative," he says.

"Were you ever?" she says. "Did you love Anita when you
had me?"

"Of course I did," he says. "Didn't you know that?"

"It doesn't matter what I know," she says, as angry and
petulant as a child. "How come you don't feed me birdseed?"
she says. "How come you don't feed the carrier pigeon?"

He pauses until he understands what she is talking about. "The letters just go one way," he says.

"Do you have too much *dignity* to answer them, or is it too risky to reveal anything?"

"Honey," he says, lowering his voice, "I don't have anything to say."

"That you loved her and now you don't?" she says. "That's what isn't worth saying?"

He's brought his knees up to his chin. The scab by his elbow is pale when he clasps his arm around his knees.

"Well, I think that's bullshit," she says. She looks at me. "And I think you're bullshit, too. You don't care about the bond between women. You just care about hanging on to him. When you kissed me, it was patronizing."

There are tears now. Tears that are ironic, because there is so much water everywhere. Today she's angry and alone, and I float between them knowing exactly how each one feels and, like the little girl Alison suspended above Dan's head, knowing that desire that can be more overwhelming than love —the desire, for one brief minute, simply to get off the earth.

RUNNING DREAMS

Barnes is running with the football. The sun strikes his white pants, making them shine like satin. The dog runs beside him, scattering autumn leaves, close to Barnes's ankles. By the time they get from the far end of the field to where Audrey and I are sitting, the dog has run ahead and tried to trip him three times, but Barnes gives him the football anyway. Barnes stops suddenly, holds the football out as delicately as a hostess offering a demitasse cup, and drops it. The dog, whose name is Bruno, snaps up the football—it is a small sponge-rubber model, a toy—and runs off with it. Barnes, who is still panting, sits on the edge of Audrey's chaise, lifts her foot, and begins to rub her toes through her sock.

"I forgot to tell you that your accountant called when you were chopping wood this morning," she says. "He called to tell you the name of the contractor who put in his neighbor's pool. I didn't know you knew accountants socially."

"I knew his neighbors," Barnes says. "They're different neighbors now. The people I knew were named Matt and Zera

Cartwright. Zera was always calling me to ask for Librium. They moved to Kentucky. The accountant kept in touch with them."

"There's so much about your life I don't know," Audrey says. She pulls off her sock and turns her foot in his hand. The toenails are painted red. The nails on her big toes are perfectly oval. Her heels have the soft skin and roundness of a baby's foot, which is miraculous to me, because I know she used to wear high heels to work every day in New York. It also amazes me that there are people who still paint their toenails when summer is over.

Predictably, Bruno is trying to bury the football. I once saw Bruno dig a hole for an inner tube, so the football will only be a minute's trouble. Early in the summer, Barnes came back to the house late at night—he is a surgeon—and gave the dog his black bag. If Audrey hadn't been less drunk than the rest of us, and able to rescue it, that would have been buried, too.

"Why do we have to build a pool?" Audrey says. "All that horrible construction noise. What if some kid drowns in it? I'm going to wake up every morning and go to the window and expect to see some little body—"

"You knew how materialistic I was when you married me. You knew that after I got a house in the country I'd want a pool, didn't you?" Barnes kisses her knee. "Audrey can't swim, Lynn," he says to me. "Audrey hates to learn new things."

We already know she can't swim. She's Martin's sister, and I've known her for seven years. Martin and I live together— or did until a few months ago, when I moved. Barnes has known her almost all her life, and they've been married for six months now. They were married in the living room of this house, while it was still being built, with Elvis Presley on the stereo singing "As Long as I Have You." Holly carried a bouquet of cobra lilies. Then I sang "Some Day Soon"—

Audrey's favorite Judy Collins song. The dog was there, and a visiting Afghan. The stonemason forgot that he wasn't supposed to work that day and came just as the ceremony was about to begin, and decided to stay. He turned out to know how to foxtrot, so we were all glad he'd stayed. We had champagne and danced, and Martin and I fixed crêpes.

"What if we just tore the cover off that David Hockney book," Audrey says now. "The one of the man floating face down in a pool, that makes him look like he's been pressed under glass? We could hang it from the tree over there, instead of wind chimes. I don't want a swimming pool."

Barnes puts her foot down. She lifts the other one and puts it in his hand.

"We can get you a raft and you can float around, and I can rub your feet," he says.

"You're never here. You work all the time," Audrey says.

"When the people come to put in the pool, you can hold up your David Hockney picture and repel them."

"What if they don't understand that, Barnes? I can imagine that just causing a lot of confusion."

"Then you lose," he says. "If you show them the picture and they go ahead and put in the pool anyway, then either it's not a real cross or they're not real vampires." He pats her ankle. "But no fair explaining to them," he says. "It has to be as serious as charades."

Martin tells me things that Barnes has told him. In the beginning, Martin didn't want his sister to marry him, but Barnes was also his best friend and Martin didn't want to betray Barnes's confidences to him, so he asked me what I thought. Telling me mattered less than telling her, and I had impressed him long ago with my ability to keep a secret by not telling him his mother had a mastectomy the summer he went to Italy. He only found out when she died, two years later, and then he found out accidentally. "She didn't want you to know," I said. "How could you keep that a secret?" he said. He loves me and hates me for things like that. He loves me because I'm the kind of person people come to. It's an attribute he wishes he had, because he's a teacher. He teaches history in a private school. One time, when we were walking through Chelsea late at night, a nicely dressed old lady leaned over her gate and handed me a can of green beans and a can opener and said, "Please." On the subway, a man handed me a letter and said, "You don't have to say anything, but please read this paragraph. I just want somebody else to see it before I rip it up." Most of these things have to do with love, in some odd way. The green beans did not have to do with love.

Martin and I are walking in the woods. The poison ivy is turning a bright autumnal red, so it's easy to recognize. As we go deeper into the woods we see a tree house, with a ladder made of four boards nailed to the tree trunk. There are empty beer bottles around the tree, but I miss the most remarkable thing in the scene until Martin points it out: a white balloon wedged high above the tree house, where a thin branch forks. He throws some stones and finally bounces one off the balloon, but it doesn't break it or set it free. "Maybe I can lure it down," he says, and he picks up an empty Michelob bottle, holds it close to his lips, and taps his fingers on the glass as if he were playing a horn while he blows a slow stream of air across the top. It makes an eerie, hollow sound, and I'm glad when he stops and drops the bottle. He's capable of surprising me as much as I surprise him. We lived together for years. A month ago, he came to the apartment I was subletting late one night, after two weeks of not returning my phone calls at work and keeping his phone pulled at home—came over and hit the buzzer and was standing there smiling when I looked out the window. He walked up the four flights, came in still smiling, and said, "I'm going to do something you're really going to like." I was ready to hit him if he tried to touch me, but he took me lightly by the wrist, so that I knew that was the only part of my body he'd touch, and sat down and pulled me into the chair with him, and whistled the harp break to "Isn't She Lovely." I had never heard him whistle before. I had no idea he knew the song. He whistled the long, complex interlude perfectly, and then sat there, silently, his lips warm against the top of my hair.

Martin pushes aside a low-hanging branch, so I can walk by. "You know what Barnes told me this morning?" he says. "He sees his regular shrink on Monday mornings, but a few weeks ago he started seeing a young woman shrink on Tuesdays and not telling either of them about the other. Then he said he was thinking about giving both of them up and buying a camera."

"I don't get it."

"He does that—he starts to say one thing, and then he adds some non sequitur. I don't know if he wants me to question him or just let him talk."

"Ask."

"You wouldn't ask."

"I'd probably ask," I say.

We're walking on leaves, through bright-green fern. From far away now, he tosses another stone, but it misses the branch; it doesn't go near the balloon.

"You know what it is?" Martin says. "He never *seems* vague or random about anything. He graduated first in his class from medical school. All summer, the bastard hit a home run every time he was up at bat. He's got that charming, self-deprecating way of saying things—the way he was talking about the swimming pool. So when he seems to be opening up to me, it would be unsophisticated for me to ask what going to two shrinks and giving up both of them and buying a camera is all about."

"Maybe he talks to you because you don't ask him questions."

Martin is tossing an acorn in the air. He pockets it, and squeezes my hand.

"I wanted to make love to you last night," he says, "but I knew she'd be walking through the living room all night."

She did. She got up every few hours and tiptoed past the fold-out bed and went into the bathroom and stayed there, silently, for so long that I'd drift back to sleep and not realize she'd come out until I heard her walking back in again. Audrey has had two miscarriages in the year she's been with Barnes. Audrey, who swore she'd never leave the city, never have children, who hung out with poets and painters, married the first respectable man she ever dated—her brother's best friend as well—got pregnant, and grieved when she lost the first baby, grieved when she lost the second.

"Audrey will be all right," I say, and push my fingers through his.

"We're the ones I'm worried about," he says. "Thinking about them stops me from talking about us." He puts his arm around me as we walk. Our skin is sweaty—we have on too many clothes. We trample ferns I'd avoid if I were walking alone. With his head pressed against my shoulder, he says, "I need for you to talk to me. I'm out of my league with you people. I don't know what you're thinking, and I think you must be hating me."

"I told you what I thought months ago. You said you needed time to think. What more can I do besides move so you have time to think?"

He is standing in front of me, touching the buttons of his wool shirt that I wear as a jacket, then brushing my hair behind my shoulders.

"You went, just like that," he says. "You won't tell me what your life is like."

He moves his face toward mine, and I think he's going to kiss me, but he only closes his eyes, puts his forehead against mine. "You know all my secrets," he whispers, "and when we're apart I feel like they've died inside you."

At dinner, we've all had too much to drink. I study Martin's face across the table and wonder what secrets he had in mind. That he's afraid of driving over bridges? Afraid of gas stoves? That he can't tell a Bordeaux from a Burgundy?

Barnes has explained, by drawing a picture on a napkin, how a triple-bypass operation is done. Audrey accidentally knocks over Barnes's glass, and the drawing of the heart blurs under the spilled water. Martin says, "That's a penis, Doctor." Then he scribbles on my napkin, drips water on it, and says, "That is also a penis." He is pretending to be taking a Rorschach test.

Barnes takes another napkin from the pile in the middle of the table and draws a penis. "What's that?" he says to Martin.

"That's a mushroom," Martin says.

"You're quite astute," Barnes says. "I think you should go into medicine when you get over your crisis."

Martin wads up a napkin and drops it in the puddle running across the table from Barnes's napkin. "Did you ever have a crisis in *your* life?" he says to him, mopping up.

"Not that you observed. There were a few weeks when I thought I was going to be second in my class in med school."

"Aren't you embarrassed to be such an overachiever?" Martin says, shaking his head in amazement.

"I don't think about it one way or another. It was expected of me. When I was in high school, I got stropped by my old man for every grade that wasn't an A."

"Is that true?" Audrey says. "Your father beat you?"

"It's true," Barnes says. "There are a lot of things you don't know about me." He pours himself some more wine. "I can't stand pain," he says. "That's part of why I went into medicine. Because I think about it all the time anyway, and doing what I do I can be grateful every day that it's somebody else's suffering. When I was a resident, I'd go to see the patient after surgery and leave the room and puke. Nurses puke sometimes. You hardly ever see a doctor puke."

"Did you let anybody comfort you then?" Audrey says. "You don't let anybody comfort you now."

"I don't know if that's true," Barnes says. He takes a drink of wine, raising the glass with such composure that I wouldn't know he was drunk if he wasn't looking into the goblet at the same time he was drinking. He puts the glass back on the table. "It's easier for me to talk to men," he says. "Men will only go so far, and women are so single-minded about soothing you. I've always thought that once I started letting down I might lose my energy permanently. Stay here and float in a swimming pool all day. Read. Drink. Not keep going."

"Barnes," Audrey says, "this is awful." She pushes her bangs back with one hand.

"Christ," Barnes says, leaning over and taking her hand from her face. "I sound like some character out of D. H. Lawrence. I don't know what I'm talking about." He gets up. "I'm going to get the other pizza out of the oven."

On the way into the kitchen, he hits his leg on the coffee table. Geodes rattle on the glass tabletop. On the table, in a wicker tray, there are blue stones, polished amethysts, inky-black pebbles from a stream, marbles with clouds of color like smoke trapped inside. The house is full of things to touch—silk flowers you have to put a finger on to see if they're real, snow domes to shake, Audrey's tarot cards. Audrey is looking at Martin now with the same bewildered look that she gets when she lays out the tarot cards and studies them. Martin takes her hand. He is still holding her hand when Barnes comes back, and only lets go when Barnes begins to lower the pizza to the center of the table.

"I'm sorry," Barnes says. "It's not a good time to be talking about my problems, is it?"

"Why not?" Martin says. "Everybody's been their usual witty and clever self all weekend. It's all right to talk about real things."

"Well, I don't want to make a fool of myself anymore," Barnes says, cutting the pizza into squares. "Why don't you talk about what it's like to have lived with Lynn for so many years and then suddenly she's famous." Barnes puts a piece of pizza on my plate. He serves a piece to Martin. Audrey holds her fingers above her plate. For a drunken minute, I don't realize she's saying she doesn't want more food—her fingers are hovering lightly, the way they do when she picks up a tarot card.

"Last Monday I put in an all-nighter," Barnes says to me. "Matty Klein was with me. We were riding down Park Avenue afterwards, and your song came on the radio. We were both so amazed. Not at what we'd just pulled off in five hours of surgery but that there we were in the back of a cab with the sun coming up and you were singing on the radio. I'm still used to the way you were singing with Audrey in the kitchen a while ago—the way you just sing, and she sings along. Then I realized in the cab that that wasn't private anymore." He takes another drink of wine. "Am I making any sense?" he says.

"It makes perfect sense," Martin says. "Try to explain that to her."

"It's not private," I say. "Other things are private, but that's just me singing a song."

Barnes pushes his chair back from the table. "I'll tell you what I never get over," he says. "That I can take my hands out of somebody's body, wash them, get in a cab, go home, and hardly wait to get into bed with Audrey to touch her, because that's so mysterious. In spite of what I do, I haven't found out anything."

"Is this leading up to your saying again that you don't know why I've had two miscarriages?" Audrey says.

"No, I wasn't thinking about that at all," Barnes says.

"I'll tell you what *I* thought it was about," Martin says. "*I* thought that Barnes wanted me to tell everybody why I've freaked out now that Lynn's famous. It doesn't seem very . . . timely of me to be pulling out now."

"When did I say that what I wanted was to be famous?" I say.

"I can't do it," Audrey says. "It's too hard to pretend to be involved in what other people are talking about when all I can think about are the miscarriages."

She is the first to cry, though any of us might have been.

Bruno, the dog, has shifting loyalties. Because Martin threw the football for him after dinner, he has settled by our bed in the living room. His sleep is deep, and fitful: paws flapping, hard breaths, a tiny, high-pitched yelp once as he exhales. Martin says that he is having running dreams. I close my eyes and try to imagine Bruno's dream, but I end up thinking about all the things he probably doesn't dream about: the blue sky, or the hardness of the field when the ground gets cold. Or, if he noticed those things, they wouldn't seem sad.

"If I loved somebody else, would that make it easier?" Martin says.

"Do you?" I say.

"No. I've thought that that would be a way out, though. That way you could think I was just somebody you'd misjudged."

"Everybody's changing so suddenly," I say. "Do you realize that? All of a sudden Barnes wants to open up to us, and you want to be left alone, and Audrey wants to forget about the life she had in the city and live in this quiet place and have children."

"What about you?" he says.

"Would it make sense to you that I've stopped crying and feeling panicky because I'm in love with somebody else?"

"I'll bet that's true," he says. I feel him stroking the dog. This is what he does to try to quiet him without waking him up—gently rubbing his side with his foot. "Is it true?" he says.

"No. I'd like to hurt you by having it be true, though."

He reaches for the quilt folded at the foot of the bed and pulls it over the blanket.

"That isn't like you," he says.

He stops stroking the dog and turns toward me. "I feel so locked in," he says. "I feel like we've got to come out here every weekend. I feel it's inevitable that there's a 'we.' I feel guilty for feeling bad, because Barnes's father beat him up, and my sister lost two babies, and you've been putting it all on the line, and I don't feel like I'm keeping up with you. You've all got more energy than I do."

"Martin—Barnes was dead-drunk, and Audrey was in tears, and before it was midnight I had to admit I was exhausted and go to bed."

"That's not what I mean," he says. "You don't understand what I mean."

We are silent, and I can hear the house moving in the wind. Barnes hasn't put up the storm windows yet. Air leaks in around the windows. I let Martin put his arm around me for the warmth, and I slide lower in the bed so that my shoulders are under the blanket and quilt.

"What I meant is that I'm not entitled to this," Martin says. "With what he goes through at the hospital, he's entitled to get blasted on Saturday night. She's got every right to cry. Your head's full of music all the time, and that wears you down, even if you aren't writing or playing." He whispers, even more quietly, "What did you think when he said that about his father beating him?"

"I wasn't listening to him any more than you two were. You know me. You know I'm always looking for a reason why it was all right that my father died when I was five. I was thinking maybe it would have turned out awful if he had lived. Maybe I would have hated him for something."

Martin moves his head closer to mine. "Let me go," he says, "and I'm going to be as unmovable as that balloon in the tree."

Bruno whimpers in his sleep, and Martin moves his foot up and down Bruno's body, half to soothe himself, half to soothe the dog.

I didn't know my father was dying. I knew that something was wrong, but I didn't know what dying was. I've always known simple things: how to read the letter a stranger hands me and nod, how to do someone a favor when they don't have my strength. I remember that my father was bending over—stooped with pain, I now realize—and that he was winter-pale, though he died before cold weather came. I remember standing with him in a room that seemed immense to me at the time, in sunlight as intense as the explosion from a flashbulb. If someone had taken that photograph, it would have been a picture of a little girl and her father about to go on a walk. I held my hands out to him, and he pushed the fingers of the gloves tightly down each of my fingers, patiently, pretending to have all the time in the world, saying, "This is the way we get ready for winter."

LIKE GLASS

In the picture, only the man is looking at the camera. The baby in the chair, out on the lawn, is looking in another direction, not at his father. His father has a grip on a collie—trying, no doubt, to make the dog turn its head toward the lens. The dog looks away, no space separating its snout from the white border. I wonder why, in those days, photographs had borders that looked as if they had been cut with pinking shears.

The collie is dead. The man with a pompadour of curly brown hair and with large, sloping shoulders was alive, the last time I heard. The baby grew up and became my husband, and now is no longer married to me. I am trying to follow his line of vision in the picture. Obviously, he'd had enough of paying attention to his father or to the dog that day. It is a picture of a baby gazing into the distance.

I have a lot of distinct memories of things that happened while I was married, but lately I've been thinking about two things that are similar, although they have nothing in common. We lived on the top floor of a brownstone. When we

decided to separate and I moved out, Paul changed the lock
on the door. When I came back to take my things, there was
no way to get them. I went away and thought about it until
I didn't feel angry anymore. By then it was winter, and cold
leaked in my windows. I had my daughter, and other things,
to think about. In the cold, though, walking around the
apartment in a sweater most people would have thought thick
enough to wear outside, or huddling on the sofa under an old
red-and-brown afghan, I would start feeling romantic about
my husband.

One afternoon—it was February 13, the day before Valentine's Day—I had a couple of drinks and put on my long
green coat with a huge hood that made me look like a monk
and went to the window and saw that the snow had melted
on the sidewalk: I could get away with wearing my comfortable rubber-soled sandals with thick wool socks. So I went
out and stopped at Sheridan Square to buy *Hamlet* and
flipped through until I found what I was looking for. Then
I went to our old building and buzzed Larry. He lives in the
basement—what is called a garden apartment. He opened the
door and unlocked the high black iron gate. My husband had
always said that Larry looked and acted like Loretta Young;
he was always exuberant, he had puffy hair and crinkly eyes,
and he didn't look as if he belonged to either sex. Larry was
surprised to see me. I can be charming when I want to be,
so I acted slightly bumbly and apologetic and smiled to let
him know that what I was asking was a silly thing: could I
stand in his garden for a minute and call out a poem to my
husband? I saw Larry looking at my hands, moving in the
pockets of my coat. The page torn from *Hamlet* was in one
pocket, the rest of the book in the other. Larry laughed. How
could my husband hear me, he asked. It was February. There
were storm windows. But he let me in, and I walked down
his long, narrow hallway, through the back room that he used
as an office, to the door that led out to the back garden. I

pushed open the door, and his gray poodle came yapping up to my ankles. It looked like a cactus, with maple leaves stuck in its coat.

I picked up a little stone—Larry had small rocks bordering his walkway, all touching, as if they were a chain. I threw the stone at my husband's fourth-floor bedroom window, and hit it—*tonk!*—on the very first try. Blurrily, I watched the look of puzzlement on Larry's face. My real attention was on my husband's face, when it appeared at the window, full of rage, then wonder. I looked at the torn-out page and recited, lilt-ingly, Ophelia's song: " 'Tomorrow is Saint Valentine's day / All in the morning betime, / And I a maid at your window, / To be your Valentine.' "

"Are you *insane?*" Paul called down to me. It was a shout, really, but his voice hung thin in the air. It floated down.

"I did it," Larry said, coming out, shivering, cowering as he looked up to the fourth floor. "I let her in."

I could smell jasmine when the wind blew. I had put on too much perfume. Even if he did take me in, he'd back off; he'd never let me be his valentine. What he noticed, of course, when he'd come downstairs to lead me out of the garden, seconds later, was the Scotch on my breath.

"This is all wrong," I said, as he pulled me by the hand past Larry, who stood holding his barking poodle in the hall-way. "I only had two Scotches," I said. "I just realized when the wind blew that I smell like a flower garden."

"You bet it's all wrong," he said, squeezing my hand so hard it almost broke. Then he shook off my hand and walked up the steps, went in and slammed the door behind him. I watched a hairline crack leap across all four panes of glass at the top of the door.

The other thing happened in happier times, when we were visiting my sister, Karin, on Twenty-third Street. It was the first time we had met Dan, the man she was engaged to, and we had brought a bottle of champagne. We drank her wine first, and ate her cheese and told stories and heard stories and smoked a joint, and sometime after midnight my husband went to the refrigerator and got out our wine—Spanish champagne, in a black bottle. He pointed the bottle away from him, and we all squinted, silently watching. At the same instant that the cork popped, as we were all saying "Hooray!" or "That does it!"—whatever we were saying—we heard glass raining down, and Paul suddenly crouched, and then we looked above him to see a hole in the skylight, and through the hole black sky.

I've just told these stories to my daughter, Eliza, who is six. She used to like stories to end with a moral, like fairy tales, but now she thinks that's kid's stuff. She still wants to know what stories mean, but now she wants me to tell her. The point of the two stories—well, I don't know what the point is, I'm always telling her. That he broke the glass by mistake, and that the cork broke the glass by a miracle. The point is that broken glass is broken glass.

"That's a joke ending," she says. "It's dumb." She frowns.

I cop out, too tired to think, and then tell her another part of the story to distract her: Uncle Dan and Aunt Karin told the superintendent that the hole must have come from something that fell from above. He knew they were lying— nothing was above them—but what could he say? He asked them whether they thought perhaps meteorites shrank to the size of gumballs falling through New York's polluted air. He hated not only his tenants but the whole city.

She watches me digress. She reaches for the cologne on her night table and lifts her long blond hair, and I spray her neck. She takes the bottle and sprays her wrists, rubs them together, holds out her wrists for me to smell. I make a silly face and pretend to be dazed by such a wonderful smell. I stroke her hair until she is silent, and tiptoe out, still moving as if I'm walking through broken glass.

· · ·

Once a week, for a couple of hours, I read to a man named Norman, who is blind. In the year I've been doing it, he and I have sort of become friends. He usually greets me with something like "So what's new with your life?" He sits behind his desk and I sit beside it, in a chair. This is the way a teacher and pupil should sit, and I've fallen into the pattern of letting him ask.

He gets up to open the window. It's always too hot in his little office. His movements are exaggerated, like a bird's: the quickly cocked head, the way he grips the edge of his desk when he's bored. He grips the edge, releases his hold, grabs again, like a parrot shifting on its bar. Norman has never seen a bird. He has an eight-year-old daughter, who likes to describe things to him, although she is a prankster and sometimes deliberately lies, he has told me. He buys her things from the joke shop on the corner of the street where he works. He takes home little pills that will make drinks bubble over, buzzers to conceal in the palm of your hand, little black plastic flies to freeze in ice cubes, rubber eyeglass rims attached to a fat nose and a bushy mustache. "Daddy, now I'm wearing my big nose," she says. "Daddy, I put a black fly in your ice cube, so spit it out if it sinks in your drink, all right?" My daughter and I have gone to two dinners at their house. My daughter thinks that his daughter is a little weird. The last time we visited, when the girls were playing and Norman was washing dishes, his wife showed me the hallway she had just wallpapered. It took her forever to decide on the wallpaper, she told me. We stood there, dwarfed by wallpaper imprinted with the trunks of shiny silver trees that her husband would never see.

What's new with me? My divorce is final.

My husband remembers the circumstances of the photograph. I told him it was impossible—he was an infant. No, he was a child when the picture was taken, he said—he just looked small because he was slumped in the chair. He remembers it all distinctly. Rufus the dog was there, and his father, and he was looking slightly upward because that was where his mother was, holding the camera. I was amazed that I had made a mystery of something that had such a simple answer. It is a picture of a baby looking at its mother. For the millionth time he asks why must I make myself morose, why call in the middle of the night.

Eliza is asleep. I sit on the edge of her bed in the half-darkness, tempting fate, fidgeting with a paperweight with bursts of red color inside, tossing it in the air. One false move and she will wake up. One mistake and glass shatters. I like the smoothness of it, the heaviness as it slaps into my palm over and over.

Today when I went to Norman, he was sitting on his window ledge, with his arms crossed over his chest. He had been uptown at a meeting that morning, where a man had come up to him and said, "Be grateful for the cane. Everybody who doesn't take hold of something has something take hold of them." Norman tells me this, and we are both silent. Does he want me to tell him, the way Eliza wants me to summarize stories, what I think it means? Since Norman and I are adults, I answer my silent question with another question: What do you do with a shard of sorrow?

GREENWICH
TIME

"I'm thinking about frogs," Tom said to his secretary on the phone. "Tell them I'll be in when I've come up with a serious approach to frogs."

"I don't know what you're talking about," she said.

"Doesn't matter. I'm the idea man, you're the message taker. Lucky you."

"Lucky you," his secretary said. "I've got to have two wisdom teeth pulled this afternoon."

"That's awful," he said. "I'm sorry."

"Sorry enough to go with me?"

"I've got to think about frogs," he said. "Tell Metcalf I'm taking the day off to think about them, if he asks."

"The health plan here doesn't cover dental work," she said.

Tom worked at an ad agency on Madison Avenue. This week, he was trying to think of a way to market soap shaped like frogs—soap imported from France. He had other things on his mind. He hung up and turned to the man who was waiting behind him to use the phone.

"Did you hear that?" Tom said.

"Do what?" the man said.

"Christ," Tom said. "Frog soap."

He walked away and went out to sit across the street from his favorite pizza restaurant. He read his horoscope in the paper (neutral), looked out the window of the coffee shop, and waited for the restaurant to open. At eleven-forty-five he crossed the street and ordered a slice of Sicilian pizza, with everything. He must have had a funny look on his face when he talked to the man behind the counter, because the man laughed and said, "You sure? Everything? You even look surprised yourself."

"I started out for work this morning and never made it there," Tom said. "After I wolf down a pizza I'm going to ask my ex-wife if my son can come back to live with me."

The man averted his eyes and pulled a tray out from under the counter. When Tom realized that he was making the man nervous, he sat down. When the pizza was ready, he went to the counter and got it, and ordered a large glass of milk. He caught the man behind the counter looking at him one more time—unfortunately, just as he gulped his milk too fast and it was running down his chin. He wiped his chin with a napkin, but even as he did so he was preoccupied, thinking about the rest of his day. He was heading for Amanda's, in Greenwich, and, as usual, he felt a mixture of relief (she had married another man, but she had given him a key to the back door) and anxiety (Shelby, her husband, was polite to him but obviously did not like to see him often).

When he left the restaurant, he meant to get his car out of the garage and drive there immediately, to tell her that he wanted Ben—that somehow, in the confusion of the situation, he had lost Ben, and now he wanted him back. Instead, he found himself wandering around New York, to calm himself so that he could make a rational appeal. After an hour or so, he realized that he was becoming as interested in the city

as a tourist—in the tall buildings; the mannequins with their
pelvises thrust forward, almost touching the glass of the store
windows; books piled into pyramids in bookstores. He passed
a pet store; its front window space was full of shredded newspaper and sawdust. As he looked in, a teenage girl reached
over the gate that blocked in the window area and lowered
two brown puppies, one in each hand, into the sawdust. For
a second, her eye met his, and she thrust one dog toward him
with a smile. For a second, the dog's eye also met his. Neither
looked at him again; the dog burrowed into a pile of paper, and
the girl turned and went back to work. When he and the girl
caught each other's attention, a few seconds before, he had
been reminded of the moment, earlier in the week, when a
very attractive prostitute had approached him as he was walking past the Sheraton Centre. He had hesitated when she
spoke to him, but only because her eyes were very bright—
wide-set eyes, the eyebrows invisible under thick blond bangs.
When he said no, she blinked and the brightness went away.
He could not imagine how such a thing was physically possible; even a fish's eye wouldn't cloud over that quickly, in
death. But the prostitute's eyes had gone dim in the second
it took him to say no.

He detoured now to go to the movies: *Singin' in the Rain.*
He left after Debbie Reynolds and Gene Kelly and Donald
O'Connor danced onto the sofa and tipped it over. Still smiling about that, he went to a bar. When the bar started to
fill up, he checked his watch and was surprised to see that
people were getting off work. Drunk enough now to wish for
rain, because rain would be fun, he walked to his apartment
and took a shower, and then headed for the garage. There
was a movie house next to the garage, and before he realized
what he was doing he was watching *Invasion of the Body
Snatchers.* He was shocked by the dog with the human head,
not for the obvious reason but because it reminded him of

the brown puppy he had seen earlier. It seemed an omen—
a nightmare vision of what a dog would become when it was
not wanted.

Six o'clock in the morning: Greenwich, Connecticut. The
house is now Amanda's, ever since her mother's death. The
ashes of Tom's former mother-in-law are in a tin box on top
of the mantel in the dining room. The box is sealed with wax.
She has been dead for a year, and in that year Amanda has
moved out of their apartment in New York, gotten a quickie
divorce, remarried, and moved into the house in Greenwich.
She has another life, and Tom feels that he should be careful
in it. He puts the key she gave him into the lock and opens
the door as gently as if he were disassembling a bomb. Her
cat, Rocky, appears, and looks at him. Sometimes Rocky
creeps around the house with him. Now, though, he jumps
on the window seat as gently, as unnoticeably, as a feather
blown across sand.

Tom looks around. She has painted the living-room walls
white and the downstairs bathroom crimson. The beams in
the dining room have been exposed; Tom met the carpenter
once—a small, nervous Italian who must have wondered why
people wanted to pare their houses down to the framework.
In the front hall, Amanda has hung photographs of the wings
of birds.

Driving out to Amanda's, Tom smashed up his car. It was
still drivable, but only because he found a tire iron in the
trunk and used it to pry the bent metal of the left front
fender away from the tire, so that the wheel could turn. The
second he veered off the road (he must have dozed off for an
instant), the thought came to him that Amanda would use the
accident as a reason for not trusting him with Ben. While he
worked with the tire iron, a man stopped his car and got out
and gave him drunken advice. "Never buy a motorcycle," he

said. "They spin out of control. You go with them—you don't have a chance." Tom nodded. "Did you know Doug's son?" the man asked. Tom said nothing. The man shook his head sadly and then went to the back of his car and opened the trunk. Tom watched him as he took flares out of his trunk and began to light them and place them in the road. The man came forward with several flares still in hand. He looked confused that he had so many. Then he lit the extras, one by one, and placed them in a semicircle around the front of the car, where Tom was working. Tom felt like some saint, in a shrine.

When the wheel was freed, he drove the car to Amanda's, cursing himself for having skidded and slamming the car into somebody's mailbox. When he got into the house, he snapped on the floodlight in the back yard, and then went into the kitchen to make some coffee before he looked at the damage again.

In the city, making a last stop before he finally got his car out of the garage, he had eaten eggs and bagels at an all-night deli. Now it seems to him that his teeth still ache from chewing. The hot coffee in his mouth feels good. The weak early sunlight, nearly out of reach of where he can move his chair and still be said to be sitting at the table, feels good where it strikes him on one shoulder. When his teeth don't ache, he begins to notice that he feels nothing in his mouth; where the sun strikes him, he can feel the wool of his sweater warming him the way a sweater is supposed to, even without sun shining on it. The sweater was a Christmas present from his son. She, of course, picked it out and wrapped it: a box enclosed in shiny white paper, crayoned on by Ben. "B E N," in big letters. Scribbles that looked like the wings of birds.

Amanda and Shelby and Ben are upstairs. Through the doorway he can see a digital clock on the mantel in the next room, on the other side from the box of ashes. At seven, the alarm will go off and Shelby will come downstairs, his gray hair, in the sharpening morning light, looking like one of those cheap abalone lights they sell at the seashore. He will stumble around, look down to make sure his fly is closed; he will drink coffee from one of Amanda's mother's bone-china cups, which he holds in the palms of his hands. His hands are so big that you have to look to see that he is cradling a cup, that he is not gulping coffee from his hands the way you would drink water from a stream.

Once, when Shelby was leaving at eight o'clock to drive into the city, Amanda looked up from the dining-room table where the three of them had been having breakfast—having a friendly, normal time, Tom had thought—and said to Shelby, "Please don't leave me alone with him." Shelby looked perplexed and embarrassed when she got up and followed him into the kitchen. "Who gave him the key, sweetheart?" Shelby whispered. Tom looked through the doorway. Shelby's hand was low on her hip—partly a joking sexual gesture, partly a possessive one. "Don't try to tell me there's anything you're afraid of," Shelby said.

Ben sleeps and sleeps. He often sleeps until ten or eleven. Up there in his bed, sunlight washing over him.

Tom looks again at the box with the ashes in it on the mantel. If there is another life, what if something goes wrong and he is reincarnated as a camel and Ben as a cloud and there is just no way for the two of them to get together? He wants Ben. He wants him now.

The alarm is ringing, so loud it sounds like a million madmen beating tin. Shelby's feet on the floor. The sunlight shining a rectangle of light through the middle of the room. Shelby will walk through that patch of light as though it were a rug rolled out down the aisle of a church. Six months ago, seven, Tom went to Amanda and Shelby's wedding.

Shelby is naked, and startled to see him. He stumbles,

grabs his brown robe from his shoulder and puts it on, asking Tom what he's doing there and saying good morning at the same time. "Every goddam clock in the house is either two minutes slow or five minutes fast," Shelby says. He hops around on the cold tile in the kitchen, putting water on to boil, pulling his robe tighter around him. "I thought this floor would warm up in summer," Shelby says, sighing. He shifts his weight from one side to the other, the way a fighter warms up, chafing his big hands.

Amanda comes down. She is wearing a pair of jeans, rolled at the ankles, black high-heeled sandals, a black silk blouse. She stumbles like Shelby. She does not look happy to see Tom. She looks, and doesn't say anything.

"I wanted to talk to you," Tom says. He sounds lame. An animal in a trap, trying to keep its eyes calm.

"I'm going into the city," she says. "Claudia's having a cyst removed. It's all a mess. I have to meet her there, at nine. I don't feel like talking now. Let's talk tonight. Come back tonight. Or stay today." Her hands through her auburn hair. She sits in a chair, accepts the coffee Shelby brings.

"More?" Shelby says to Tom. "You want something more?"

Amanda looks at Tom through the steam rising from her coffee cup. "I think that we are all dealing with this situation very well," she says. "I'm not sorry I gave you the key. Shelby and I discussed it, and we both felt that you should have access to the house. But in the back of my mind I assumed that you would use the key—I had in mind more . . . emergency situations."

"I didn't sleep well last night," Shelby says. "Now I would like it if I didn't feel that there was going to be a scene to start things off this morning."

Amanda sighs. She seems as perturbed with Shelby as she is with Tom. "And if I can say something without being jumped on," she says to Shelby, "because, yes, you *told* me

not to buy a Peugeot, and now the damned thing won't run
—as long as you're here, Tom, it would be nice if you gave
Inez a ride to the market."

"We saw seven deer running through the woods yesterday," Shelby says.

"Oh, cut it out, Shelby," Amanda says.

"Your problems I'm trying to deal with, Amanda," Shelby
says. "A little less of the rough tongue, don't you think?"

Inez has pinned a sprig of phlox in her hair, and she walks
as though she feels pretty. The first time Tom saw Inez, she
was working in her sister's garden—actually, standing in the
garden in bare feet, with a long cotton skirt sweeping the
ground. She was holding a basket heaped high with iris
and daisies. She was nineteen years old and had just arrived
in the United States. That year, she lived with her sister and
her sister's husband, Metcalf—his friend Metcalf, the craziest
man at the ad agency. Metcalf began to study photography,
just to take pictures of Inez. Finally his wife got jealous and
asked Inez to leave. She had trouble finding a job, and
Amanda liked her and felt sorry for her, and she persuaded
Tom to have her come live with them, after she had Ben.
Inez came, bringing boxes of pictures of herself, one suitcase,
and a pet gerbil that died her first night in the house. All the
next day, Inez cried, and Amanda put her arms around her.
Inez always seemed like a member of the family, from the first.

By the edge of the pond where Tom is walking with Inez,
there is a black dog, panting, staring up at a Frisbee. Its mas-
ter raises the Frisbee, and the dog stares as though transfixed
by a beam of light from heaven. The Frisbee flies, curves,
and the dog has it as it dips down.

"I'm going to ask Amanda if Ben can come live with me,"
Tom says to Inez.

"She'll never say yes," Inez says.

"What do you think Amanda would think if I kidnapped Ben?" Tom says.

"Ben's adjusting," she says. "That's a bad idea."

"You think I'm putting you on? I'd kidnap you with him."

"She's not a bad person," Inez says. "You think about upsetting her too much. She has problems, too."

"Since when do you defend your cheap employer?"

His son has picked up a stick. The dog, in the distance, stares. The dog's owner calls its name: "Sam!" The dog snaps his head around. He bounds through the grass, head raised, staring at the Frisbee.

"I should have gone to college," Inez says.

"College?" Tom says. The dog is running and running. "What would you have studied?"

Inez swoops down in back of Ben, picks him up and squeezes him. He struggles, as though he wants to be put down, but when Inez bends over he holds on to her. They come to where Tom parked the car, and Inez lowers Ben to the ground.

"Remember to stop at the market," Inez says. "I've got to get something for dinner."

"She'll be full of sushi and Perrier. I'll bet they don't want dinner."

"You'll want dinner," she says. "I should get something."

He drives to the market. When they pull into the parking lot, Ben goes into the store with Inez, instead of to the liquor store next door with him. Tom gets a bottle of cognac and pockets the change. The clerk raises his eyebrows and drops them several times, like Groucho Marx, as he slips a flyer into the bag, with a picture on the front showing a blue-green drink in a champagne glass.

"Inez and I have secrets," Ben says, while they are driving home. He is standing up to hug her around the neck from the back seat.

Ben is tired, and he taunts people when he is that way. Amanda does not think Ben should be condescended to: she reads him R. D. Laing, not fairy tales; she has him eat French food, and only indulges him by serving the sauce on the side. Amanda refused to send him to kindergarten. If she had, Tom believes, if he was around other children his age, he might get rid of some of his annoying mannerisms.

"For instance," Inez says, "I might get married."

"Who?" he says, so surprised that his hands feel cold on the wheel.

"A man who lives in town. You don't know him."

"You're dating someone?" he says.

He guns the car to get it up the driveway, which is slick with mud washed down by a lawn sprinkler. He steers hard, waiting for the instant when he will be able to feel that the car will make it. The car slithers a bit but then goes straight; they get to the top. He pulls onto the lawn, by the back door, leaving the way clear for Shelby and Amanda's car to pull into the garage.

"It would make sense that if I'm thinking of marrying somebody I would have been out on a date with him," Inez says.

Inez has been with them since Ben was born, five years ago, and she has gestures and expressions now like Amanda's —Amanda's patient half-smile that lets him know she is half charmed and half at a loss that he is so unsophisticated. When Amanda divorced him, he went to Kennedy to pick her up when she returned, and her arms were loaded with pineapples as she came up the ramp. When he saw her, he gave her that same patient half-smile.

At eight, they aren't back, and Inez is worried. At nine, they still aren't back. "She did say something about a play yesterday," Inez whispers to Tom. Ben is playing with a puzzle in the other room. It is his bedtime—past it—and he has the concentration of Einstein. Inez goes into the room again, and he listens while she reasons with Ben. She is quieter than Amanda; she will get what she wants. Tom reads the newspaper from the market. It comes out once a week. There are articles about deer leaping across the road, lady artists who do batik who will give demonstrations at the library. He hears Ben running up the stairs, chased by Inez.

Water is turned on. He hears Ben laughing above the water. It makes him happy that Ben is so well adjusted; when he himself was five, no woman would have been allowed in the bathroom with him. Now that he is almost forty, he would like it very much if he were in the bathtub instead of Ben— if Inez were soaping his back, her fingers sliding down his skin.

For a long time, he has been thinking about water, about traveling somewhere so that he can walk on the beach, see the ocean. Every year he spends in New York he gets more and more restless. He often wakes up at night in his apartment, hears the air-conditioners roaring and the woman in the apartment above shuffling away her insomnia in satin slippers. (She has shown them to him, to explain that her walking cannot possibly be what is keeping him awake.) On nights when he can't sleep, he opens his eyes just a crack and pretends, as he did when he was a child, that the furniture is something else. He squints the tall mahogany chest of drawers into the trunk of a palm tree; blinking his eyes quickly, he makes the night light pulse like a buoy bobbing in the water and tries to imagine that his bed is a boat, and that he is setting sail, as he and Amanda did years before, in Maine, where Perkins Cove widens into the choppy, ink-blue ocean.

Upstairs, the water is being turned off. It is silent. Silence for a long time. Inez laughs. Rocky jumps onto the stairs, and one board creaks as the cat pads upstairs. Amanda will not let him have Ben. He is sure of it. After a few minutes, he hears Inez laugh about making it snow as she holds the can of talcum powder high and lets it sift down on Ben in the tub.

Deciding that he wants at least a good night, Tom takes off his shoes and climbs the stairs; no need to disturb the quiet of the house. The door to Shelby and Amanda's bedroom is open. Ben and Inez are curled on the bed, and she has begun to read to him by the dim light. She lies next to him on the vast blue quilt spread over the bed, on her side with her back to the door, with one arm sweeping slowly through the air: "*Los soldados hicieron alto a la entrada del pueblo....*"

Ben sees him, and pretends not to. Ben loves Inez more than any of them. Tom goes away, so that she will not see him and stop reading.

He goes into the room where Shelby has his study. He turns on the light. There is a dimmer switch, and the light comes on very low. He leaves it that way.

He examines a photograph of the beak of a bird. A photograph next to it of a bird's wing. He moves in close to the picture and rests his cheek against the glass. He is worried. It isn't like Amanda not to come back, when she knows he is waiting to see her. He feels the coolness from the glass spreading down his body. There is no reason to think that Amanda is dead. When Shelby drives, he creeps along like an old man.

He goes into the bathroom and splashes water on his face, dries himself on what he thinks is Amanda's towel. He goes back to the study and stretches out on the daybed, under the open window, waiting for the car. He is lying very still on an unfamiliar bed, in a house he used to visit two or three times a year when he and Amanda were married—a house always decorated with flowers for Amanda's birthday, or smelling of newly cut pine at Christmas, when there was angel hair arranged into nests on the tabletops, with tiny Christmas balls glittering inside, like miraculously colored eggs. Amanda's mother is dead. He and Amanda are divorced. Amanda is married to Shelby. These events are unreal. What is real is the past, and the Amanda of years ago—that Amanda whose image he cannot get out of his mind, the scene he keeps remembering. It had happened on a day when he had not expected to discover anything; he was going along with his life with an ease he would never have again, and, in a way, what happened was so painful that even the pain of her leaving, and her going to Shelby, would later be dulled in comparison. Amanda—in her pretty underpants, in the bedroom of their city apartment, standing by the window—had crossed her hands at the wrists, covering her breasts, and said to Ben, "It's gone now. The milk is gone." Ben, in his diapers and T-shirt, lying on the bed and looking up at her. The mug of milk waiting for him on the bedside table—he'd drink it as surely as Hamlet would drink from the goblet of poison. Ben's little hand on the mug, her breasts revealed again, her hand overlapping his hand, the mug tilted, the first swallow. That night, Tom had moved his head from his pillow to hers, slipped down in the bed until his cheek came to the top of her breast. He had known he would never sleep, he was so amazed at the offhand way she had just done such a powerful thing. "Baby—" he had said, beginning, and she had said, "I'm not your baby." Pulling away from him, from Ben. Who would have guessed that what she wanted was another man— a man with whom she would stretch into sleep on a vast ocean of blue quilted satin, a bed as wide as the ocean? The first time he came to Greenwich and saw that bed, with her watching him, he had cupped his hand to his brow and looked far across the room, as though he might see China.

The day he went to Greenwich to visit for the first time after the divorce, Ben and Shelby hadn't been there. Inez was there, though, and she had gone along on the tour of the redecorated house that Amanda had insisted on giving him.

Tom knew that Inez had not wanted to walk around the house with them. She had done it because Amanda had asked her to, and she had also done it because she thought it might make it less awkward for him. In a way different from the way he loved Amanda, but still a very real way, he would always love Inez for that.

Now Inez is coming into the study, hesitating as her eyes accustom themselves to the dark. "You're awake?" she whispers. "Are you all right?" She walks to the bed slowly and sits down. His eyes are closed, and he is sure that he could sleep forever. Her hand is on his; he smiles as he begins to drift and dream. A bird extends its wing with the grace of a fan opening; *los soldados* are poised at the crest of the hill. About Inez he will always remember this: when she came to work on Monday, after the weekend when Amanda had told him about Shelby and said that she was getting a divorce, Inez whispered to him in the kitchen, "I'm still your friend." Inez had come close to him to whisper it, the way a bashful lover might move quietly forward to say "I love you." She had said that she was his friend, and he had told her that he never doubted that. Then they had stood there, still and quiet, as if the walls of the room were mountains and their words might fly against them.

THE
BURNING
HOUSE

Freddy Fox is in the kitchen with me. He has just washed
and dried an avocado seed I don't want, and he is leaning
against the wall, rolling a joint. In five minutes, I will not be
able to count on him. However: he started late in the day,
and he has already brought in wood for the fire, gone to the
store down the road for matches, and set the table. "You mean
you'd know this stuff was Limoges even if you didn't turn
the plate over?" he called from the dining room. He pretended
to be about to throw one of the plates into the kitchen, like a
Frisbee. Sam, the dog, believed him and shot up, kicking the
rug out behind him and skidding forward before he realized
his error; it was like the Road Runner tricking Wile E. Coyote
into going over the cliff for the millionth time. His jowls sank
in disappointment.

"I see there's a full moon," Freddy says. "There's just nothing that can hold a candle to nature. The moon and the stars,
the tides and the sunshine—and we just don't stop for long
enough to wonder at it all. We're so engrossed in ourselves."
He takes a very long drag on the joint. "We stand and stir

the sauce in the pot instead of going to the window and gazing at the moon."

"You don't mean anything personal by that, I assume."

"I love the way you pour cream in a pan. I like to come up
behind you and watch the sauce bubble."

"No, thank you," I say. "You're starting late in the day."

"My responsibilities have ended. You don't trust me to help
with the cooking, and I've already brought in firewood and
run an errand, and this very morning I exhausted myself by
taking Mr. Sam jogging with me, down at Putnam Park.
You're sure you won't?"

"No, thanks," I say. "Not now, anyway."

"I love it when you stand over the steam coming out of a
pan and the hairs around your forehead curl into damp little
curls."

My husband, Frank Wayne, is Freddy's half brother. Frank
is an accountant. Freddy is closer to me than to Frank. Since
Frank talks to Freddy more than he talks to me, however, and
since Freddy is totally loyal, Freddy always knows more than
I know. It pleases me that he does not know how to stir sauce;
he will start talking, his mind will drift, and when next you
look the sauce will be lumpy, or boiling away.

Freddy's criticism of Frank is only implied. "What a gra-
cious gesture to entertain his friends on the weekend," he says.

"Male friends," I say.

"I didn't mean that you're the sort of lady who doesn't draw
the line. I most certainly did not mean that," Freddy says. "I
would even have been surprised if you had taken a toke of
this deadly stuff while you were at the stove."

"O.K.," I say, and take the joint from him. Half of it is
left when I take it. Half an inch is left after I've taken two
drags and given it back.

"More surprised still if you'd shaken the ashes into the
saucepan."

"You'd tell people I'd done it when they'd finished eating,

and I'd be embarrassed. You can do it, though. I wouldn't be embarrassed if it was a story you told on yourself."

"You really understand me," Freddy says. "It's moon-madness, but I have to shake just this little bit in the sauce. I have to do it."

He does it.

Frank and Tucker are in the living room. Just a few minutes ago, Frank returned from getting Tucker at the train. Tucker loves to visit. To him, Fairfield County is as mysterious as Alaska. He brought with him from New York a crock of mustard, a jeroboam of champagne, cocktail napkins with a picture of a plane flying over a building on them, twenty egret feathers ("You cannot get them anymore—strictly illegal," Tucker whispered to me), and, under his black cowboy hat with the rhinestone-studded chin strap, a toy frog that hopped when wound. Tucker owns a gallery in SoHo, and Frank keeps his books. Tucker is now stretched out in the living room, visiting with Frank, and Freddy and I are both listening.

". . . so everything I've been told indicates that he lives a purely Jekyll-and-Hyde existence. He's twenty years old, and I can see that since he's still living at home he might not want to flaunt his gayness. When he came into the gallery, he had his hair slicked back—just with water, I got close enough to sniff—and his mother was all but holding his hand. So fresh-scrubbed. The stories I'd heard. Anyway, when I called, his father started looking for the number where he could be reached on the Vineyard—very irritated, because I didn't know James, and if I'd just phoned James I could have found him in a flash. He's talking to himself, looking for the number, and I say, 'Oh, did he go to visit friends or—' and his father interrupts and says, 'He was going to a gay pig roast. He's been gone since Monday.' *Just like that.*"

Freddy helps me carry the food out to the table. When we are all at the table, I mention the young artist Tucker was talking about. "Frank says his paintings are really incredible," I say to Tucker.

"Makes Estes look like an Abstract Expressionist," Tucker says. "I want that boy. I really want that boy."

"You'll get him," Frank says. "You get everybody you go after."

Tucker cuts a small piece of meat. He cuts it small so that he can talk while chewing. "Do I?" he says.

Freddy is smoking at the table, gazing dazedly at the moon centered in the window. "After dinner," he says, putting the back of his hand against his forehead when he sees that I am looking at him, "we must all go to the lighthouse."

"If only *you* painted," Tucker says. "I'd want you."

"You couldn't have me," Freddy snaps. He reconsiders. "That sounded halfhearted, didn't it? Anybody who wants me can have me. This is the only place I can be on Saturday night where somebody isn't hustling me."

"Wear looser pants," Frank says to Freddy.

"This is so much better than some bar that stinks of cigarette smoke and leather. Why do I do it?" Freddy says. "Seriously—do you think I'll ever stop?"

"Let's not be serious," Tucker says.

"I keep thinking of this table as a big boat, with dishes and glasses rocking on it," Freddy says.

He takes the bone from his plate and walks out to the kitchen, dripping sauce on the floor. He walks as though he's on the deck of a wave-tossed ship. "Mr. Sam!" he calls, and the dog springs up from the living-room floor, where he had been sleeping; his toenails on the bare wood floor sound like a wheel spinning in gravel. "You don't have to beg," Freddy says. "Jesus, Sammy—I'm just giving it to you."

"I hope there's a bone involved," Tucker says, rolling his eyes to Frank. He cuts another tiny piece of meat. "I hope your brother does understand why I couldn't keep him on.

He was good at what he did, but he also might say just *any-thing* to a customer. You have to believe me that if I hadn't been extremely embarrassed more than once I never would have let him go."

"He should have finished school," Frank says, sopping up sauce on his bread. "He'll knock around a while longer, then get tired of it and settle down to something."

"You think I died out here?" Freddy calls. "You think I can't hear you?"

"I'm not saying anything I wouldn't say to your face," Frank says.

"I'll tell you what I wouldn't say to your face," Freddy says. "You've got a swell wife and kid and dog, and you're a snob, and you take it all for granted."

Frank puts down his fork, completely exasperated. He looks at me.

"He came to work once this stoned," Tucker says. *"Comprenez-vous?"*

"You like me because you feel sorry for me," Freddy says.

He is sitting on the concrete bench outdoors, in the area that's a garden in the springtime. It is early April now—not quite spring. It's very foggy out. It rained while we were eating, and now it has turned mild. I'm leaning against a tree, across from him, glad it's so dark and misty that I can't look down and see the damage the mud is doing to my boots.

"Who's his girlfriend?" Freddy says.

"If I told you her name, you'd tell him I told you."

"Slow down. What?"

"I won't tell you, because you'll tell him that I know."

"He knows you know."

"I don't think so."

"How did you find out?"

"He talked about her. I kept hearing her name for months,

and then we went to a party at Garner's, and she was there, and when I said something about her later he said, 'Natalie who?' It was much too obvious. It gave the whole thing away."

He sighs. "I just did something very optimistic," he says. "I came out here with Mr. Sam and he dug up a rock and I put the avocado seed in the hole and packed dirt on top of it. Don't say it—I know: can't grow outside, we'll still have another snow, even if it grew, the next year's frost would kill it."

"He's embarrassed," I say. "When he's home, he avoids me. But it's rotten to avoid Mark, too. Six years old, and he calls up his friend Neal to hint that he wants to go over there. He doesn't do that when we're here alone."

Freddy picks up a stick and pokes around in the mud with it. "I'll bet Tucker's after that painter personally, not because he's the hottest thing since pancakes. That expression of his— it's always the same. Maybe Nixon really loved his mother, but with that expression who could believe him? It's a curse to have a face that won't express what you mean."

"Amy!" Tucker calls. "Telephone."

Freddy waves goodbye to me with the muddy stick. " 'I am not a crook,' " Freddy says. "Jesus Christ."

Sam bounds halfway toward the house with me, then turns and goes back to Freddy.

It's Marilyn, Neal's mother, on the phone.

"Hi," Marilyn says. "He's afraid to spend the night."

"Oh, no," I say. "He said he wouldn't be."

She lowers her voice. "We can try it out, but I think he'll start crying."

"I'll come get him."

"I can bring him home. You're having a dinner party, aren't you?"

I lower my voice. "Some party. Tucker's here. J.D. never showed up."

"Well," she says. "I'm sure that what you cooked was good."

"It's so foggy out, Marilyn. I'll come get Mark."

"He can stay. I'll be a martyr," she says, and hangs up before I can object.

Freddy comes into the house, tracking in mud. Sam lies in the kitchen, waiting for his paws to be cleaned. "Come on," Freddy says, hitting his hand against his thigh, having no idea what Sam is doing. Sam gets up and runs after him. They go into the small downstairs bathroom together. Sam loves to watch people urinate. Sometimes he sings, to harmonize with the sound of the urine going into the water. There are footprints and pawprints everywhere. Tucker is shrieking with laughter in the living room. ". . . he says, he says to the other one, 'Then, dearie, have you ever played *spin* the bottle?'" Frank's and Tucker's laughter drowns out the sound of Freddy peeing in the bathroom. I turn on the water in the kitchen sink, and it drowns out all the noise. I begin to scrape the dishes. Tucker is telling another story when I turn off the water: ". . . that it was Onassis in the Anvil, and nothing would talk him out of it. They told him Onassis was dead, and he thought they were trying to make him think he was crazy. There was nothing to do but go along with him, but, God—he was trying to goad this poor old fag into fighting about Stavros Niarchos. You know—Onassis's *enemy*. He thought it was *Onassis*. In the *Anvil*." There is a sound of a glass breaking. Frank or Tucker puts *John Coltrane Live in Seattle* on the stereo and turns the volume down low. The bathroom door opens. Sam runs into the kitchen and begins to lap water from his dish. Freddy takes his little silver case and his rolling papers out of his shirt pocket. He puts a piece of paper on the kitchen table and is about to sprinkle grass on it, but realizes just in time that the paper has absorbed water from a puddle. He balls it up with his thumb, flicks it to the floor, puts a piece of rolling paper where the table's dry and shakes a line of grass down it. "You smoke this," he says to me. "I'll do the dishes."

"We'll both smoke it. I'll wash and you can wipe."

"I forgot to tell them I put ashes in the sauce," he says.

"I wouldn't interrupt."

"At least he pays Frank ten times what any other accountant for an art gallery would make," Freddy says.

Tucker is beating his hand on the arm of the sofa as he talks, stomping his feet. ". . . so he's trying to feel him out, to see if this old guy with the dyed hair knew *Maria Callas.* Jesus! And he's so out of it he's trying to think what opera singers are called, and instead of coming up with '*diva*' he comes up with '*duenna.*' At this point, Larry Betwell went up to him and tried to calm him down, and he breaks into song —some aria or something that Maria Callas was famous for. Larry told him he was going to lose his *teeth* if he didn't get it together, and . . ."

"He spends a lot of time in gay hangouts, for not being gay," Freddy says.

I scream and jump back from the sink, hitting the glass I'm rinsing against the faucet, shattering green glass everywhere.

"What?" Freddy says. "Jesus Christ, what is it?"

Too late, I realize what it must have been that I saw: J.D. in a goat mask, the puckered pink plastic lips against the window by the kitchen sink.

"I'm sorry," J.D. says, coming through the door and nearly colliding with Frank, who has rushed into the kitchen. Tucker is right behind him.

"Oooh," Tucker says, feigning disappointment, "I thought Freddy smooched her."

"I'm sorry," J.D. says again. "I thought you'd know it was me."

The rain must have started again, because J.D. is soaking wet. He has turned the mask around so that the goat's head stares out from the back of his head. "I got lost," J.D. says. He has a farmhouse upstate. "I missed the turn. I went miles. I missed the whole dinner, didn't I?"

"What did you do wrong?" Frank asks.

"I didn't turn left onto 58. I don't know why I didn't realize my mistake, but I went *miles*. It was raining so hard I couldn't go over twenty-five miles an hour. Your driveway is all mud. You're going to have to push me out."

"There's some roast left over. And salad, if you want it," I say.

"Bring it in the living room," Frank says to J.D. Freddy is holding out a plate to him. J.D. reaches for the plate. Freddy pulls it back. J.D. reaches again, and Freddy is so stoned that he isn't quick enough this time—J.D. grabs it.

"I thought you'd know it was me," J.D. says. "I apologize." He dishes salad onto the plate. "You'll be rid of me for six months, in the morning."

"Where does your plane leave from?" Freddy says.

"Kennedy."

"Come in here!" Tucker calls. "I've got a story for you about Perry Dwyer down at the Anvil last week, when he thought he saw Aristotle Onassis."

"Who's Perry Dwyer?" J.D. says.

"That is not the point of the story, dear man. And when you're in Cassis, I want you to look up an American painter over there. Will you? He doesn't have a phone. Anyway—I've been tracking him, and I know where he is now, and I am *very* interested, if you would stress that with him, to do a show in June that will be *only* him. He doesn't answer my letters."

"Your hand is cut," J.D. says to me.

"Forget it," I say. "Go ahead."

"I'm sorry," he says. "Did I make you do that?"

"Yes, you did."

"Don't keep your finger under the water. Put pressure on it to stop the bleeding."

He puts the plate on the table. Freddy is leaning against the counter, staring at the blood swirling in the sink, and smoking the joint all by himself. I can feel the little curls on my forehead that Freddy was talking about. They feel heavy on my skin. I hate to see my own blood. I'm sweating. I let J.D. do what he does; he turns off the water and wraps his hand around my second finger, squeezing. Water runs down our wrists.

Freddy jumps to answer the phone when it rings, as though a siren just went off behind him. He calls me to the phone, but J.D. steps in front of me, shakes his head no, and takes the dish towel and wraps it around my hand before he lets me go.

"Well," Marilyn says. "I had the best of intentions, but my battery's dead."

J.D. is standing behind me, with his hand on my shoulder.

"I'll be right over," I say. "He's not upset now, is he?"

"No, but he's dropped enough hints that he doesn't think he can make it through the night."

"O.K.," I say. "I'm sorry about all of this."

"Six years old," Marilyn says. "Wait till he grows up and gets that feeling."

I hang up.

"Let me see your hand," J.D. says.

"I don't want to look at it. Just go get me a Band-Aid, please."

He turns and goes upstairs. I unwrap the towel and look at it. It's pretty deep, but no glass is in my finger. I feel funny; the outlines of things are turning yellow. I sit in the chair by the phone. Sam comes and lies beside me, and I stare at his black-and-yellow tail, beating. I reach down with my good hand and pat him, breathing deeply in time with every second pat.

"*Rothko?*" Tucker says bitterly, in the living room. "Nothing is great that can appear on greeting cards. Wyeth is that way. Would 'Christina's World' look bad on a cocktail napkin? You know it wouldn't."

I jump as the phone rings again. "Hello?" I say, wedging

the phone against my shoulder with my ear, wrapping the dish towel tighter around my hand.

"Tell them it's a crank call. Tell them anything," Johnny says. "I miss you. How's Saturday night at your house?"

"All right," I say. I catch my breath.

"Everything's all right here, too. Yes indeed. Roast rack of lamb. Friend of Nicole's who's going to Key West tomorrow had too much to drink and got depressed because he thought it was raining in Key West, and I said I'd go in my study and call the National Weather Service. Hello, Weather Service. How are you?"

J.D. comes down from upstairs with two Band-Aids and stands beside me, unwrapping one. I want to say to Johnny, "I'm cut. I'm bleeding. It's no joke."

It's all right to talk in front of J.D., but I don't know who else might overhear me.

"I'd say they made the delivery about four this afternoon," I say.

"This is the church, this is the steeple. Open the door, and see all the people," Johnny says. "Take care of yourself. I'll hang up and find out if it's raining in Key West."

"Late in the afternoon," I say. "Everything is fine."

"Nothing is fine," Johnny says. "Take care of yourself."

He hangs up. I put the phone down, and realize that I'm still having trouble focusing, the sight of my cut finger made me so light-headed. I don't look at the finger again as J.D. undoes the towel and wraps the Band-Aids around my finger.

"What's going on in here?" Frank says, coming into the dining room.

"I cut my finger," I say. "It's O.K."

"You did?" he says. He looks woozy—a little drunk. "Who keeps calling?"

"Marilyn. Mark changed his mind about staying all night. She was going to bring him home, but her battery's dead. You'll have to get him. Or I will."

"Who called the second time?" he says.

"The oil company. They wanted to know if we got our delivery today."

He nods. "I'll go get him, if you want," he says. He lowers his voice. "Tucker's probably going to whirl himself into a tornado for an encore," he says, nodding toward the living room. "I'll take him with me."

"Do you want me to go get him?" J.D. says.

"I don't mind getting some air," Frank says. "Thanks, though. Why don't you go in the living room and eat your dinner?"

"You forgive me?" J.D. says.

"Sure," I say. "It wasn't your fault. Where did you get that mask?"

"I found it on top of a Goodwill box in Manchester. There was also a beautiful old birdcage—solid brass."

The phone rings again. I pick it up. "Wouldn't I love to be in Key West with you," Johnny says. He makes a sound as though he's kissing me and hangs up.

"Wrong number," I say.

Frank feels in his pants pocket for the car keys.

J.D. knows about Johnny. He introduced me, in the faculty lounge, where J.D. and I had gone to get a cup of coffee after I registered for classes. After being gone for nearly two years, J.D. still gets mail at the department—he said he had to stop by for the mail anyway, so he'd drive me to campus and point me toward the registrar's. J.D. taught English; now he does nothing. J.D. is glad that I've gone back to college to study art again, now that Mark is in school. I'm six credits away from an M.A. in art history. He wants me to think about myself, instead of thinking about Mark all the time. He talks as though I could roll Mark out on a string and let him fly off, high above me. J.D.'s wife and son died in a car crash.

His son was Mark's age. "I wasn't prepared," J.D. said when we were driving over that day. He always says this when he talks about it. "How could you be prepared for such a thing?" I asked him. "I am now," he said. Then, realizing he was acting very hardboiled, made fun of himself. "Go on," he said, "punch me in the stomach. Hit me as hard as you can." We both knew he wasn't prepared for anything. When he couldn't find a parking place that day, his hands were wrapped around the wheel so tightly that his knuckles turned white.

Johnny came in as we were drinking coffee. J.D. was looking at his junk mail—publishers wanting him to order anthologies, ways to get free dictionaries.

"You are so lucky to be out of it," Johnny said, by way of greeting. "What do you do when you've spent two weeks on *Hamlet* and the student writes about Hamlet's good friend Horchow?"

He threw a blue book into J.D.'s lap. J.D. sailed it back.

"Johnny," he said, "this is Amy."

"Hi, Amy," Johnny said.

"You remember when Frank Wayne was in graduate school here? Amy's Frank's wife."

"Hi, Amy," Johnny said.

J.D. told me he knew it the instant Johnny walked into the room—he knew that second that he should introduce me as somebody's wife. He could have predicted it all from the way Johnny looked at me.

For a long time J.D. gloated that he had been prepared for what happened next—that Johnny and I were going to get together. It took me to disturb his pleasure in himself—me, crying hysterically on the phone last month, not knowing what to do, what move to make next.

"Don't do anything for a while. I guess that's my advice," J.D. said. "But you probably shouldn't listen to me. All I can do myself is run away, hide out. I'm not the learned professor.

You know what I believe. I believe all that wicked fairy-tale crap: your heart will break, your house will burn."

Tonight, because he doesn't have a garage at his farm, J.D. has come to leave his car in the empty half of our two-car garage while he's in France. I look out the window and see his old Saab, glowing in the moonlight. J.D. has brought his favorite book, *A Vision*, to read on the plane. He says his suitcase contains only a spare pair of jeans, cigarettes, and underwear. He is going to buy a leather jacket in France, at a store where he almost bought a leather jacket two years ago.

In our bedroom there are about twenty small glass prisms hung with fishing line from one of the exposed beams; they catch the morning light, and we stare at them like a cat eyeing catnip held above its head. Just now, it is 2 A.M. At six-thirty, they will be filled with dazzling color. At four or five, Mark will come into the bedroom and get in bed with us. Sam will wake up, stretch, and shake, and the tags on his collar will clink, and he will yawn and shake again and go downstairs, where J.D. is asleep in his sleeping bag and Tucker is asleep on the sofa, and get a drink of water from his dish. Mark has been coming into our bedroom for about a year. He gets onto the bed by climbing up on a footstool that horrified me when I first saw it—a gift from Frank's mother: a footstool that says "Today Is the First Day of the Rest of Your Life" in needle-point. I kept it in a closet for years, but it occurred to me that it would help Mark get up onto the bed, so he would not have to make a little leap and possibly skin his shin again. Now Mark does not disturb us when he comes into the bedroom, except that it bothers me that he has reverted to sucking his thumb. Sometimes he lies in bed with his cold feet against my leg. Sometimes, small as he is, he snores.

Somebody is playing a record downstairs. It's the Velvet Underground—Lou Reed, in a dream or swoon, singing "Sunday Morning." I can barely hear the whispering and tinkling of the record. I can only follow it because I've heard it a hundred times.

I am lying in bed, waiting for Frank to get out of the bathroom. My cut finger throbs. Things are going on in the house even though I have gone to bed; water runs, the record plays. Sam is still downstairs, so there must be some action.

I have known everybody in the house for years, and as time goes by I know them all less and less. J.D. was Frank's adviser in college. Frank was his best student, and they started to see each other outside of class. They played handball. J.D. and his family came to dinner. We went there. That summer—the summer Frank decided to go to graduate school in business instead of English—J.D.'s wife and son deserted him in a more horrible way, in that car crash. J.D. has quit his job. He has been to Las Vegas, to Colorado, New Orleans, Los Angeles, Paris twice; he tapes post cards to the walls of his living room. A lot of the time, on the weekends, he shows up at our house with his sleeping bag. Sometimes he brings a girl. Lately, not. Years ago, Tucker was in Frank's therapy group in New York, and ended up hiring Frank to work as the accountant for his gallery. Tucker was in therapy at the time because he was obsessed with foreigners. Now he is also obsessed with homosexuals. He gives fashionable parties to which he invites many foreigners and homosexuals. Before the parties he does TM and yoga, and during the parties he does Seconals and isometrics. When I first met him, he was living for the summer in his sister's house in Vermont while she was in Europe, and he called us one night, in New York, in a real panic because there were wasps all over. They were "hatching," he said—big, sleepy wasps that were everywhere. We said we'd come; we drove all through the night to get to Brattleboro. It was true: there were wasps on the undersides of plates, in the plants, in the folds of curtains. Tucker was so upset that he was out behind the house, in the cold Vermont morning, wrapped like an Indian in a blanket, with only his pajamas on underneath. He was sitting in a lawn chair, hiding behind a bush, waiting for us to come.

And Freddy—"Reddy Fox," when Frank is feeling affectionate toward him. When we first met, I taught him to ice-skate and he taught me to waltz; in the summer, at Atlantic City, he'd go with me on a roller coaster that curved high over the waves. I was the one—not Frank—who would get out of bed in the middle of the night and meet him at an all-night deli and put my arm around his shoulders, the way he put his arm around my shoulders on the roller coaster, and talk quietly to him until he got over his latest anxiety attack. Now he tests me, and I retreat: this man he picked up, this man who picked him up, how it feels to have forgotten somebody's name when your hand is in the back pocket of his jeans and you're not even halfway to your apartment. Reddy Fox —admiring my new red silk blouse, stroking his fingertips down the front, and my eyes wide, because I could feel his fingers on my chest, even though I was holding the blouse in front of me on a hanger to be admired. All those moments, and all they meant was that I was fooled into thinking I knew these people because I knew the small things, the personal things.

Freddy will always be more stoned than I am, because he feels comfortable getting stoned with me, and I'll always be reminded that he's more lost. Tucker knows he can come to the house and be the center of attention; he can tell all the stories he knows, and we'll never tell the story we know about him hiding in the bushes like a frightened dog. J.D. comes back from his trips with boxes full of post cards, and I look at all of them as though they're photographs taken by him, and I know, and he knows, that what he likes about them is their flatness—the unreality of them, the unreality of what he does.

Last summer, I read *The Metamorphosis* and said to J.D.,
"Why did Gregor Samsa wake up a cockroach?" His answer
(which he would have toyed over with his students forever)
was "Because that's what people expected of him."

They make the illogical logical. I don't do anything, be-
cause I'm waiting, I'm on hold (J.D.); I stay stoned because
I know it's better to be out of it (Freddy); I love art because
I myself am a work of art (Tucker).

Frank is harder to understand. One night a week or so ago,
I thought we were really attuned to each other, communicat-
ing by telepathic waves, and as I lay in bed about to speak I
realized that the vibrations really existed: they were him,
snoring.

Now he's coming into the bedroom, and I'm trying again
to think what to say. Or ask. Or do.

"Be glad you're not in Key West," he says. He climbs into
bed.

I raise myself up on one elbow and stare at him.

"There's a hurricane about to hit," he says.

"What?" I say. "Where did you hear that?"

"When Reddy Fox and I were putting the dishes away. We
had the radio on." He doubles up his pillow, pushes it under
his neck. "Boom goes everything," he says. "Bam. Crash.
Poof." He looks at me. "You look shocked." He closes his eyes.
Then, after a minute or two, he murmurs, "Hurricanes upset
you? I'll try to think of something nice."

He is quiet for so long that I think he has fallen asleep.
Then he says, "Cars that run on water. A field of flowers,
none alike. A shooting star that goes slow enough for you to
watch. Your life to do over again." He has been whispering in
my ear, and when he takes his mouth away I shiver. He
slides lower in the bed for sleep. "I'll tell you something really
amazing," he says. "Tucker told me he went into a travel
agency on Park Avenue last week and asked the travel agent
where he should go to pan for gold, and she told him."

"Where did she tell him to go?"

"I think somewhere in Peru. The banks of some river in Peru."

"Did you decide what you're going to do after Mark's birthday?" I say.

He doesn't answer me. I touch him on the side, finally.

"It's two o'clock in the morning. Let's talk about it another time."

"You picked the house, Frank. They're your friends downstairs. I used to be what you wanted me to be."

"They're your friends, too," he says. "Don't be paranoid."

"I want to know if you're staying or going."

He takes a deep breath, lets it out, and continues to lie very still.

"Everything you've done is commendable," he says. "You did the right thing to go back to school. You tried to do the right thing by finding yourself a normal friend like Marilyn. But your whole life you've made one mistake—you've surrounded yourself with men. Let me tell you something. All men—if they're crazy, like Tucker, if they're gay as the Queen of the May, like Reddy Fox, even if they're just six years old —I'm going to tell something about them. Men think they're Spider-Man and Buck Rogers and Superman. You know what we all feel inside that you don't feel? That we're going to the stars."

He takes my hand. "I'm looking down on all of this from space," he whispers. "I'm already gone."

ABOUT THE AUTHOR

ANN BEATTIE's most recent book was the novel *Falling in Place* (1980). In addition to having written two novels, she is the author of three short-story collections and her fiction appears frequently in *The New Yorker* and other magazines. She occasionally teaches writing at the University of Virginia and lives, with her dog, in New York City.